The Considerate Killer

Books by Lene Kaaberbøl and Agnete Friis

The Nina Borg Thrillers

The Boy in the Suitcase

Invisible Murder

Death of a Nightingale

The Considerate Killer

By Agnete Friis

What My Body Remembers

The Summer of Ellen

The Considerate Killer

LENE KAABERBØL

AND

AGNETE FRIIS

Translated from the Danish by Elisabeth Dyssegaard

Published by
Soho Press, Inc.
227 W 17th Street
New York, NY 10011

Library of Congress Cataloging-in-Publication Data

Kaaberbøl, Lene.
[Betænksomme morder. English]
The considerate killer / Lene Kaaberbol and Agnete Friis ; translated from the Danish by Elisabeth Dyssegaard.

ISBN 978-1-61695-801-5
eISBN 978-1-61695-529-8

1. Denmark—Fiction. I. Friis, Agnete. II. Dyssegaard, Elisabeth Kallick, translator. III. Title.
PT8177.21.A24B4813 2016
839.813'8—dc23 2015009881

Printed in the United States of America

10 9 8 7 6 5 4 3 2

The Considerate Killer

THE CONFESSIONAL WAS empty. Otherwise he wouldn't have gone in. It was hushed and dim—almost cool after the moist, stinking tropical heat of Manila's streets—and he could smell the beeswax the women of the congregation used when they polished the dark wooden panels. His right hand moved involuntarily in an ancient pattern—forehead to chest, left shoulder to right shoulder—but he didn't know how to begin. Then it came, abruptly and without preamble.

"I have to kill someone," he whispered at the small curtain and the confessional's empty side. "I'm not sure I can do it. But I can't not do it. Help me!"

He would have been terrified if there had been an answer. Instead the silence swallowed his words without giving him anything in return, and when after a few minutes he got up and left, he felt neither lighter of heart nor less fearful.

THE SECOND BLOW hit Nina on the back of the neck, right where the skull meets the cervical vertebrae. She fell forward. The cement rose to meet her, and she was already so numb that the abrupt contact didn't hurt. She lay on the parking garage's grubby, oil-stinking concrete deck, incapable of creating a connection between her bruised brain and the arms and legs she should have been mobilizing in order to save herself.

She had dropped the SuperBest bags with the first blow. A can of diced tomatoes rolled across the concrete, so close that she could have touched it if her arms and hands were still functioning, and right in the center of her foggy field of vision an object hit the floor with a drawn-out metallic clatter—an iron pipe, dark-brown with rust, as if it had been lying outside for years in some nettle-covered trash heap behind a shed.

Someone dropped to his knees beside her.

"Sorry," mumbled a soft, stumbling voice in an odd sing-song English. "Sorry. It won't take long, I promise . . ."

What wouldn't take long?

"Ama namin," the voice whispered, in a rapid rush, *"Sumsalangi Ka, Sambahin ang ngalan Mo . . ."*

Nina had heard the words before. She wasn't sure where or what they meant, but somewhere in the increasing darkness in her skull, small bubbles of memory rose and burst, small explosions of sensory impressions from the past. Heat. Buzzing flies. The stench of corpses. Distant, inconsolable weeping.

"Mapasaamin ang kaharian Mo . . ."

The Lord's Prayer, she suddenly thought. *That's the Lord's Prayer*. But she couldn't remember in what language.

"*Sundin ang loob Mo, dito sa lupa, para nang sa langit . . .*"

Why was someone kneeling beside her on the damp cold concrete and reciting the Lord's Prayer?

"Wait . . ." she mumbled. Or tried to, but her tongue was as senseless as the rest of her.

"Sorry, sorry," repeated the voice. "Amen."

Something dark and smelling of leather was placed across Nina's face, shutting out almost all the light. There was the sound of footsteps. An engine started, revving up angrily. The roar receded, then came nearer again. She could hear the sound of the tires rolling across the concrete, closer and closer.

I should move, thought Nina. *Crawl away. Do something. Save myself.*

She couldn't.

But instead of the shattering contact with tires, undercarriage and engine power she had expected, there was the scream of metal against metal and a muffled crash. The sound of the engine ceased. Into the sudden stillness came the sound of an agitated voice with a Viborg accent.

"What the *hell* are you doing? Watch out . . . Hey, I'm talking to you!"

Not to me, thought Nina. *Not me. I don't have to answer.*

The other man, the apologetic one, apparently didn't mean to answer either. There was the sound of a rattling cough from an over-choked engine, then it settled once again into smooth efficiency, and with shrieking tires and screaming brakes a car—*the* car, thought Nina—left the Saint Mathias Mall.

"What the . . ." Hesitant steps came closer. "Hello . . . Are you okay?"

The external darkness disappeared when someone removed the leather jacket covering her face. Instead, an inner darkness moved in inexorably.

"Fuck . . ." she heard the Viborg voice say, an instant before she ceased to hear anything at all.

"SØREN KIRKEGAARD?"

"Yes?" Søren automatically reached for his notebook. There was an official quality to the unfamiliar voice at the other end of the line that triggered his professional instincts. He had been a policeman for most of his adult life, and an intelligence officer in the Danish PET for nearly fifteen years, and he was quite used to meticulously registering the details of other people's disasters. But the next words shattered his expectations and froze his hand in midair above the pad.

"Next of kin to Nina Borg?"

Next of kin. Oh, God. She's dead. Only dead people have "next of kin."

"Yes," he said hoarsely.

"I'm calling from Viborg General Hospital. Nina Borg has been hospitalized here following an assault, and unfortunately she is unconscious."

Not dead. It was not only the dead, he thought with relief; patients had "next of kin" as well. But—assault? Unconscious?

"What happened?" he asked.

"I don't know the circumstances," said the voice carefully. "It's a police matter. But I can tell you that she is on Ward A24, our ICU, under observation for a fractured skull. If you go to the ward's reception desk . . ."

"I'm in Copenhagen," he said. "It'll take me a few hours to get there." Tirstrup? Billund? No, Karup. Karup had to be the closest airport. Or was it faster simply to get in the car and drive? *Unconscious*. That could mean all kinds of things. "Can't you tell me a little more now?" he asked and thought of the long drive across Fyn, and then Jutland, or the unbearable wait in the airport, without knowing, without having any idea how . . .

"I'm in administration," said the voice, not without a certain degree of compassion. "Unfortunately, I only know what it says in the papers. Observation for a fractured skull."

Observation—that sounded somewhat reassuring. If the skull had been seriously smashed, then it wouldn't just be "observation," would it?

"I'll be there," he said.

Then he remembered that he wasn't the only one with a stake in this. There were people who had a greater right, a closer relationship to Nina than he did. Children. Family.

"Has her husband—I mean her ex-husband been informed? And her mother?"

Nina was in Viborg because of her mother. Because of her mother's illness. In fact, why had they called him? Only now did he realize that this was odd. If Nina wasn't conscious, then how did they know . . . ?

"This is the only number I have been given," said the voice. "It was in her diary under 'in case of emergency.'"

"I'll call the others," said Søren.

• • •

HE CALLED THE ex-husband first. It took a little while to find the number, time he felt he could ill afford. His instincts clamored for him to throw himself behind the wheel and just drive. But Morten was the father of her children.

There was an odd echo in the background of the call. Clattering steps, shouts, the shrill sound of sneakers squealing against a gym floor. Handball? Badminton?

"Yes?"

Søren explained. For several seconds, there was silence on the line, except for the sports backdrop.

"Oh, damn it. Not again. What am I supposed to tell the children?"

Søren assumed it was a rhetorical question. He was amazed at the anger in Morten's voice, as if this was something Nina had done on purpose to hurt her family. But the key to that anger had to lie in the "not again." It was Morten who had initiated the divorce. He was the one who could not live with Nina's involvement in other people's disasters and the danger in which she repeatedly put herself—sometimes along with her family—as a consequence of what her daughter called her "save the world" gene. In the end, Morten had felt that he had no choice but to rescue Ida and Anton from Nina's personal war zone.

"She didn't exactly do it on purpose," said Søren.

"No," said Morten and did not sound particularly mollified. "It's never on purpose. She just can't help herself."

"I'm on my way there," said Søren and let an unspoken question hang in the air.

"Good," said Morten. "It's great that someone still has the

energy. Tell her that she should call the children as soon as she is able."

"Aren't you being a bit harsh?" Søren couldn't help asking.

"Possibly. But it's . . . let me see . . . the fifth or the sixth time in the last few years, if you count a few episodes from the Coal-House Camp. She's been attacked, she's had radiation poisoning, someone took a shot at her . . . She was the reason my daughter was attacked and kidnapped and . . . and placed in a hole in the ground, in an oil tank where she could have been asphyxiated . . ." Morten's voice had acquired a tremor, and Søren sympathized. He remembered that particular episode more clearly than he liked, since he was the one who had pulled Ida out of that dark hole in the ground, out of what might otherwise have been a living grave. The expression in her eyes had stayed with him for days.

Morten interrupted his tally with what was clearly a great effort. "Just tell her to call," he then said. "I won't tell the children until she can speak to them herself."

NINA'S MOTHER WAS more compassionate, though her first reaction was almost identical:

"Oh, no. Not again."

She apparently knew who Søren was, so although he had never met her—Nina and he had not proceeded that far in their hesitant partnering—Nina had at least told her mother that he existed.

"I'm sorry," he said. "But at least 'under observation for a fractured skull' isn't the same as a fractured skull."

"No," said Hanne Borg. "I suppose not."

"I'll call as soon as I know more," he said.

"I can call the hospital myself," said Nina's mother. "You just get going. And if you need a bed, I have a spare room."

She didn't *sound* sick, but then, no one said you had to sound like the final act of *La Traviata* just because you had been diagnosed with cancer.

FINALLY, HE WAS free to leave. He chose the highway in the end; he didn't have patience for the alternative. And while kilometer after kilometer disappeared under the Hyundai's hood, he wondered what he should make of that "next of kin." It was at once touching and surprising to him that she had thought of him in this way.

They had "dated"—he winced a bit at the adolescent connotations, but what else could you call it?—yet had proceeded no further into the minefield of personal relations. He was not sure what she wanted with him. Sex, yes. Love? He couldn't quite tell. She didn't have as much as a toothbrush in his house in Rødovre and no one had so far mentioned cohabitation. Perhaps it was only now that it occurred to him that this was what he wanted—completely and without reservations. To be a couple. Married or not, he didn't much care which, but to share a home, to live together, to obey and honor and love, until the last breath of life left his feeble failing body.

Feeble. That was precisely the way he felt now, and perhaps the deeper reason he hadn't pushed harder than he had. He felt more mortal than usual, more decrepit. It was not just the bullet that had made a mess of his lungs and ribcage, and the first convalescence that had taken much longer than he had hoped.

He had made it to his feet again, made it back into his chair as group leader in the PET. It had been a struggle, but he could manage. Or he thought so until . . .

Until Torben, at his most boss-like, had put Søren out to grass, sent him home with orders not to return for at least three months. Anger, anger at the unfairness still rumbled inside him. How could Torben have betrayed him in that way?

He hadn't told Nina. Wrongheaded masculine pride, perhaps. He would have to drop that now, he supposed. If they really *were* "next of kin." And if he had to explain why he had been able to drop everything at a moment's notice to go to Viborg to sit by her bedside.

Assaulted.

He pictured her slight, boyish figure, the dark hair cut so short that it followed the shape of her skull like a soft, auburn shadow. It probably didn't make much of a difference how long your hair was if someone decided to hit you in the head with a baseball bat, or whatever they had used. All the same, it seemed to him to make her extra vulnerable and the attack more brutal.

Who had done it? And why? Was it random, or was it because Nina was Nina? Both Morten and Hanne seemed automatically to assume the latter, but even stubborn and at times highly exasperating Red Cross nurses could be the victims of random violence. He had to speak to the local police. Find out what had happened, and how they were handling the case. The desire to act, to *do* something, was overwhelming.

He coaxed a few more miles per hour out of the Hyundai and changed lanes to pass a Polish long-haul. Adrenaline made his hands vibrate faintly against the steering wheel, and somewhere in his chest was a tight nervous pain that for once has nothing to do with the physical scarring.

HE REACHED VIBORG just shy of midnight. There had been an accident near Fredericia that backed up the traffic all the way across the Lillebaelt Bridge. The intensive care unit was dimly lit and oddly womb-like. There were no windows facing the outside world, only a glass wall separating it from the central observation point from which the output from all the various apparata in the ward was monitored. Sounds were faint and muffled, soft beeps and distant steps, lowered voices. Through the glass, he could see how the eyes of the duty staff slid constantly from one monitor to the next, their faces lit more by the screens than by the dim lamps. It reminded him sharply of the atmosphere inside a surveillance van.

Nina was alone in a unit called OBS 4. At the sight of her slight figure in the hospital bed, his heart took an entirely unauthorized tumble in his scarred chest. He knew it was illogical—that you in fact did not love with your heart, but rather with your brain and a complex series of hormonal signals. Still, he could not free himself from the thought that she had gained access to the most vulnerable part of him when she—to save his life and allow the punctured lung room to expand again—had plunged first a knife and then part of a ballpoint pen into his chest. With great precision and ruthlessness, in exactly the right place. "Wow," the young ambulance doctor had commented, "she sure hit that one right on the nail." And then, when he realized that Søren had heard him, "Sorry, but that's one of the most effective acute interventions I've ever seen. You can thank her for the fact that you are still alive."

He knew that. While he had lain there in the snow, feeling the ability to breathe being taken from him, heartbeat by heartbeat, he had had time to think about death. Not Death with a capital D, personified in the somewhat theatrical guise of the Grim Reaper, but the simple, concrete, and omnipresent biological process that would shut down all his vital signs. For his part there had been no dark tunnel and bright light, no out-of-body experience. Absolutely no sense of anything but struggle, pain, and suffering, and somewhere a point in time when the suffering would end, when everything that he considered his—an active body, a functioning brain, a consciousness or a soul or whatever you preferred to call it—when all of that would cease to be *him* and turn instead into random decomposable matter headed for biology's recycling system.

Nina had saved him from that point of death. It was perhaps not too surprising that the experience had left certain inerasable grooves in his inner universe.

Sure, he had noticed her before that. There was something about her stubbornness, her intensity, the too-slender body, and those eyes . . . particularly those eyes, dark grey like a sky before a storm, with an unfathomably vivid gaze that he felt compelled to meet, even at moments when it would have been wiser not to. Certainly, he had seen her, and been curious. Interested. But it was only after the knife had gone in that she had acquired this ability to hurt him. The ability to make his abdomen contract, the ability to make his hands turn into fists reflexively if he thought any kind of danger, imaginary or real, threatened her.

Right now his fists were clenched so hard that his fingers were getting numb. With an effort, he unclenched them one by one.

She lay on her side, probably so the weight of her head would not put pressure on the shaved area on the back of her head and the damage that was hidden under a white gauze compress as large as a standard sheet of paper. A raw and crusty abrasion covered most of one cheek, and the hollows of her eyes were so bruised and swollen that the eyes were just greasy slits. A bit of clear fluid leaked from one nostril and dripped down onto the flat pillow under her head, where there was already a damp spot.

Søren was relieved to see that she was breathing on her own, but otherwise there wasn't much to celebrate.

"Nina, damn it," he said quietly, without any hope that she could hear him. "What have you gotten yourself in to now?"

At that instant he recognized Morten's anger and understood it completely. Nina had probably never had the occasion to force a kitchen knife into her ex-husband's chest, but she had undoubtedly made him feel a similar pain every time she had thrown herself in front of an on-rushing catastrophe without considering the consequences. There had to be limits to how many stabs of that knife one could survive before one started to protect oneself.

And Morten was not alone. He had Ida and Anton to consider.

Søren hesitantly touched Nina's hand and hardly knew himself whether it was to caress it or to register her symptoms. Chilled, he observed, but not ice-cold. Not the cold that comes when the blood is retreating from the body's outer extremities because the inner organs are fighting off death.

Stable, they had said. Not critical. She had been hit twice; the first blow had landed quite high and had bounced off the skull to a certain extent, but the second was of more concern—it had gone in at the base of the cranium, and the full unblunted force of it had made the brain slap hard against its bony case. And, yes, there was a crack. A fractured skull was now the official diagnosis—a so-called basilar skull fracture.

"We can see a bit of fluid from the nose and the ears, so there must be a lesion in the brain membrane," a helpful intensive care nurse had explained. "Usually it stops by itself, but we have to keep an eye on it. And we'd like to see signs of consciousness soon. If you could just sit and talk to her, that would be very helpful. Hearing is often restored long before any of the other senses."

He obediently sat down, but at first could not get a word out. What was he supposed say? Should he scold her? Reassure her? Tell her that he "was here," as if that circumstance alone would suddenly make all the horrors go away?

"Nina," he said quietly, "it's me, Søren." He felt like a complete idiot. But if the nurse was right and it could in some way help Nina to hear his voice, then so be it. "I . . . came to see how you're doing. So I'll just sit here and . . . talk a little. So you know that I'm here."

THE PHILIPPINES, FOUR YEARS EARLIER

IT MEANT NOTHING. The interview. It was a formality of the kind that no one seriously worried about, except maybe his father, and of course Vincent himself. But his father had always doubted God too much, or so his mother said, and what Vincent was feeling was probably just a kind of stage fright. His place in medical school was as good as certain.

"You are gifted," said his mother. "And your scholarship comes from the church. That means that you are both gifted *and* of good moral character. God will help us."

Vincent tried to hold on to that thought. His mother, God, and the fact that that all previous applicants with the St. Joseph's Church Scholarship had been accepted and had passed with distinction—white coats, families bawling with happiness.

Nothing could go wrong.

Vincent sat in the sweltering lobby of the university, trying not to fidget.

It was one of Manila's finest universities, and graduating from it practically guaranteed a job—perhaps even an international one. But the decor was far from fashionable. The broad stone staircase to the auditoriums on the second floor was scratched and dull, and the paint on the bannister was peeling. Portraits of the school's previous presidents graced the beige walls: men and women in suits, wearing serious smiles. The school's current president wasn't up there yet, but Vincent had heard that he was both a doctor and a professor and that he appreciated proper dress. Vincent's mother had provided him with an ironed white shirt and newly pressed dark pants for the occasion, and on the entire trip in the jeepney, the open truck-bus from San Marcelino to Manila, he had stored the unfamiliar outfit neatly folded in his suitcase along with shorts, sandals, a couple of clean T-shirts and the present for his cousin Maria. Later he had changed his clothes in the restroom of a bowling alley.

Now he sat as motionless as he could manage in the costume, his arms held away from his body so the sweat stains wouldn't become too noticeable. The pages of the book he was attempting to read were damp from contact with his hands.

Two hours ago there had been more guys sitting or standing around. Dark pants, white shirts, and glistening foreheads. There had been girls too, of course—most in business suits and skirts, but also a few in expensive-looking jeans, sneakers, shirts and discreet makeup. Not a single one had looked a day over eighteen, and Vincent was willing to bet next semester's allowance that they were all fresh from high school with top grades, because you needed those to get in, but also with money. Rich kids, most of them, respectable and well-connected, from Manila or the wealthy suburbs. And they had all been called in before him.

The only person left besides himself was a giant of a guy who sat a few empty seats away, reading the *Manila Times* while he calmly chewed his way through a bag of cashews.

"Would you like one?" he asked when he noticed Vincent's look.

"No, thanks." Just the thought of the salty, dried nuts made his throat constrict even further.

The guy just nodded.

"Victor," he said and stretched out a large hand. He could comfortably reach across the empty seats.

"Vincent," said Vincent and offered his hand.

Victor's grip was soft and dry and without any macho attempt to demonstrate his strength. Vincent wondered how his own hand felt—damper than usual, definitely, but could his panic be detected?

Victor did not seem to notice anything. He just offered him another small nod, as if this was merely another item on some inner to-do list: say hello politely—check. Vincent was envious of his apparent serenity.

He wished it was over and done with. He knew that they would ask him about "his motivation for becoming a doctor" and about his "personal character," as had been somewhat vaguely indicated in the letter from the faculty. What kind of personal characteristics they were hoping to find, he had no idea, even though he had had plenty of time to think about it lying awake the night before.

He had always been told that he was gifted and that he worked hard. He had studied so strenuously for his exams last week that you would have been able to wake him up at any point in the night to make him recite the properties of the elements, explain the Coriolis effect, and demonstrate differential equations. But whatever being of "good moral character" meant, it seemed less tangible, and all he had to go by were Father Abuel's injunctions to keep sex inside holy wedlock, honor your parents, and so forth.

He was a virgin, which could not be said to be entirely his own doing. Bea was the one who had kept cool for them both on the rare occasions when they had been alone together and had kissed for so long that everything had gone up in flames. He was not sure he could credit those bonus points to his own moral account.

And there were those damnably autonomous nightly erections followed by just as damnable ejaculations, with or without his own active intervention, a sin that according to the church was almost as severe as sex outside of marriage. If purity and fidelity were counted as a subject, he was not at all sure he would pass, and he shrank from confessing such embarassments to Father Abuel. The priest had taken a vow of silence, of course, but it still felt as if the sinful words might somehow leak from the confessional and find their own way to Bea during the Sunday mass in San Marcelino. Also, it was Father Abuel who had written the recommendation that finally had secured the St. Joseph scholarship for Vincent. It did in fact say that Vincent was "of good moral character" and that he pursued "a Christian way of life." After that, Vincent had stopped going to confession entirely.

As far as honoring your parents went, he was doing better. Quite respectably, in fact. He did what he was told. It wasn't really that difficult. Any idiot could do homework until ten every evening. It was easy. Or had been in elementary and high school anyway, with his mother providing a newly ironed school uniform, clean T-shirts, and three meals a day.

So he was, when he summed it up, hard-working and quite intelligent and he honored his mother and father, as it was written in the Bible. He could not think of any other positive personal characteristics. There wasn't really anything to hold on to, he thought, other than the information on his identity card. Vincent Bernardo. Twenty years old, engaged to Bea; son of his parents and big brother to Mimi. Not poor, but far from rich. Whether this was enough to get him accepted into St. Francis College of Medicine, he had no idea.

"Hey!"

Vincent jumped.

The heavy, dark door to the street had been opened and a young man stepped into the hall. His face was narrow and boyish, and his body had not yet found its mature proportions. Still, he did not look as if he was Vincent's age. It was his posture, Vincent decided. He carried himself with the confidence and weight of a grown man who knew his own worth.

He looked directly at Vincent and raised his chin impatiently. "How long have you been sitting here?"

Vincent looked at his watch and quickly did the math. Five sweaty hours had passed. According to the letter from the university, he had had an appointment at one, but apparently all the other candidates had as well.

"Crap," said the newcomer explosively.

He let himself drop into the chair next to Vincent, fiddling restlessly with a cigarette. He was wearing two gold rings—one on the ring finger and an extra wide one on his thumb. While that in itself was not so unusual, still there was something unmistakably sleek, something of the dandy, about him.

A kind of natural arrogance in the way he folded his slender arms behind his neck, his legs slightly apart, and in the restless boredom he exuded.

"I hate waiting," he said. "Every minute we spend in these chairs is a goddamn waste of precious time. Waste of life. If you live to be eighty, you have about forty-two million minutes to use, and that may sound like a lot, my friend, but if you've been sitting here for five hours, that's three hundred of them just gone out the window. Poof. Time swallowed by nothing. As if it weren't bad enough that we have to spend five years of our lives in this place afterward. Insult to injury, I tell you."

He jerked his jeweled thumb toward the glass door to the auditorium on the other side of the lobby and smiled. And it was a smile that lit up his features irresistibly, warm and wide in the narrow face. Vincent could feel his usual defenses melting away. The guy would have been a shoo-in for a Philippine remake of *Dead Poets Society*. His sparkle, his energy, his upper-class confidence. Carpe diem, seize the day and all of that. Vincent knew his Latin from church.

"I've been reading," Vincent said, holding out his book, a primer on pediatrics, borrowed from the library back home in San Marcelino. Despite his secret uncertainties about getting in, he had attacked the first year's curriculum with his usual diligence; the required reading ran to a daunting number of pages, even for him.

The guy grinned even more broadly, though Vincent would have sworn that wasn't possible.

"You're the type who worries too much," he said. "We're not even in yet. Are you nervous?"

Vincent shrugged. "A little," he said and carefully dried his palms on his pants. His cheap shirt felt glued to his back.

Actually nervous wasn't the right word. Waiting for the interview, or rather, for the letter that would arrive in a few days, was like standing at the top of the tower on Mount Samat, gazing across forested slopes and luminous green rice fields out to sea, where the container ships floated under a sky grey as dust, far out in Manila Bay.

If he got in, this whole world would still exist, and look the same.

If he was rejected, it would disappear in the blink of an eye. He was to become a doctor. He had always been going to become a doctor. Any other future was literally unimaginable.

The carpe-diem guy ran a hand through his longish black hair. There was a bit of European or perhaps American in him, Vincent guessed. His nose was big and had a slight hook like the beak of a bird of prey, but his skin was dusky and his eyes dark, narrow and sparkling with hidden, friendly laughter. He didn't seem nervous. Just a bit restless. To judge by the knife-sharp pleats in his pants and the bright white, newly ironed shirt, he hadn't been waiting for five hours.

Vincent smiled politely, leaned forward and returned his attention to the part of his book that he was studying—a chart showing normal blood pressures for children ages zero to fifteen. There were a lot of numbers, but he could memorize them if he read the chart a few times, wrote the numbers in his notebook and practiced by closing the book and repeating them to himself.

It didn't come easy, that kind of thing. Learning things by heart took several passes; he had to work at it.

"So you want to be a doctor? Why?"

Vincent looked up at Carpe Diem and felt momentarily confused. This was not the same as being asked by the board about his "motivation" and coming up with some appropriate phrases. The man seemed genuinely to question why Vincent wanted this. He had never been asked that before, not in that way. It was the kind of thing that didn't need an explanation because it was so obvious. It was a good job, you earned a lot of money, and you were . . . respected. His parents had saved for his education since he was a little boy.

"I . . ." Vincent cleared his throat. "That's always been my plan."

The guy nodded as if he had said something really wise.

"I think I know what you mean," he said. "It's that thing about helping others, right? To make a difference? That's what I want to do too. There are way too many people here in the Philippines who only think about money. I have a . . . girlfriend, who is studying here. We want to work for Doctors Without Borders, and so on."

The guy rotated the unlit cigarette again between his fingers and sighed deeply.

"Aw, fuck it," he then said. Dug out a lighter, lit the cigarette and took a couple of intense, deep drags.

"I don't think you're allowed to smoke here," said Vincent and pointed to the sign above them. The guy sent him a searching gaze. Kindly.

"It's nice of you to worry about me," he said. "Do you smoke?"

He dug around in his pants pocket, pulled out a package of cigarettes and gave Vincent an encouraging nod. He had a tattoo on the back of his hand. Something written in exquisitely drawn Arabic letters.

"You can just take one for later if you don't want to smoke here."

Vincent shook his head.

"I don't smoke."

The guy jumped up from his chair and strode with light steps across the floor, his cigarette still hanging from the corner of his mouth. The blue smoke drifted up toward the badly functioning air conditioner and disappeared.

"Very sensible," he said. "I should stop too. I dive, you know. Free diving without oxygen. It's the coolest thing in the world. Better than sex and drugs. Have you tried it?"

Vincent shook his head while he followed Carpe Diem's restless wandering with his eyes.

"What a waste of time," the guy sighed, kicked lightly at a couple of chair legs. "I'll buy you a beer afterward, okay? For every minute we spend in here, we need to spend at least three on cigarettes, whiskey, and naked ladies. That's the only way to bring the universe back into cosmic balance. I've studied astrology for several years to reach this conclusion. I'm not kidding. This is precious knowledge I'm sharing with you."

Vincent couldn't help laughing, which made the guy jump up on a chair and spread his arms. Ash from his cigarette sprinkled the floor.

"I'll wait for you after my interview, okay? At the Cabana Bar on the other side of the street. We've got to celebrate this, damn it."

The big guy, Victor, had followed the exchange without saying a word. Now he got up and stretched to his full height. It was only at this point that Vincent fully understood how enormous he was. The man was at least 190 centimeters tall, but his height was less impressive than his bulk. Everything about him was wide and looked as if had been built with three levels of reinforcement. His forehead was wide, his chest was wide, his wrists were wide and his calves so powerfully muscular that they were the size of Vincent's thighs. His hair was cut close to the dark skin.

"I'm in," he said and crumpled his snack bag. "I'll need a beer after this."

"A beer?" The carpe-diem guy whistled, clearly impressed and with eyes slightly narrowed against the smoke. "You look like it'll take something a lot stronger than beer to get you drunk. You're built like an ox, damn it. But . . . perfect. What's your name?"

"Victor."

"And you, my rule-following friend?"

Carpe Diem looked questioningly at Vincent, and he had time to think that he didn't know what they were celebrating, but that this was completely beside the point. The guy's energy was infectious here in the middle of the boring yellow-and-beige front hall, and why shouldn't he have a beer? His exams were over and he wasn't going back to San Marcelino for a few days. With complete disregard for the fact that he had not yet actually been accepted into the medical school, his mother's cousin Maria had promised to help him find a room while he was in Manila, but the house hunting wouldn't start until tomorrow. For once he could actually permit himself a break from textbooks and expectations.

"Okay," he said and was rewarded with an immediate and happy grin from his new friend.

"Vadim," the guy said and held out his hand. "A pleasure to meet you, Vincent."

Their eyes met, and Vincent later thought that it had been a kind of love at first sight. Not the romantic kind, not the way he felt about Bea. Of course not. There wasn't the pull of sexual excitement or dark longings—just an overpowering curiosity and an intense wish to get to know him better. Vadim. The sense of having met a person who was going to take up space in your life. That kind of love.

Of course this wasn't something he articulated to himself on the spot, more a sort of retroactive rationalization when he thought back on the first meeting of the V-Team.

It was love.

Vincent, Victor, and Vadim.

THERE WAS NO real transition. One moment she was nowhere, for all intents and purposes did not even exist. In the next . . . she was there. Here. Wherever "here" might be. From somewhere nearby came a quiet voice, somewhat hoarse, which for some reason found it necessary to give her a detailed description of the room.

". . . it's still pretty warm here. I've taken off my sweater, and I'm still sweating. But it's probably for your sake that they turn the heat up so high, so that you won't get cold. It's actually quite calm and nice, considering. The walls are dark blue, and the curtains are . . . you would probably call them violet, a kind of . . . dark purple. Then there's some . . . linoleum. I think that's what it is. On the floor. Sort of . . . charcoal grey. It's probably practical and easy to clean."

It was Søren. But why on earth was he sitting there telling her about the flooring?

Where was she?

A nauseating tug of uncertainty went through her. Something had happened, but she didn't know what. The sounds underlying Søren's quiet voice shouted "HOSPITAL," in very large letters, and her headache weighed in at about an eight on the NRS scale—so bad that it was hard to think of anything else—but she *had* to think. Why couldn't she remember what had happened?

Head trauma is often accompanied by retrograde amnesia, a textbook voice informed her helpfully from somewhere in her brain's back catalog. But what head trauma?

She tried to open her eyes, but it was as if there wasn't room in her eye sockets.

"By the way, Morten and the kids said to give you their love," said Søren in the middle of his absurd description of the room. "They'll visit when you're feeling a bit better. Or . . . you can call them. Soon, right?"

The children. Ida. Anton. She was supposed to pick up Anton after school. Morten would be furious because—

No. Morten didn't get furious anymore. The divorce had been finalized, and Morten was usually just grumpy, cold and resigned. And besides, he could hardly expect her to pick up Anton when she was in the hospital.

In Viborg. She wasn't in Copenhagen at all, she was in Viborg, with her mother. She had taken a three-month temp job as a nurse with a local GP: lots of blood work and so-called lifestyle consultations—usually boiling down to "eat less, exercise more, and stop smoking"—and absolutely no drama. Deadly dull, not to put too fine a point to it, and all in order to "be there," that vague form of caring which consisted mostly of being nearby if something went wrong.

But what had gone wrong now was apparently not her mother's treatment for the breast cancer her oncologist called, with careful optimism, "one of the less aggressive types."

A traffic accident? Screeching brakes and shattered glass?

There was a nervous twitch in some inner alarm center, but no clear memory appeared.

"It would be great if you could wake up," said Søren. "It would be extremely nice to see you. Or feel you. Maybe you could squeeze my hand? Just a little?"

Oh, God. He was sitting there talking like a lonely waterfall because they had told him to. That's how they always instructed the next of kin—"*Talk to her, she might be able to hear you.*" This wasn't exactly wrong; she *could* in fact hear him, even though establishing control over her eyelids and finer motor functions seemed to be beyond her still. But it was also a tactic that was supposed to give the next of kin a sense of purpose and a job to do, so that they stayed with the patient instead of taking all their desperate worries to the overburdened staff.

Head trauma. How bad was it? No respirator, and while her thoughts did not line up in neat straight lines, she *was* able to think, speculate, articulate, remember . . . mostly. So . . . probably not life threatening in spite of the vague sensation of . . . of dread. Of having come much too close to death.

It was worrisome that she couldn't work out how to move. What if she was paralyzed? What if this sensation of the body as a heavy, unresponsive prison of flesh was . . . permanent?

No, damn it. She ignored her headache and focused all her concentration, all her power on an attempt to use her left hand to grip Søren's fingers. She never discovered whether she succeeded, because the pain would not be forced back; it rose up like a violent dark flood and tore her back with it into nothingness.

• • •

THE SECOND TIME was better. There were voices around her. Activity.

"Her eyes," said Søren. "It doesn't look . . . very nice. Did someone hit her in the face, or . . . ?"

"Not directly. It's what we call a raccoon-eye hematoma. It's an effect of the fractured skull."

She still felt heavier than usual. Her eyelids were fat and sticky, but she managed to establish a form of control over the lower part of her face.

"I'm thirsty," she said.

"Nina!" Søren exclaimed. "I'm sorry, but I couldn't hear . . . What did you say?"

"Thirsty!"

"Yes. Um . . . Could she have something to drink?"

"It's best to wait until you've got things a bit more under control, Nina," said the nursing staff voice. "You don't actually have a *need* for liquids; we put in a drip. Your mouth is just dry, so you *feel* thirsty. We can moisten your lips a little. How are you feeling otherwise?"

"Headache," she said irritably. She was perfectly able to determine whether she could drink. Or . . . was she? She didn't want to choke—just the thought of coughing started a pounding in her battered skull.

"That's understandable. Now that you are conscious, we can look into treating the pain. You were hit twice in the back of the head, and one of the blows created a small fracture. You need to relax for a while, but the prognosis is good."

Relief slid through her in the form of a heavy dullness. The battle had been canceled; she could relax. She wouldn't need the adrenaline reserves after all. She yawned carefully and felt a secondary soreness in her jaw.

"Just give me a little water," she said, somewhat more clearly. "I promise not to cough."

"A little bit, then," said the voice. "You can have more later."

A fat plastic straw was pushed in between her lips, and she sucked carefully. Even the sucking sent waves through her entire cranium and made it hurt even more. But at least her mouth immediately felt less mummified—it was easier to move her tongue, easier to swallow. Small victories, very small victories, but right now she'd take what she could get.

"The local police would like to speak with you," said Søren. "When you feel ready."

"Why?" she asked stupidly.

"Because you were the victim of an assault. Did you see who did it?"

Assault. A couple of blows to the head. It didn't make any sense.

"No," she said. "I didn't see anything."

The instant she said it, fear returned. It wasn't even a fight-or-flight reaction. It was worse. It was the hopeless passive terror of the prey when there's nothing more to be done except wait for death.

Stop, she whispered silently to herself. *There's nothing to be afraid of. You're safe here.*

She could hear her own pulse crackle in her ears. Her body did not believe her reassurances; it knew better.

• • •

THE YOUNG DETECTIVE sergeant reminded Søren of one of his own officers, Gitte. Who wasn't his at all, of course, even though he couldn't help feeling a certain possessive pride because he was the one who had originally hired her.

It wasn't that they looked so very similar—the DS from Mid-West Jutland Police was somewhat smaller and darker and did not have quite Gitte's impressive swimmer's physique. But she had trimmed her hair just as short; she was just as young, and just as determinedly intelligent.

"In the last few months we've seen a rise in the numbers of robberies and assaults," she explained. "Both break-ins and street crimes like the one your friend experienced. We'd like to establish whether or not there is a connection to any of the other cases."

He sensed that she was a little unsure about how to treat him. Was he a colleague or merely a relation of the victim? He had introduced himself at once and had stressed that his interest in "the case" was exclusively civilian in nature. The rest of the police force commonly had a strained relationship to the PET, and Søren didn't feel like contributing to the general paranoia.

"Nina's memory of the assault is pretty foggy," he said. "At least at this point. But you'll see that for yourself when she wakes up."

They both glanced through the glass door into the room—no longer in the intensive care unit, but an ordinary ward—where Nina now lay fast asleep. Mid-West Jutland Police had not rushed over as soon as they heard that the "victim" was conscious, but some hours later Detective Sergeant Caroline Westmann had arrived, armed with smartphone, case files, and ambition.

"I can come back later," she said.

"She'll probably wake up in a little while," said Søren. "She generally doesn't sleep for hours at a stretch. If you have the time . . ."

He didn't want her to leave. Not until he had extracted a little more information from her.

"Are there any witnesses?" he asked.

She hesitated—again this uncertainty: colleague or outsider?—but apparently decided to allow professional courtesy to win the day.

"A couple whose car was hit when the perpetrator made his escape," she said. "And a few shoppers who saw him drive away. None of them have been able to give us a proper description, though they're pretty much in agreement that there was only one. Right now the car is our best lead."

"Does this fit into your pattern?" he asked. "A singe perp?"

"No," she admitted. "In the other attacks two or three attackers were involved. They appear to be foreigners."

"Their nationality?"

"We don't know. The victim of one of the break-ins thought that his attackers spoke an eastern European language, but he wasn't completely sure. They pulled a plastic bag over his head at the very beginning. He could have suffocated."

"Was that the intention?"

"We don't know. Maybe just random brutality. Maybe they just didn't care whether the victim survived or not."

"Was a bag put over Nina's head?"

"No. But he placed a jacket over her face. A leather jacket, which he left behind, probably because he was interrupted."

"A jacket? That must have given you something?"

"It wasn't originally made in Denmark, but . . . it's hard to say how much that means these days."

"DNA?"

She nodded with some reluctance.

"Yes. A few hairs, and some sweat stains. So if it is actually his jacket . . ."

"Any matches?"

"We haven't received the results yet."

"Do you have any DNA from the other cases?"

"Saliva from a few cigarette stubs, but we're not even sure that they belong to anyone from the gang. Otherwise, they've been pretty careful."

He had the urge to take notes, but knew that it would most likely cause the stream of information to dry up. It was one thing to keep him informed in order to be polite, but something else entirely to let him take part in the investigation.

"What about the car, the one he was driving? You said you have something on that?"

"Yes . . . We have a description and some paint traces from the collision. We think it was stolen—at least we've got a report on a black VW Passat that fits the bill. So . . . find the car, and we may find other leads. Or even the perp."

The optimism in Westmann's voice had a hard-won quality to it. Most likely, thought Søren, the attacker had dumped VW car as soon as he was able, and the young DS knew that perfectly well. That this jaundiced assessment of her own chances did not cause her to give up was admirable in his eyes.

He had once been just as enthusiastic. About a hundred years ago.

Damn it, he thought. *They'll never find him if that's all they've got.* And what if . . . what if it wasn't a random robbery? What if it was personal and deliberate and directed at Nina?

If that was the case, there was every reason to expect the man to try again.

THE PHILIPPINES, THREE YEARS EARLIER

STRANGE THAT IT could be so easy to travel.

Five hours ago Vincent and Bea had been sitting in a taxi on the way to the airport in Manila, watching the glitteringly hot tin roofs of the slums slip by outside. No stinking jeepney and sweaty T-shirts for them. Just cool air conditioning, a very short line at the check-in and then a bite to eat while they waited to board. Now they lay in matching orange striped lawn chairs, gazing out across the Pacific, even though it had really just been the plan for Bea to stay with her cousin in Manila for a week or so. Vincent had planned trips to the movies, meals at some cheap restaurants, and strolls along the marina. Nice enough, but perhaps a little lacking in home comforts. Female visitors to his six-by-nine closet of a dorm room were *bawal*: strictly forbidden. But then Vadim had turned up with his big smile and the promise of surfing and flame-red sunsets, waving free tickets to Samal, the family's resort near Davcao City. Both Vincent and Victor must join him, he insisted, and Bea was, of course, welcome as well.

The waves beat faintly and rhythmically against the beach, and when Vincent closed his eyes it seemed almost hypnotic.

They were holding hands, he and Bea. They had crooked their fingers together over the gap between the chairs. Bea's hand was still wet after her most recent dip in the water. She was wearing the new bikini that Vadim had given her when they met him and his girlfriend at the airport.

At the sight of Diana and the super-expensive designer skirt carelessly wrapped around her slender hips, Bea's self-confidence had plummeted.

"I don't have . . . those kinds of clothes," she whispered to Vincent.

Vadim wasn't supposed to hear her, but he did.

"All you need on Samal is a swimsuit," he said. He measured her expertly with his eyes and bought the robin's-egg blue Dolce & Gabbana on the spot. It meant nothing to Vadim that this was an expensive brand and that the bikini cost the equivalent of a month's spending money for Vincent. It wasn't arrogance, more a form of blindness developed through a lifetime in his father's marble palace.

Now Bea reclined in her chair, looking the very picture of upper-class elegance, just like the girls they had seen by the resort pool—only more beautiful. Her skin glowed golden in the sun, and in unguarded moments Vincent couldn't help glancing at her slender, smooth thighs and the robin's-egg bikini, which hid what bikinis were supposed to hide and no more. Bea had small high breasts. Her stomach was flat and smooth with discreetly drawn stomach muscles. Just above the edge of the bikini bottoms there was a delicate dark birthmark, which he desperately longed to touch. He had never seen her like this before. Almost naked.

Feeling yet another erection coming on, he turned over onto his stomach and raised himself up on his elbows.

"Do you like it?"

Bea sat up and looked across the water, fingering her narrow gold necklace—a gift he had given her on the one-year anniversary of their engagement.

"It's beautiful here, Vincent. And I like your friends, but . . . It's so different. As if you suddenly moved to a different planet. It seems wrong. How do you hold on to yourself when you live in a place where no one knows who you are? Your family . . . everyone you have always known."

She was so serious. He smiled, leaned across the narrow gap between the two lawn chairs and kissed her carefully on the mouth. Her lips were endlessly soft and tasted of salt after the dip in the Pacific.

"With a bit of luck," he said, "this will also be our world one day. When I finish my degree and start to make money. You might as well get used to it."

"You think so?"

She looked at the distant ocean-going ships with a serious expression.

Even though he was only two years older than she was, he sometimes thought of Bea as a child. She was still living with her parents while she studied to become a nurse. Ate with her parents in the evening and played with the dog before going to sleep under the slow-turning ceiling fan. Her childhood room was still completely unchanged, with the little desk against one wall, the bed against the other, and her textbooks piled neatly on the bedside table next to the lamp.

Vadim called them from the wide porch of the house, as he emerged balancing a couple of neon-colored drinks. Soft pop music drifted through the open patio doors.

"Are you coming?"

Bea and Vincent got up. He was already a bit groggy from the heat and the sharp light across the sea. Bea, on the other hand, walked with a dancer's balanced steps, a thin beach shawl wrapped around the blue bikini. He could see her dark, soft silhouette through the light material, and he felt a touch of something that had to be happiness. A sense that he was finally young in the way he ought to be. With a lightness that he had observed in others. Carefree as he had never felt before.

Perhaps Vadim could see it.

"How sweet you look together," he said. "Young love's dream."

He was already halfway through his own drink, and Vincent suspected him of having had a few while he and Bea were at the beach. His narrow dark eyes wore the musing expression that usually showed up in the course of a sodden evening, and he spoke more and more like a character from an American movie. Even under normal circumstances Vadim spiced up his speech with more English expressions than most Filipinos, but it was especially noticeable when he was feeling emotional or drunk, which with him was often the same thing. Vadim was pure love when mixed with alcohol. Soft as a kitten.

Diana and Victor were already sitting in a pair of broad, upholstered chairs, Victor with a collection of notes and a beer standing at his feet, Diana with a tattered English paperback. She was a year ahead of them, but Vadim had apparently known her as far back as high school, and their relationship seemed . . . complicated. Diana did not have Vadim's lightness, but was beautiful and earnest and wore T-shirts with peace signs and political slogans like "Corruption Stinks," "Fight Poverty" and "Health for All." She had started a health clinic out in the slums in Las Pinas City together with a couple of older students. There was something dogged, and contagious about her rebellious frontal attack on the entire world, but when Vincent saw Vadim and Diana kiss and weave their fingers together on the stone wall in the university's garden, it was like observing a wordless and chronically undecided power struggle. Diana's gravity against Vadim's constant attempts at lightness. Occasionally Vincent thought he could see a deep wonder in Diana's gaze when she looked at Vadim. As if she had to search for the reason for the obvious attraction between them. But then Vadim would grab her ponytail, pull her head back and kiss her on the neck and collarbone until she, bursting with laughter, had to capitulate. Until next time.

Vadim handed them each a drink.

"Drink, my young friends," he said and they all five raised their glasses. Bea drank carefully and with a small wrinkle on her nose. Vincent wasn't sure if she had ever tasted alcohol before, except of course for the altar wine every Sunday at church, but that didn't really count. Father Abuel had the reputation for diluting the blood of Jesus Christ quite a bit, out of consideration for the delicate souls of his congregation.

Vincent bent down and kissed Bea's delicately curved ear.

"Be careful with that stuff," he said. "It's strong."

"I know," she said and smiled. "But I'm with you—so what could happen?"

• • •

AFTERWARD VADIM ORDERED takeaway from the restaurant a bit further down the beach. They had hauled some of the solid mahogany furniture from the living room almost all the way down to the water's edge: the dining room table, five chairs, and a three-armed candelabra that might or might not be silver. Vadim had just shrugged when Bea asked him. He didn't know and clearly didn't care. Happy and indifferent.

They ate butter-fried carp with sweet potatoes, and Vadim plucked out the small white pearls of the carp's eyes and gave an enthusiastic lecture on ophthalmology before he plopped them in his white wine and emptied the glass with the triumphant expression of a magician. Diana had lit a cigarette and appeared to be far away in her own thoughts, but Bea was laughing, lighthearted and carefree, and leaned against Vincent with a bright smile.

Her skin was burning hot against his bare arms, and in a glimpse he caught Vadim giving him a complicit I-told-you-she-would-like-it kind of smile, which he returned. The beach and the dark sea wobbled around him, but it was a pleasant inebriation, the kind that only expanded time and made you want to smile at everything.

He placed a hand on Bea's thigh and carefully moved his fingers toward the robin's-egg blue fabric under the beach shawl, and she let him do it. Even spread her thighs a little. She wasn't quite sober either.

"The mosquitoes are coming to devour us," said Vadim and got up. "I think it's time to move inside."

He was right. In the gathering dusk, they could hear the whining hum of little wings.

They walked barefooted across the sands to the house, Bea right in front of Vincent, so he couldn't help staring at the swaying pertness of her ass. He suddenly felt dizzy and very far from home. It was the alcohol, perhaps, but also the sound of the ocean and the black starry sky above them.

THE HOUSE'S SECOND floor lounge was enormous, the floor made of cool, smoothly polished stone. Aerosmith was playing from the hidden speakers, Aerosmith and fucking Usher with "Nice & Slow," one long, rhythmic coupling. Vincent's entire body buzzed with alcohol and the heat that emanated from Bea's body. They sat next to each other in one of the deep sofas that faced the wall-to-wall picture windows. It was already getting so dark that the sea could only be made out as a slightly deeper blackness under the evening sky. Bea had pulled her slender and sun-browned feet up into the sofa and sat with her head on Vincent's shoulder. With his fingertips, he stroked her black hair and her exposed neck and throat.

Victor had gone to bed, and they could hear Vadim and Diana speaking quietly downstairs. Diana laughed, soft and low. Vincent imagined the battle that was unfolding between them. Vadim, dancing around Diana, trying to puncture her gravity. Diana rarely laughed for long or with all her heart, but when she did, Vadim looked like a poodle that had finally been rewarded after a furious round of prancing on its hind legs, playing dead, and wearing a tutu.

Being addicted to Diana's laughter was hard work.

It was quiet for a while. They must be kissing, thought Vincent, but then Diana must have disappeared alone into one of the room's downstairs, because a little later Vadim appeared by the stairs, a glass of rum in his left hand, and threw himself full length onto the sofa that stood kitty-corner to theirs. He saluted Vincent and Bea, and then looked out at the Pacific.

He suddenly looked tired, thought Vincent, like an actor when the makeup was removed and the lights in the studio turned off. That classic movie scene in front of the dressing-room mirror when all the ugliness and sorrow appears.

"I hope you'll be very happy," said Vadim and lifted his glass just precisely high enough that it turned into a toast. "Vincent, you're my best friend. Perhaps the only one. And I hope you'll be happy together. I envy you. You're so damn . . . I love you."

He sounded so serious and had adopted such a sad hangdog look that Vincent couldn't help laughing. The rum and white wine had not quite done him in yet. Besides, it was comical that Vadim would envy him anything at all. Here, of all places, where they were lying surrounded by the luxury that was Vadim's life.

"Stop laughing, cow face."

Vadim hurled a pillow at Vincent and hit him dead center so that the rum in Vincent's glass spilled and made a dark spot on the couch, but at least Vadim looked like himself again. There was light and laughter in the crooked gaze. The exhaustion was erased.

"I think I'm done for tonight," he said and got up. "I'll leave the house to you two lovebirds, if you think you can behave properly. No ruining the furniture."

He blinked at Bea, who smiled slowly and a bit absently. She had gotten some of the light sticky rum on her hands and unselfconsciously licked her fingers clean like a child.

Once Vadim had closed the door to his room behind him, they gazed at each other for a long moment.

"You should go to bed, Bea," said Vincent, getting somewhat shakily to his feet. "It's late."

She nodded, but remained sitting, looking up at him. Expectantly.

"Don't you want to kiss me at all?" she asked.

He backed away.

"Yes, are you crazy?" he said and again felt the burning sensation spread through his body. The half-erection, which had lurked all evening, the entire day with Bea, in fact, kicked off and became more insistent.

"But I think it's best if we don't. You know . . . We've had too much to drink."

"We're getting married soon," she said and took his hands. Pulled him down toward her. "I'd like to."

The last bit she whispered against his ear, and her scent broke something in him and made him sink down next to her. Let his hand slide up her thigh again. This time all the way up to the robin's-egg blue and further still. She moaned faintly and spread her legs, so he could slip a finger into the moist heat of her while he kissed her. He touched her, and she moved softly under his hand. Everything swam around him and inside him. They were supposed to wait. They had promised each other that they would wait. That she would be a virgin on their wedding night. It meant something to her, and she was drunk now.

Oh, God.

More than he was.

He was the one who needed to stop. He was the man who had to live up to his responsibility—everything his family and Bea expected from him. He should stop right now, but instead he pulled the ridiculous beach shawl off her and loosened the bikini top so he could look at her beautiful breasts, slightly lighter than her stomach and shoulders after the afternoon at the beach. Her nipples were large and dark against the light skin.

How could he stop now? Aerosmith had begun again, an urgent wail telling him not to fall asleep, not to close his eyes.

He pressed her down on to the couch with his entire weight and pulled off his swimming trunks; removed the robin's-egg blue scraps while Bea arched her back and turned her face into the shadow, so the tendons on her slender neck were taut and exposed. A slight almost inaudible sound escaped her. She drew him down and pushed his face against her shoulder and neck while he penetrated her with slow and infinite caution.

A door was opened somewhere in the huge house. Vincent heard and didn't hear. His body had taken over. Could not be stopped.

Bea had closed her eyes, but Vincent saw it. Saw him. Vadim, who for a brief moment stood in the half-open door. Then he slid away again, disappearing in the very instant that Vincent himself came in a long and painful shudder.

IT WAS AFTERNOON and really too hot to be in the sun when Vincent, Victor and Vadim sailed out from the beach in Vadim's little flat-bottomed speedboat the next day. The wind had freshened once they were clear of the cove, and the boat leaped and slapped against the waves like an animal squirming beneath them.

Vincent had never been a keen sailor, and after his complete and utter failure to master a surfboard that morning, he would have preferred to stay in the house with Bea. They had not talked about what had happened in the night. They had merely gotten up, searching awkwardly for their clothing, neither looking at the other. Later, there had been an almost equally awkward breakfast, and then the disastrous surf lesson on the beach in claustrophobically tight wet suits.

Victor had gone shopping at the market in the morning and had returned with chili, rice, garlic, mung beans, and coconut milk. He prepared lunch, which he served on the porch. He didn't like restaurant food, he said. It was too expensive and not good enough. Victor was in fact an excellent cook. They drank a couple of beers with the food, and Vincent finally managed to catch Bea's gaze and hold it until they both blushed and had to look down.

Afterward Diana had invited Bea along for a bit of sightseeing in the little resort town, which clearly bothered Vadim. He had been looking forward to seeing her pull on her wet suit again, he complained. Diana just laughed and teasingly tweaked the elastic on his white swim trunks.

"You'll have to manage without us," she said. "We need to buy glass beads and cockleshells. Bracelets. You know—girl things."

"Dear God," groaned Vadim dramatically and pulled her hard toward him. "You're killing me, girl. Stay here."

Diana kissed him and pulled free, and she and Bea went into

the house to change. Shortly afterward, the front door clicked, and they could see the girls walking side by side along the beach toward town, Diana with a cigarette in one slender hand. Their long hair fluttered in the wind.

"Then let's go diving," said Vadim definitively. "Hunting. Like real men do."

The diving equipment was stowed in a couple of boxes in the bottom of the boat. No oxygen or anything like that. That was too complicated, said Vadim. What they needed was some weights, a mask, flippers, and a harpoon. With a bit of luck they'd be able to spear their dinner down in the deep.

Vincent doubted that. He was a decent swimmer as a result of the many afternoons by the river at home, but he did not like to dive. He didn't like the water's pressure against his body and eardrums. It made him feel trapped.

Vadim steered the boat along the coast until they reached the shelter of the steep, forested slope. High above their heads dark green treetops leaned out across the water, and a couple of monkeys rustled among the branches, appearing and disappearing with an insulted cackling. The water was turquoise under the boat.

"How deep do you think it is?" asked Vadim.

He chucked the anchor overboard, and with a faint whir the chain began to disappear into the deep.

Vincent leaned over the railing and looked down. Despite the deepening blue under the fragmented surface he could clearly see the sandy bottom, with small tufts of coral and vegetation. A black-and-white sea snake swam past in perfect S-curves and disappeared in the deeper shadows underneath the cliff.

"Five meters, maybe a little more?" he volunteered.

Vadim began to rummage around in the diving gear in the boxes.

"It's almost nine meters deep," he said and smiled. "I've gone diving here a couple of times. It's a cool place. Lots of fish both close to the cliff and a little further out."

He pointed to a dark blue shadow which revealed the presence of a sandbank with yet more coral. Then he threw diving goggles and flippers into Victor's arms.

The big man smiled broadly and pulled a Coke out of the ice chest.

"I'll stay up here and watch the boat. That suits me."

"Wimps won't get any fish tonight," said Vadim and slapped his shoulder casually. "Why the hell won't you dive? It's against nature for a Filipino."

Victor shrugged. He was from Angeles, a few hundred kilometers north of Manila and far from the coast.

"I grew up in a rice paddy," he said with not even a tiny sign of apology, and as if that was a sufficient explanation. Then he moved to sit next to outboard of the little powerboat. His weight made the boat tip dangerously.

"Then it'll be you and me, Vincent," said Vadim and handed Vincent his equipment. Diving goggles, flippers and a belt with lead weights.

"Is this really necessary?" Victor had picked up one of the lead belts and weighed it in his hand.

Vadim looked at him with irritation.

"Yes, unless you have huge balls of steel. Who's the expert here, you or me? I wasn't aware you had done a lot of diving courses in that rice paddy if yours."

"No, but . . ."

"It gives you better balance in the water. And Vincent will descend faster. He'll need the extra time, he doesn't have as much experience as me."

A warm wind swept across the boat and ruffled the surface of the water faintly. Vincent had started to sweat a lot. The T-shirt he had pulled on to shield his already sunburned shoulders was almost soaked through with sweat.

"I can't dive nine meters," he said then. "I can barely hold my breath for nine seconds. If I can get down there at all, I won't have time to get up again."

"Don't worry." Vadim put an arm around Vincent's shoulder and smiled encouragingly. "I'll be down there, and I've done it lots of times. You don't even smoke. You'll be fine. Just two quick dives down to the bottom here and then we'll snorkel the reefs afterward. Catch a little dinner."

Vincent hesitated.

He didn't know much about diving, but nine meters couldn't be entirely without danger. He seemed to have heard that you didn't get the bends when you dived without oxygen, but a fast ascent from so great a depth could cause other problems. Blackouts. Or in his case, running out of time and air. God, he really hated diving.

"Come on. Do it for me." Vadim slapped him teasingly across the neck. "Have I ever asked you for anything before?"

There was a smile in his voice but deeper down Vincent thought he could hear something else, a kind of . . . desperation. The same desperation he heard in his mother's voice when she begged him to visit more often. *Come on, do it for me, for us. Show that you love me. And your father. And Mimi, who misses you. I'll make* kare-kare. *You never get that in Manila.*

He shook his head lightly and looked at Vadim, who was putting on the big, clumsy flippers with practiced moves. He himself sat stiffly and without moving, his bare feet immersed in the shallow water at the bottom of the motorboat.

"Can't we just snorkel?" he asked, but could immediately tell that Vadim thought he had said the wrong thing. His friend's eyes were narrow and focused on what he was doing, but the jaw muscles worked in his sun-browned face.

"You'll love it," he said. "It's the wildest high when you get down there. Better than drugs. Better than sex."

For a second he looked directly at Vincent and called forth an unwelcome flashback from the night before. The sensation in his body as he came, and saw Vadim standing like a shadow in the doorway.

Vincent lowered his gaze. Had the odd thought that this was the price that had to be paid because he had slept with Bea while Vadim had gone to bed alone. He had to prove his loyalty, just like those times when Vadim remained sitting in Cabana Club until five o'clock in the morning and Vincent had to stay there with him and match him drink for drink, though it made his innards heave.

"You're my only true friend," Vadim would say, drunk and crooked, with love pouring from his entire body. "A friend isn't there for the money, but because you'd do anything . . ." Here he would narrow his eyes and sniff. "Because you'd do *anything* for each other, right?"

"Okay," he muttered. "Let's do it then."

"Do you know how to equalize the pressure?" Vadim looked at him. His gaze was concentrated and inward looking.

"Yes, I think so."

"Good. Do it often. Don't wait until you feel the pressure."

Vadim sat on the edge of the boat with his back to the water. He pulled off one of his gold rings and held it out. The wide one that he wore on his thumb.

"An inheritance from my grandfather," he said. "His wedding ring. He used to wear it on his ring finger. American. He was as big as Victor."

Victor nodded approvingly and opened cola number two.

"Big men wear big jewelry."

"Yes, and that's what we are diving for," said Vadim.

He pulled his mask over his face, and it was impossible to read his expression when he held his hand out and let go of the ring right above the anchor line.

Vincent stared at him.

"Are you crazy?" he said. "It'll be impossible to find down there."

Vadim nodded.

"Yes, if we don't hurry. Sand moves quickly on the bottom. Hurry up and put on those weights or you'll have no chance to make it. Come on."

Vincent buckled the lead belt across his hips and fumbled with the plastic lock on the dog collar–like chain that was supposed to improve his balance in the water. It felt impossibly heavy.

Vadim nodded briefly, swung himself over the edge and slowly lowered himself into the water. His long, lean biceps rippled under his dark, sun-chafed skin. He inhaled deeply a couple of times, rolled forward and dove under the surface with powerful strokes. Then he began to pull himself downward on the anchor line. Vincent could see him as a vertical line in the water, heading straight for the bottom, his white swim trunks bright in the gradually darkening blue.

Vincent threw a quick look at Victor. His friend's face was stone calm. His sunglasses were pushed up on his forehead, and he had his hand on the boat's tiller.

"Don't look at me," he said, spreading his arms. "You and he are the ones who do the stupid stuff. I just come along. And . . . he's probably got it under control."

"You'll keep an eye on us, right?"

"Yes," said Victor. "But there's not much I can do if something goes wrong. Stay here. He'll come up again when he needs air."

How long had it been? Thirty seconds, a minute?

He could see Vadim swimming along the bottom. Calm, lazy movements of the flippers. He was so far down that he looked like a child.

Vincent tipped himself over the boat's railing, and the water closed around him with a fierceness that instinctively made him fight his way upward. Or try to. The lead belt was too heavy, and even though he worked with both arms and legs, he sank slowly but surely toward the bottom. He reminded himself that this was in fact the idea and turned so he could work with it rather than against it. Direction down. Stiff kicks. Sunlight from the real world above him formed luminous columns in the clear water.

He could already feel that he needed to breathe. His initial hopeless struggle to reach the surface had used his oxygen. He thought about taking just one deep breath, and about the fact that he couldn't. There was a pressure in his chest, and knowing he couldn't take that one breath only made it worse.

Think of something else. Find that fucking ring and reach the surface again.

He observed with a certain relief that his long fall was over. The bottom was right beneath him now. He could stretch out his hands and touch the sand around the small, sharp anchor and the line that went up to the boat high above them.

He turned over and caught sight of Vadim a little further away. He lay calmly, almost apathetically, above the sandy bottom and let his fingers run across it, making long, soft lines which were erased almost the second he drew them.

Vincent rolled over on his stomach and began to do the same. Every time he moved there was the sound of thunder in his ears. A couple of sizeable fish floated lazily past him. Blue-finned jacks and scorpion fish with empty, staring, flat eyes and mouths that opened and closed with hypnotic slowness.

How long could Vadim hold his breath? Two or three minutes, maybe more. He himself felt a massive pressure against his head and chest, but the initial panic had subsided.

He let his fingers glide through the sand. Felt warm water and small, fine grains under his fingertips and then, he could hardly believe it, something smooth and round that glimmered dully and got away from him when he first tried to grab it. Could he be that lucky on his first dive?

He let his hand run across the place again, but in his eagerness he stirred up a cloud of sand which swirled slowly in the warm water and for a moment made it impossible for him to orient himself. He felt . . . high. New fish glided by him, smaller this time, a school of golden, streamlined creatures that circled around him. The pressure in his chest grew and grew, but the sand was settling and had left the bottom a bit darker, so the bright ring could now be made out with the naked eye.

He reached out his hand, carefully this time, and had just placed the ring solidly on his own thumb when his chest gave an involuntary and cramp-like jerk, an attempt to breathe and even the pressure. He was just barely able to fight his body's intense impulse.

The world around him had turned a dusty grey. He had left the bottom and was surrounded by water on all sides now and in a brief confused and panicked moment he lost his sense of up and down. Then he saw Vadim's body floating in the sunlight above him—on his way up.

Vincent had stayed down too long.

His chest kicked again, and he instinctively reached his arms above his head and stretched toward the light. Lashed out with his arms and legs. But nothing happened. He stayed where he was, floating right above the bottom of the sea.

The lead belt, he thought. I have to get that belt off.

He fumbled with the buckle, which slipped under his soft and slippery fingers. Impossible to open. Fucking impossible. He hurt inside now, and someplace far, far down in his consciousness he began to cry. Because he was lost. Because he was going to die and would never see Bea again.

An enormous school of black-and-white-striped damsel fish danced around him now, and his chest gulped in a bit of salt water. He couldn't prevent it. Dark blotches began to creep across his vision. Then something hard and living hit his shoulder and knocked him backward the second before all light disappeared from the world.

"YOU'RE AN IDIOT. You know that, right?"

Vadim's voice and the blue sky. A boat that rocked beneath him, and a painful contraction in his abdomen which made him curl up and vomit. The taste of saltwater and stomach acid.

"Vincent?"

Victor's face slid in front of the blue sky. His gaze was serious, and he placed his fingers against Vincent's throat and counted his pulse beats quietly out loud with the sun surrounding his head like a halo. The light was so sharp that Vincent had to squint.

"It was Big V who got you up," said Vadim. He stood right behind Victor and fiddled with the diving gear. "What on earth were you doing, fumbling around down there on the bottom? You could have got yourself killed."

"The belt . . ." It hurt his throat to talk. Actually it hurt in his entire skull and also in his chest. "I couldn't get the belt off."

Vadim lifted his head and looked at him with a half smile.

"But you got the ring, my man. Well fought. Brothers in arms, eh!"

"We're not at war."

Victor's voice sounded cold and severe, unusually so.

Vincent closed his eyes and remained lying in the bottom of the boat, letting the sun bake his body while they drifted across the shallow part of the reef. Vadim jumped in with his harpoon and reappeared shortly afterward with two large silver-colored milkfish that still wriggled on the spear when he threw them down to Vincent on the bottom of the boat. The long, powerful tail fins flapped against the hull.

Vadim climbed out with the water dripping from his slippery body and his knee-length bathing trunks and then, as on a sudden impulse, he bent over Vincent and tousled his hair.

"I love you, man," he said darkly. "Never doubt it."

They sat silently on the way home across the darkening oil-smooth water.

"HELLO, NINA-GIRL."

He came in the door, hung his windbreaker on the hook, and then opened his arms as wide as he could, as if there had to be room not just for her but also for the rest of the world. His eyes were warm and happy. It was a good day.

"Daddy?" Her heart did an uncertain summersault, because she thought . . . there was something . . . wasn't he . . .

But her longing wiped away all reservations. She melted into an embrace that pushed both the fear of dying and the headache into the background. His hands were warm. He smelled a little of sweat and even more of freshly worked wood. He must have come directly from his shop class, the subject he liked to teach best of all. That was where he let loose and charmed even the most uncertain students into using a hammer and a plane with self-confidence and the joy of creation.

"What's wrong with you, little one?" he asked. "You look so sad."

"Where have you been?" she asked instead of answering. "I've missed you."

"Yes, but I'm here now. Didn't you think I'd come back?"

She clutched at his shirt, clenching her hands around fistfuls of soft material.

"I was afraid you wouldn't," she whispered. "Don't scare me like that again."

"Sweetheart. You know you can trust me. You won't get rid of me that easily." He laughed quietly and ruffled her hair with one hand without loosening his embrace.

Oh, to be so loved. To be held like this. To be safe like this.

"Our Father," he whispered into her hair. "Who art in heaven . . ."

A rush of sheer terror raced through her. She tore herself loose and stared up into his face. He smiled so the wrinkles around his eyes appeared. She wanted to ask him why he did it, why he was praying for her, he who had never so much as said grace before dinner through her entire childhood, but another voice broke in and made her sense of reality totter.

"Nina Borg?"

She opened her eyes with difficulty and felt a nauseating physical dislocation. Dream, it was a dream. There was no smell of fresh wood here, only disinfectant and bedpan pee. For a terrible, teetering moment she tried to hold on, but he was gone. The naked, raw loss hit her as if she had only just been told that he was dead. The loss and the fear, the terror she had felt . . . *Our Father.* Why? Her feelings were sloshing around chaotically, and she fumbled for some slight grip on reality.

"Yes," she said hoarsely. "What is it?"

"My name is Caroline Westmann. I'm a detective sergeant with the Mid-West Jutland Police. I wondered if I might speak with you?"

Nina lay motionless for a moment while she waited for her focus to improve. Detective sergeant? Head trauma. She had been hit on the head, they said. Assaulted.

"Okay," she said. "What do you want to know?"

She was young, the detective sergeant. Short, chestnut-brown hair, freckles and the charming hint of an overbite that had defied all attempts of overzealous orthodontists to correct it. An eager, alert gaze. Jeans and a vaguely nautical red-and-white-striped sweater.

"First and foremost, I'd like to know what happened."

Nina closed her eyes again. It was too hard to keep them open.

"I don't know," she said. "I remember absolutely nothing."

"You had been grocery shopping," persisted the detective sergeant. "In the Saint Mathias Mall. Do you remember that?"

Viborg. She was in Viborg again. Home again. Was that why her father appeared in her dream?

"More or less," she admitted. "I . . . we were out of milk. I was cooking. My mother is unfortunately seriously ill." The last part sounded stiff and wrong, as if it was an excuse she had fabricated herself for some teacher's note.

Stop it. She wasn't in school any longer. Teacher's note? *Damn it, Nina.* No one even wrote notes any longer; these days you used the school's intranet.

She tried to capture her floundering thoughts. Honestly, it was as if all rationality and capacity for concentration had leaked out of her along with the brain fluid they said she had lost.

"Nina's mother is being treated for breast cancer," Søren prompted from someplace in the room. "Nina is here to support her through the chemotherapy. Normally we live near Copenhagen."

We? Since when had she become a part of such an inclusive

and intimate plural? Anyone would think they cohabited . . . But she didn't protest. She was glad he was here.

"You had shopped at SuperBest, we could see from your groceries. And then you went down to the parking deck . . ."

Sounds and images returned stickily and reluctantly. The slam of a car door echoing between concrete walls. Small, greasy pools of oil and rainwater glinting in the fluorescent tube lights. The SuperBest bags held lean ground beef, peppers, and canned tomatoes, and she wondered whether they had onions or whether she should have bought some.

That was it. The film ended.

"I remember shopping," she said. "I remember that I went down in to the parking garage. But no more. There *is* no more."

The microsounds from Westmann's side of the bed took on a touch of resignation—a faint creaking from the frame of the visitor chair, an intake of breath that wasn't quite a sigh but still deeper than normal.

"You still had your wallet," said the detective sergeant. "But we couldn't find a cell phone. Could it have been stolen?"

"Maybe. No, wait—I was charging it. At the clinic where I work. I must have forgotten it. It's probably still there."

"Did you have anything else valuable with you?"

"I don't think so."

"Could there be a motive other than robbery?"

"How would I know?" she snarled. "I wasn't the one who did it."

A hand covered hers. Not the detective sergeant's; it was Søren, who was trying to rein in her antipathy. The first time they met each other, he had warned her that he had the power to put her in jail as a hostile witness if she didn't cooperate. How on earth had they gotten from that to the relationship they had now—whatever that might be?

The warmth from his hand created a fixed point, something she could respond to physically in the midst of her uncertainty and powerlessness. She slowly turned her own hand so that their palms met.

"I don't know," she said, a bit more politely. "I can't imagine any other reasons. It has to be random. Sometimes people are just attacked randomly, for no good reason. Aren't they?"

"Unfortunately, yes." Chair legs scraped against the floor, and Nina opened her eyes again. The detective sergeant had risen to her feet. "I'd like to come back when you are feeling a little better," said Caroline Westmann. "I hope that will be soon."

She left. Nina turned her head—this time without feeling as if it was falling off—and looked at Søren. He was tired. His shoulders slumped, his skin somehow fell more heavily around the bones of his face. She felt a sharp and unexpected tenderness, a desire to make everything all better. But at the heels of the tenderness came a renewed sense of loss and sorrow because you *couldn't* kiss away all the pain, no matter how long and how desperately you tried.

He had taken off his glasses and sat polishing them distractedly in the dark blue fabric of his T-shirt.

"Is it true you don't remember anything?" he asked. "Or was it just that you didn't feel like answering?"

"I have a fractured skull," she snapped. "I can't remember shit."

"Okay. Just asking."

The tears came suddenly and intensely, without giving her the chance to control them, and the longing opened in her like a hopeless abyss, a doomsday hole in the world that everything could disappear into. Her father was dead; he wasn't coming back. Dreams *lied*. A damned, corrosive lie that shook her more than the head trauma, the basal fracture and the leaking brain fluid could explain.

Søren handed her a paper napkin. Without saying a word, thank God.

THE FLOWERS ARRIVED an hour after Søren had left.

"Should I put them here?" asked the nursing assistant. "Or is the window ledge better?"

"This is fine," said Nina and quickly moved a newspaper and a glass to make room. "Who are they from?"

The NA smiled professionally. She was around fifty, grey-haired and steely, but in a friendly way.

"There was a card, I think," she said. "It must have fallen off when I put them in water . . . Just a moment, I'll find it."

She disappeared out of the room and Nina could hear her Crocs pattering down the hall. The bouquet was enormous, an explosion of waxen white calla lilies wrapped in pink tissue paper. They looked like something made out of marzipan and the heavy scent they emitted prompted a mixed association of florist, funeral parlor, and air freshener. Perhaps she should ask to have them placed in the window after all.

The NA came pattering back and handed her a small white card.

"I found it!" she said triumphantly. "I *knew* I had seen it . . ."

"Thank you," murmured Nina.

The card was, not surprisingly, from a local florist. *Viola. Bouquets for every occasion!* proclaimed one side of it, followed by an address and a phone number. On the other side a few words in English had been carefully typed: *His peace passeth understanding.*

There was no name. Nothing to indicate who the sender was.

His peace passeth understanding? It had to be biblical. Some sect that did missionary work in a slightly bizarre way? Like the Social Democrats and their red roses . . . but no. The sects stuck little pamphlets into people's hands, printed on cheap paper; they didn't shower them with elaborate bouquets. There had to be several hundred kroner's worth of flowers here. It made no sense. She stared hostilely at the white, wax-like petals surrounding each fat, yellow, incredibly genital-looking . . . what was it they were called? It wasn't just an overgrown stamen. Spadix. That was it. They couldn't be from Søren, could they? No, she decided. Not with that card.

It wasn't just the toilet air freshener effect that bothered her. She felt somehow invaded by those damned lilies and their Bible-quoting card.

Maybe they aren't for me at all.

The moment she had the thought, a rush of relief raced through her. No, of course they weren't. That was the explanation. No one who knew her at all would think to send *that* greeting.

She caught a glimpse of the aid through the open door and forgot that she wasn't really supposed to get out of bed alone yet—dizziness, the risk of falling, and so on.

"Hey," she shouted in a fairly controlled manner. "Wait a second . . . I think there's been a mistake."

The NA stopped and came back.

"A mistake?" she asked.

"Yes. Those can't be for me . . ."

"But they are," said the NA. "I accepted the delivery myself." Her tone suggested that this kind of mistake did not happen on her watch.

"Yes but . . . who from?"

"Didn't it say on the card?"

"No."

"There was a messenger," said the NA. "A young man, I don't think he spoke Danish. But he showed me a note with your name on it. Nina Borg. So there's no doubt."

"Give them to someone else," said Nina. "I . . . would prefer not to keep them."

"But why not? It's a beautiful bouquet. And so big . . ." There was a hint of disapproval in the NA's tone. A suggestion that she found Nina's behavior both peculiar and ungrateful. Nina didn't care.

"I'm allergic," she lied. "Put them in the common room if no one else wants them."

It helped to get them out of her sight, though the scent hung in the air for quite a while. She looked at the card one more time before crumpling it up. Peace? That was pretty much the last thing she felt.

HANNE BORG DID not look like a woman with one foot in the grave—and hopefully she wasn't, Søren quickly corrected himself. The short brown hair must be a wig, but you had to look closely to suspect it. Her eyes were some degrees lighter than Nina's, but had a little of the same intensity.

"Welcome," she said. "I'm actually *very* pleased that you'll be staying here while you are in Viborg."

In spite of her clearly sincere invitation, Søren had at first thought that he would prefer a hotel room. It felt fairly transgressive—of his own limits *and* Nina's—to move in with his "mother-in-law" without having met her before. But then he had remembered that there was a reason that Nina had gone home to Viborg. It was tough to go through chemotherapy like Hanne Borg's alone, and there was the added complication that Nina's mother didn't like to drive. If nothing else he could act as chauffeur and help with shopping and the like while they waited for Nina to be discharged.

"What a cozy place," he said, and meant it.

The house on Cherry Lane was part of a terraced estate from the fifties. Functional and well designed, red brick walls and tile roofs, with small, attractive, almost identical front yards, white doors and windows and a general air of being from before things went wrong. Inside, there were blond wood floors and kilim rugs, Danish Modern furniture and cheap bookshelves rubbing shoulders in eclectic harmony, piles of books and a multitude of pictures, ceramic vases and green plants.

"Is this where Nina grew up?"

"Partly," said Hanne Borg. "We moved here after Finn—Nina's father . . . after he died. It was cheaper, and I thought it would help to get away from . . . from the actual scene." She observed him as she said it, as if to measure how much he might know.

Søren knew perfectly well that Finn Christian Borg had committed suicide one September day in the eighties when Nina was twelve. But that was because it said so in one of the background files he had read and saved after their first meeting in the middle of an anti-terror case, and not because Nina had told him. Should he pretend he didn't know anything? To pretend ignorance was patently false but the opposite would make it appear that Nina had taken him further into her confidence than he had so far ventured.

"It can't have been easy," he said, as a form of compromise.

Hanne Borg smiled bitterly.

"No," she said. "It wasn't. Nina found him. But you probably know that."

"Oh . . . no, she . . . didn't tell me that."

"The old house had a bathroom in the basement. That's where he was, in the bathtub . . . For a child to see something like that . . . it's not something you get over in a hurry."

It seemed to him that there was a kind of warning in her tone—perhaps an attempt to ensure that he knew what he was getting into?

"No, I understand," he just said. "It's pretty remarkable that she . . . functions so well in a crisis now." *Terrifyingly effective* was the description that occurred to him. He would never forget the expression on her face when she rammed the knife in between his fourth and fifth rib.

"Oh, yes," said Hanne Borg. "She's excellent in a crisis."

That was all she said, but Søren didn't need glasses to read the subtext: it was life between the crises that was a challenge for Hanne's daughter.

That was probably his own Achilles heel as well. He certainly had not excelled when it came to creating a life beyond the stresses of his job. He felt he was at his best at work—his sharpest and most alive. Or . . . that was the way it had been.

"Would you like a cup of coffee?"

He pushed aside the thought of Torben and his damned sick leave and checked his watch.

"Yes, thank you, a quick cup," he said. "I have a meeting at the police station in an hour or so."

"About Nina?"

"Yes. I'd like to see if I can help the investigation along a bit. It would be nice if we could find the assailant."

CAROLINE WESTMANN WAS perhaps not exactly happy to see Søren, but she took it well.

"How is your friend?" she asked.

"Making progress," he said. "She'll probably be able to go home in a few days."

"She still doesn't remember anything about the attack?"

"No, unfortunately not."

"Ah, well. Can't be helped, I suppose."

"In some cases memory returns with time," he said. "I'm just not sure we have that time."

She waved in the direction of her colleague's empty chair, and he sat down. The office was so newly renovated that you could still smell the paint, and the bulletin boards had not yet taken on the usual patina of old agendas, memos, newspaper clippings and family photos.

"Any particular reason for this urgency?" she asked.

"I took the liberty of calling a coroner I know." Søren fished a folder out of the weekend bag that still contained everything he had managed to bring from Copenhagen. "Viborg Hospital was kind enough to forward her records, X-rays, scans, and so on."

Caroline Westmann raised one eyebrow.

"And?" she said.

"I wanted to determine the intention of the blow—was it just to pacify, or was this, in fact, an attempt to kill. The doctors in Viborg were somewhat cautious about offering an opinion."

"But your friend the coroner wasn't?" There was a clear irony in Westmann's tone.

"Oh, yes, the usual reservations. But . . ."

"But what?"

He pushed the folder across the table to her. Written conclusions, he had learned in the course of a long career, simply carried more weight than oral summations.

"The first blow would have been more than sufficient to make the victim unable to fight back. And the second blow *could* have killed her. If there had been just slightly more power behind it, if the angle had been a bit different . . ."

"I can guess where you're going with this," said Caroline Westmann. "But for now we're calling it aggravated assault, not attempted murder."

"Why?"

"Because the victim's life—according to the doctors—was not in immediate danger."

"She has a fractured skull!"

"I can only repeat what Viborg Hospital said. Neither of the blows were struck with what they would describe as 'deadly force.'"

She hadn't opened the folder. Søren fought an urge to do it for her, to force her to read the words—even though most of them were his.

"If the angle had been different . . ." he began.

"Children who grab playmates by the neck while fooling around in the school yard can put their lives at risk," she said. "That doesn't mean that they intend to kill each other."

"He hit her in the head with an iron bar. Twice! Are you suggesting he was just being playful?"

His tone had become as corrosive as it did on the occasions when had reason to call one of his people out for carelessness of the kind that *could* put lives in danger. He couldn't quite help himself, and he saw her react—because he was older, because he was of higher rank.

"No, okay, poor example," she said. "But it is really hard to say precisely when something stops being simple violence and becomes deadly force—particularly when the victim does in fact survive. You know the fine points of the law at least as well as I do."

"And it's a question of resources," he said.

"Yes, frankly, it is—a challenge with which you are also familiar!"

She looked at him with a hint of defiance, and he reminded himself that he still wanted to keep what access he had to her information. If he made her lose all sympathy for him and for Nina's case, it would be the easiest thing in the world for her to simply refuse to speak with him. He had no professional role whatsoever in her investigation, folder or no folder.

"Any news about the car?" he asked mildly.

Her shoulders relaxed a bit—she didn't like being in conflict with him, he noted. Good. He might be able to use that later.

"It was found in the parking lot behind a shopping center this morning. He had set fire to it, but the night watchman saw the flames and was able to put out the fire with a foam extinguisher before it burned altogether." She sighed. "We probably shouldn't count on finding too many DNA traces there, though."

"Any witnesses?"

She shook her head.

"It's on the outskirts of town and quite deserted after closing hours. Not a soul except the watchman and his German shepherd. But he thought he heard a car drive off—he described the sound of the engine as 'sports car–like.'"

"That doesn't give you much to work with," Søren growled.

"No. I really hope your girlfriend recovers enough to give us a lead."

Søren nodded slowly.

"So do I," he said.

NINA CONSIDERED THE lunch tray with an acute lack of enthusiasm. According to the menu that had been circulated, it was "oriental veal casserole with mashed potatoes and a symphony of seasonal vegetables," but she didn't think there was anything remotely orchestral about the spoonful of defrosted supermarket greens.

"Would you like some?" she asked her mother.

"No, thank you." Hanne Borg rummaged around in her bag and handed a cell phone to her. It was Nina's own Nokia. "Here. Daniela dropped by with it yesterday."

Daniela was one of the secretaries at the clinic. She lived not far from the house on Cherry Lane.

"Thank you." Nina put it in the night table drawer. Then she set aside to barely sampled lunch tray.

"Are you allowed to get out of bed?" her mother asked.

"Yes. As of today. They'd like me to move around a little now, in fact. The risk of thrombosis and all that."

"Why don't we go into the lounge and have a cup of coffee instead? I brought you one of my old robes."

There wasn't a soul in the lounge—most people were in their rooms, having their lunch. On the corner table stood that damned vulgar bouquet, spreading its cloying soap-like scent. Nina decisively turned her back on it, liberated a thermos from the rolling cart, and sat down by the large window facing the park. It was a grey, blustery day, but the Japanese maples flamed bright yellow and scarlet against the darker backdrop of the evergreen hedges, giving Nina a violent attack of indoor claustrophobia. She looked with envy at the lucky visitor seated on one of the lime-green benches across from the main entrance. A greenish-brown parka with a fur-lined hood made it impossible to determine whether it was a man or a woman, at least from up here. Was it already so cold that you needed polar equipment?

Nina poured coffee into two white institutional cups.

"It says 'patients only,'" her mother pointed out and with a flip of her finger indicated the Dymo strip that adorned both the thermos and its lid.

"You're a patient too," said Nina.

Her mother gave a small snort.

"Yes, I suppose I am."

"What did they say?" Her mother had come straight from a checkup in oncology.

"That I'm well enough to receive the next dose of poison."

"Good."

"Yes, I suppose so. All things considered."

Silence descended between them, heavy and brooding. Nina freely admitted that she was no expert in small talk, but her mother was usually better at it.

"What's wrong?" she finally asked.

Her mother raised her head. The wig looked so much like her own hair that it was only the unnaturally well-coiffed look that gave the game away. That and the fact that Hanne Borg had applied a bit more makeup than usual. Camouflage. Don't show weakness!

"You've got children, Nina," said her mother at last.

Nina just barely stopped the sarcastic *I know that* that was on her lips.

"What do you mean?" she asked.

"I think you know."

"No. Not really."

"Ida and Anton are coming tomorrow."

"Half-term break." Oh God, she actually *had* managed to forget. She *was* a bad mother. "With a bit of luck I'll be able to go home tomorrow," she said quickly, "or at the latest, the day after. Can you manage for that long?"

"That's not the issue."

"What do you mean then? I'm sorry if I'm a bit slow, but that can happen when someone cracks your skull." *Stupid.* Stupid, stupid, stupid comment, she knew it as soon as she'd said it.

"Nina. Do you want your sixteen-year-old daughter to ask herself why she never meant enough to her mother for you to *stop* all of that? And Anton. Anton is only nine. Do you really want to create an abyss in his life to match your own?"

"Mom!" The outburst was everything she had hoped it wouldn't be—hurt, accusing, shaky, and on the verge of tears.

"I'm sorry, sweetheart. But sooner or later you have to realize that it can't go on."

"It wasn't me . . . I didn't do a damn thing to deserve—"

"No. Not directly. Not this time. But Nina, it's no more than . . . what is it, five months? . . . since the last time you ran out on them."

"I didn't run!"

It wasn't fair. No way was that fair. She had *tried*. The entire vacation had been an attempt to see if they could make it work again, she and Morten and the kids. Morten had a conference in Manila—the Sixth Annual Offshore Oil and Gas Conference in the polished and globalized SMX Convention Center, very exciting. They'd had a week's beach vacation at a resort before the conference began, and the second week they stayed with one of Morten's business connections in a gilded, middle-class ghetto about twenty-five kilometers from the polluted congestion of the city proper, with a pool and palm trees and a housekeeper—sweet, motherly Estelle, who had fallen for Anton's blond charm within seconds.

"What would you call it then? Morten said you were gone from dawn to dusk for four days straight."

"Three. It was only three! Mom, there was an accident. A terrible one. There were so many dead and wounded, and they had no idea . . . They needed qualified people. Did you expect me to sit and twiddle my thumbs by the pool while people were dying around me?"

"Nina-girl, you *can't* save the entire—"

"*Don't call me that!*" Nice. Now she had shot out of her chair and stood with two fists floating somewhere near chin level, like a boxer with his dukes up. Her head was pounding, and she forced herself to lower her hands and breathe more calmly.

Her mother had not twitched an eyelid. She merely sat there sipping the patients-only coffee, wearing her wig and chemo camouflage, and considered Nina with a relentless and unshakable Mom-gaze.

"Nina. You have two children who are afraid of losing you, and you need to deal with that, whether you want to or not."

She had no defense. She couldn't deny it. But she really *had* tried. She had turned down several offers for overseas work; she had even quit her job at the refugee center. She no longer used her free time to help illegal immigrants who didn't dare approach the normal healthcare system. There was a clinic now where they could receive help anonymously, she had told herself sternly. She had started therapy. What more did they want? Yes, from a narrow Danish nuclear family point of view, it had been idiotic to volunteer that day in Manila. But it had happened less than five kilometers from that fucking swimming pool, and Estelle had been frantic because she had a little sister who lived in one of the apartment buildings that had collapsed. Nina hadn't exactly sought it out.

"Don't you dare get between me and my children," she finally said. "Just stay out of it! Just how brilliant were *you* as a mother? On a scale of one to ten?"

She saw the sting go in. Hanne Borg froze for the briefest of seconds and appeared unable to reply.

FIVE MINUTES LATER Nina regretted it, of course. She usually did. It was so easy to think good, loving thoughts about her mother from a distance; it was the hand-to-hand combat that did her in. She stood at the window and watched Hanne Borg leave the hospital and walk through the park toward the visitor's parking lot in the gathering autumn gloom. She was leaning into the wind, walking more slowly than usual. Not tottering, exactly, but without her usual stubborn energy. Damn it. Exactly how rotten a person did you have to be to take out your own frustrations on your cancer-stricken mother?

The parka-clad person on the bench got up—as soon as he moved, she could see that it was a man—and raised his hands to his face in a gesture that only made sense when Nina saw the tiny burst of light from a photographic flash. Then he followed Hanne Borg's stooping figure.

Nina's heart jumped, and she dug frantically in the robe pocket for her cell phone before she remembered that it was in her room. She sprinted down the hall as fast as her newly upright legs permitted, tore open the drawer and had to fiddle her way through the entire "on" procedure, pin code and everything, before she could call her mother's number.

"Mom!"

"Yes?" The wind was whistling and scratching in the phone,

but Hanne Borg's voice sounded calm and normal and slightly annoyed.

"Is . . . is someone following you?"

"Following me?" her mother repeated. "Why on earth would you think that?"

"A man. A man in a green-and-brown coat, kind of camouflage colored."

"He just walked past me," said Hanne Borg. "Nina, what's wrong? *Are* you mixed up in something?"

"No," said Nina. "I'm not. But . . . I saw him through the window. He took a picture of you and then he followed you!"

"He was probably just going the same way! He's gone now, Nina. You're getting yourself worked up over nothing."

"He took a picture of you."

"No, he didn't. He took a picture of the beautiful maple tree. Nina, stop it."

Only now did it occur to Nina that her panic didn't have any obvious or rational basis. The realization didn't make much of a difference to the alarm level in her traumatized nervous system.

"I'll call Søren," she said.

"You don't need to. He's already here; I can see the car."

"Then let me talk to him!"

It took forever, she thought, before she could hear a car door open and her mother's voice explaining.

". . . thinks she saw a man take a picture of me . . . you'd better . . ."

And then finally Søren.

"What did he look like?" he just said. Totally calm. Without offering doubting questions or accusations. Her body reacted to his voice with a mixture of endorphins and warmth, and the relief made her legs tremble.

"I couldn't see much more than the coat. He had the hood up, one of those fur-edged parka hoods . . ." she explained as precisely as she was able.

"Could you say how tall he was?"

"Not really. Taller than my mother, but . . ."

"Okay. Did he take more than one picture?"

"I only saw one flash, but I don't know if he took any without flash."

"And he was alone?"

"Yes."

She heard the car door slam, an engine starting.

"Nina, I'm going to drive your mother home now. I can't see him anywhere, and I think he's left the area. I'll mention this to Caroline Westmann when I speak with her the next time, but . . ."

"But she'll think I'm a paranoid trauma case who sees ghosts in the middle of the day." Nina had no trouble finishing the sentence for him.

"Maybe not quite," he said. "But there's not much to go on, and it *could* be a coincidence."

If he had tried to minimize it, she would probably have insisted. But she could hear that he was taking her seriously, and it calmed her unease. He was a professional, she told herself. He knew how to evaluate a risk.

"Søren," she said.

"Yes?"

"*Am* I just paranoid? Because of the blow to the head and so on . . ."

"I don't have sufficient evidence to say. There might well be a connection. We don't know why you were attacked, and we don't know whether there are individuals who continue to have hostile intentions—and might therefore possess a motive for obtaining knowledge about you and people close to you."

Hostile intentions. It should probably have alarmed her even more to hear him present that possibility, but paradoxically her pulse dropped a further few beats. Maybe it was just the relief at dragging the ghosts into the light.

"You don't think it was a random robbery?"

"I prefer to take my precautions," he said, still completely neutral, as if they were discussing the weather forecast. "And that's why you can't leave the hospital until I come to get you. Not even to go across to the newsstand or the like. Can we agree on that?"

He wasn't asking casually. He had previously given her security instructions only to have them point-blank ignored.

This time it was different. This time the target was not another human being whom she felt called to protect. If there *was* a target at all, it was her. It was an unusual and paralyzing sensation.

"Okay," she said because he was waiting for an answer.

"I mean it."

"Yes," she said. "So do I."

THE PHILIPPINES, THREE YEARS EARLIER

HE REGRETTED IT as soon as they were in Diana's car on their way to Las Pinas City, but especially when she parked the car and they got out. All three of them.

Vincent, Victor, and Diana.

A very small and badly equipped army on its way to fight . . . poverty. Nothing less. Diana had made it clear to them both that they had a responsibility, as medical students, as Filipinos, as Christians, and as human beings. Perhaps they could not relieve the suffering of the millions of poor on their own, but they could damn well—and here she had cursed—at least respect their fellow human beings enough to look them in the eye, and not just turn their backs on the whole shitty mess.

Vadim couldn't come. Obligatory family dinner. Something about his father's candidacy for the mayor's office of Manila. Business and politics were the same thing in the Philippines, Vadim said. Diana had given him a disapproving look, of the kind that made him curl up completely. Diana and Vadim's father were clearly a rock and a hard place to be caught between.

"But you two," said Diana and placed her beautiful, soft arms around Victor and Vincent. "You can come. Then I'll show you the clinic where I work on the weekends."

They had left at six in the morning to avoid the worst of the heat and traffic, and now they were standing here on the edge of chaos. A wall of low tin shacks, plastic tarps, crumbling brickwork, laundry on clotheslines, garbage, cables, and all-pervasive mud lay in front of them. The way into the shantytown was a series of claustrophobically narrow alleyways penetrating ever deeper into the whole stinking mess.

Vincent had never been this close to the slums.

He had seen beggars in the street, of course, and the squatters on the sidewalk in front of crumbling houses in Manila, but this was different. This was . . . hell. The final station for those who hadn't managed to take off their lead belts and rise to the surface.

"Intense, right?"

Diana looked as if she had read his thoughts.

"All these shacks, or rather the scraps of ground they are sitting on, are owned by middle-class or rich families. It's good business to rent them out. Did you know that?"

He shook his head.

"My father owns a strip all the way down by Manila Bay," said Diana. "It's his finest property, as he says. My jeans are paid for by these people."

She had a cigarette in her hand. She almost always did. She had once said that her father didn't like her smoking. Vincent felt fairly certain that this was why she did. Now she marched with determination among the tin shacks, zigzagged in a familiar fashion around naked children playing; old, crook-backed women; squatting men in shorts and worn flip flops; and laundry that hung like colorful garlands in the midst of all the grey and brown.

It had rained yesterday evening and even more during the night, and a fat, yellowish stream had carved a path between the houses and was oozing sluggishly toward the bay. It smelled of human excrement, and the air hung in the small passages between the houses, heavy, wet and stagnant. Vincent and Victor followed Diana as best they could. Twice Vincent almost crashed into children who were playing between the houses and darted out in front of him like small, quick-footed animals. An old toothless man sat in a doorway guarding a wicker cage filled with downy chickens that had been dyed red and purple and green. He raised the birds toward them as they walked by.

"For your children," he said and grinned encouragingly. "For the little children. Or for a funeral?"

A woman was lying on a worn couch behind him, fanning herself with a piece of cardboard. Further on, a couple of teenage boys were hanging out by a small shop window from which dried fruit, water, rice, and cola was sold.

"Here we are," said Diana and pointed at a hut that, like most of the others, was cobbled together from sheets of corrugated steel; this one, at least, had been painted at some point in recent memory. White with a red cross on one wall. Diana unlocked the solid padlock and ushered them in.

There was an examination couch. Shelves with bandages and medicine. Mostly over-the-counter stuff, pain-relief and such, but also a little penicillin and some birth control pills. The refrigerator that stood right next to the couch contained tetanus vaccine, said Diana. That was all she had been able to get ahold of this time around.

"Make yourselves a cup of coffee."

She handed them the instant coffee and cups from a cabinet and began to arrange her things. Her ponytail swung energetically while she worked.

Vincent cautiously ran a hand over the packages with bandages and antibacterial wipes.

"How long have you been doing this?"

"I started a year ago. It's the Young Christian Diamond project—they pay for the rent and most of the supplies, and I come here two days a week to put Band-Aids on lacerated feet, vaccinate when we have any vaccines, or to sew a few minor cuts and things like that. A couple of people from the tenth semester are also part of it. And a nurse from the General Hospital."

She looked around with a satisfied glint in her eye.

"Sometimes kids come all the way from the dump. They have eczema and asthma and infections. I can't do much about the asthma. But the rest . . . I do have creams. Cortisone and antibiotics."

"And birth control? Aren't you afraid of being attacked by the devout?"

Diana shrugged defiantly.

"People here are fairly pragmatic when it comes to that kind of thing. Kids are starving. That's an argument that the pope can't really refute. But I don't have enough. I only give them out to very young girls and mothers who have already had four children. In the accounts I call them iron tablets."

Victor nodded and Vincent knew that helping out here was was a dream scenario for his huge friend. He still spoke with a heavy peasant accent from Angeles and up-country, and in spite of his top grades he was often clearly uncomfortable among the wealthier students. More so than Vincent. Here, fumbling with the ramshackle clinic's electric kettle, his shoulders relaxed and he was visibly more at home.

Vincent, on the other hand, felt on edge. Poverty made him uncomfortable. It made everything ugly. Even the people who lived in it. The smell was so ripe it made nausea rise in his throat and caused him to break out into a cold sweat so that he had to sit down on the chair next to the refrigerator. He wondered if his mother and father ever thought about the fact that the profession they had so carefully chosen for him would involve him sticking his fingers up grown men's rectums, examining warts and cysts and bloody eczema in the groin. Seeing people in pain and with open cuts on their arms and legs. He doubted it. Like himself, they must have had a picture in their heads of doctors as they looked in the ads for Manila's many private clinics. White-coated, perfectly poised men and women on polished marble floors. Respectable people. People whom it was difficult to connect with a skin cancer that had completely eaten away the bridge of some poor guy's nose and was on its way up into the eye socket.

No, he didn't have the stomach for it. He would have to do something with children. Their bodies were smooth and free of defects, none of the hairiness and powerful body odors of adults. Pediatrics, or surgery in cool and sterile surroundings. Organs that were cut free and placed on steel trays, so all you could smell was iron and rubbing alcohol.

He closed his eyes for a moment and tried to envision this enchanted future. Saw himself emerging from a shiny white hospital, with his little patients waving and smiling from the ward's windows high above, no trace of any but the vaguest ailments showing in their glowing faces. Outside the sun was shining, and the leaves on the trees had fiery fall colors, like in a film from New York. Central Park.

Diana's voice brought him back to his foul-smelling reality.

"If you'll receive the first ones who show up, I'll go talk to the guy who watches the house when I'm not here. I'll be back in ten minutes."

She strolled out the door. Shorts, flip-flops and a yellow T-shirt. No makeup. But even without the upper-class trappings she emitted an enviable air of calm authority. She was a woman with a mission and the ability to carry it out.

Vincent had trouble imagining cozy family dinners with her and her slum-owning father. On the other hand, that same father was the one who was paying for her education, so maybe even Diana had to shut up once in a while.

Victor sank down onto a white plastic stool and looked around with a calm smile.

"This, Vincent. This is the life. This is what I want to do, I think." He straightened the pill boxes in the cabinet a bit. "Those clinics where everything is so polished and shiny . . . where the rich go. I don't think I could stand it."

I could, thought Vincent. But not out loud.

"But what about money?" he said instead. "Your education costs a fortune."

"I'm still free," said Victor. "My uncle doesn't expect me to pay back the money. Not even to take care of Mom and Dad. He'll take care of them, he says. We're a small family."

Victor had had the incredible luck to be sponsored by a

childless uncle in Switzerland. First through private school, and then seven years of medical school with all expenses paid. Because, as his uncle said, he was a smart boy with a good heart.

"You're lucky," mumbled Vincent, and meant it.

"You are too. Family can be a good thing too, right? They take care of you, and you take care of them. That's how it should be."

Victor slapped him in a friendly way—the rare audience with the silent peasant boy was clearly finished.

A scream outside sliced the humid air into a thousand slivers.

Vincent had never heard anyone scream in that way; he couldn't even tell whether it was a man or a woman. It sounded most of all like an animal. The scream slowly grew fainter and faded away, but only for a moment. Then it began again, and this time Vincent felt sure that it was a man. It had become a long, deep, and desperate roar.

Excited voices could be heard outside the clinic, and Vincent and Victor barely had time to get up before a man stumbled through the door. He stank of alcohol. That was the first thing that Vincent noted. Only afterward did the visual details start to sink in. The man was small, and his dirty white T-shirt hung flatly over a bony chest. In his arms he cradled an infant who was barely more than six months old. Its arms hung limply and unnaturally from the half-naked body.

"Take him."

The man handed the boy toward Victor, who took the child without hesitation, placed him on the examination couch, and carefully checked his pulse and breathing. Vincent could immediately see what Victor was thinking.

The child was dead.

But for some reason, perhaps out of respect for the man who had begun to moan and cry convulsively, Victor nonetheless bent over the infant and rhythmically squeezed the boy's chest. Tried to blow air into the nonfunctioning lungs. The tiny ribs, sharply drawn under the skin, rose and sank with each of Victor's attempts, but as soon as he stopped to return to the cardiac massage, any motion ceased.

A little group of curious bystanders had gathered in the doorway and angrily commented on the proceedings.

"Why don't they do something?"

"Who's the father?"

"He's soused. Probably just came home from the bar and strangled the whole family."

Vincent observed the man who was presumably the child's father. His tears had drawn pale lines down the dirty face. He might have worked a night shift somewhere, but had clearly had a beer on the way home. Probably more. His gaze roamed desperately over Victor and the child to finally settle on Vincent.

"There's my wife too," he said. Then he roared again. "You need to help my wife and daughter at home. They're dead. Someone killed them."

Vincent felt the eyes on him. Something was expected of him. He didn't know what it was. When was Diana coming back? Victor, who in spite of his steady work with the baby had been able to follow events, turned to look at him too, and Vincent knew that Victor could see it. His paralysis. His complete uselessness. And yet Victor's look was warm and encouraging.

"Go see what happened," he said. "Diana and I will come as

quickly as we can. Just stay calm." The man grabbed Vincent's T-shirt and pulled him close. His alcohol-laced breath was warm and pungent.

"Help," he gasped. "Help me."

Trailing a tail of neighbors, Vincent followed the man down the alley at a stumbling run, past a few dilapidated shacks, until he ducked into a crudely but solidly built brick house with a tin roof and a window that was closed with sturdy, peeling shutters. The door was wide open, and in the gloom Vincent could make out three mattresses. Two figures lay curled up as if they were sleeping.

The man began to scream again.

"I can't wake them. They're not waking up."

Vincent's nausea returned. The one he always got in response to strong smells. It was hot in the slums. There was no air conditioning here to bring relief, day or night. Dead people and animals began to smell after just a few hours, and the distance between life and decomposition was short. The two people lying on the mattresses had already begun to give off a faint sweet stench.

Vincent remained standing in the doorway as if turned to stone. Just stood there and stared until a scented angel gently nudged him aside and pushed her way past him into the house. Diana.

She checked the girl first for signs of life.

She must have been about six years old. Her hair was tangled, its neat bedtime braid now frizzy and untidy. For some reason that was what Vincent focused on. The delicate childish skull, and the way the hair was flattened where her head had come to rest on the pillow as she fell asleep. Diana held the girl's wrist with an inward-looking, concentrated expression. Then she let go and moved to the woman lying next to the child. As Diana rolled her on to her side, he caught a glimpse of a smooth and peaceful face.

Diana got up and kicked angrily at a foil tray which had been placed directly on the earthen floor. Ash and half-burned pieces of charcoal scattered across the packed dirt. A few embers flared briefly before subsiding completely.

"They're dead," she said to the man. A hand placed calmingly on his shoulder. The whites of his wide-open eyes shone in the gloom. "You have to arrange for embalming and *lamay* as fast as possible. They've already lain here for several hours."

"But we just got here," he said, confused. "We just moved in. I sold our land . . ."

The sentence hung unfinished in the air, while Diana turned on her heel and started to leave.

"I'm sorry," she said. "If you need to talk about the accident, you're welcome at the clinic another day."

Vincent followed her through a flock of curious bystanders and back to the clinic.

"Peasants," said Diana. "It happens now and then."

"What happens? They just die?"

"You could say that." Diana searched her shorts pocket for a cigarette. Lit it and stepped across a pair of emaciated cats and a muddy puddle. "It rained last night when she was making dinner. It was tough to light a fire outside. Where they come from, they probably had a hut wowen from bamboo, possibly on stilts. Lots of natural ventilation. If it rained, they could light their charcoal fire inside and stay dry. But here . . . the poor wretches apparently bought the only halfway decent house in all of Las Pinas City, and she didn't put out the coals properly."

"Carbon monoxide poisoning?"

Vincent took a deep breath.

"Yes," said Diana. "Still, there are worse ways. You just fall asleep and don't wake up. As deaths go, it doesn't get much better."

She took a long and deep drag on her cigarette, and rubbed her eyes quickly with the heel of her free hand

"Come on," she said. "Want to hand out some birth control pills?"

"STAY HERE. STAY inside. I'll get the car."

Søren left her by the main entrance and ran off with a newspaper over his head in the direction of the parking lot.

The rain trickled across the asphalt in little runnels, dragging the fallen leaves toward the sewer grate. The dark-brown walls of the hospital were covered by considerable amounts of ivy, but the flaming fall glory was fading now. *Like so much else*, thought Nina grimly. But at least she was out. Discharged, released, free. With instructions to take it easy and ample warnings about the increased risk of meningitis.

She stood in the doorway because she could barely stand to be inside any longer. It was amazing to breathe in air that didn't come from a ventilation system, and she filled her lungs and tried not to think about anything else. There were lots of people around her: staff, visitors, patients. This wasn't a deserted parking garage, and no one was lurking in the shadows with an iron bar . . .

Ida and Anton were waiting at their grandmother's. The Viborg visit had been in the cards since forever. Nina knew that Morten had planned a trip for himself, and had a strong suspicion that this holiday involved some female she had not yet met. Still, he had come close to canceling both.

"You're not doing it again," he had said. "You're not exposing them to that kind of thing one more time."

There were times when she missed Morten terribly. His body, which knew hers so well. His love for the children. His care, his warmth, his humor. The odd-ball music he had introduced her to, his complete inability to lose a board game without pouting like a five-year-old, the way he could reach Ida when she couldn't. But whether she liked it or not—and she *didn't* like it—she didn't see much of that Morten these days. It was as if he was constantly looking for confirmation that he had made the right decision. Her role as the irresponsible adrenaline-junkie seemed set in concrete, and he in turn became the cranky and corrective supervisor. She seriously doubted they would ever be one of those harmonious ex-couples who were each other's best friends.

"Then you'll just have to do without," she muttered under her breath. If they could prevent it from affecting the children, that had to be enough. Life was a bitch, and you just had to get on with it.

The cell phone growled and shuddered in her pocket. It wasn't a text, it was just an annoying alarm she had not yet figured out how to turn off—a synthetic "plop" that sounded every time one of her so-called "close friends" updated their Facebook status. But the update was from Ida, so she read it at once.

Visiting my sweet grandmother. ♥ ♥ ♥

Three pink hearts? From *Ida*? Whose favorite T-shirt was still the one that said *I'm only wearing black until they invent something darker*? What on earth was going on?

She scrolled down to see if there was more of the same, but the rest were the usual world-weary observations.

Nina knew that several psychological experts counseled parents against spying on their children on Facebook. She didn't care. After the divorce, she had thrown inhibitions like that to the wind—how else was she supposed to keep tabs on anything? Morten only told her the absolute minimum, and Ida had never been particularly informative, even before the split. Nina had been quite relieved that her friend request had been accepted . . .

In just a few weeks, she had become surprisingly more knowledgeable about her daughter's friends, activities and values. She'd already known about the roller hockey club and Ida's musical taste, which was still for the most part, but not exclusively, the doomsday rock that used to make the walls of the apartment on Østerbro vibrate. But many of the faces in the girlfriend pictures were new, and who the heck was this "Daniel" clutching a bouquet of long-stemmed birthday roses with a besotted and self-conscious expression on his smooth young high school face? A classmate, maybe? Ida had, to Nina's great surprise, applied for acceptance at Sankt Annæ, an institution known for its high standards and musical tradition, and now went to school with kids—no, young people, Nina corrected herself—from Copenhagen's cultural elite. A dawning social consciousness showed itself in the form of a "NO to Racism!" campaign and membership of more than one environmental group. Nina was not dissatisfied.

She peered into the rain. Still no Søren. How far away had he had to park? The parking conditions around the old hospital were of course completely inadequate, but still . . .

She checked her own page. Someone had posted something. She felt a freezing jolt in her stomach when she saw what it was. A biblical quote, and in English.

Fat pale lilies that smelled like a funeral. Those damned flowers popped into her head again. This quote was a bit longer:

> "*. . . they that wait upon the LORD shall renew their strength; they shall mount up with wings as eagles; they shall run, and not be weary; and they shall walk, and not faint.*" Isaiah 40:29-31. May the Lord keep you strong in your hope of Heaven. Victor.

Victor?

A second passed before it dawned on her. Victor from Manila. She remembered him mostly as a big, competent and good-natured bear of a man, a head taller than the other Filipinos she had worked with. She didn't remember him being especially religious. Or . . . well, perhaps. When they found the dead. When he was sure there was no life in the crushed and trapped bodies. Then his thick fingers made the sign of the cross, and he mumbled something in Tagalog that was probably a prayer.

He had found her on Facebook about a month ago, but this was the first time he had posted anything. And then a weirdo post like that. She tried to make sense of the archaic words Much the same kind of message as the card that had come with the bouquet.

Victor was in the Philippines. Victor couldn't have sent her flowers. Or could he? Through Interflora? Did they use small local Viborg florists? *Bouquets for every occacion.* Old-fashioned and comfortingly provincial. But how did he know she was in the hospital—and where?

Fear flopped and writhed in her stomach. The terror of the trapped animal. She took a step backward, into the lobby's busy, protective atmosphere and stayed there until Søren's Hyundai appeared in front of the steps.

THE RAIN HAD stopped, and the October sun shone warm and golden through the tall windows of the conservatory. Her mother sat in a wicker chair with a blanket around her legs sipping a glass of the devil's claw tea that her alternative medicine friend Grethe claimed would help. Who knew, maybe it was true. But it stank to high heaven and tasted awful.

They smiled carefully at each other, like two negotiators at a peace conference.

"Coffee?" asked Hanne.

"Thank you." Nina let herself slide into the wicker chair's matching companion.

"I'll get it," said Ida, astonishingly helpful, and disappeared in the direction of the kitchen. Nina could hear her speaking with Søren, who apparently was already quite at home and able to find such necessities as cake plates and forks. They had bought a pear tart on the way home. With crème fraîche, no less. It was all too staid for words, and Nina felt as if she was about to be smothered by bingo club invitations and barbecues with that nice couple next door . . .

Like her, Søren had his roots in Jutland, but it was a different kind of Jutland. Gym dances and football and hot dogs from the local grill instead of Viborg's carefully cultivated atmosphere of culture and provincial etiquette. Both of them had left those roots behind a long time ago, but whereas he seemed to be perfectably comfortable living in middle-class suburbia, she wasn't sure she'd be able to stand it.

Which might be a moot point as he hasn't actually asked you to move in, she told herself and wondered why the thought had popped up at all.

"So, how are you?" asked Hanne.

"Fine," Nina answered automatically.

"Søren says that you still can't remember what happened."

"That's true." Nina squirmed in her chair. "Mom, I . . . I'm sorry about what I said."

Hanne Borg raised her tea glass as if to make a toast.

"I guess your saying it instead of just thinking it is progress of a kind," she commented drily.

The door slammed and there was a rapid clatter of nine-year-old footsteps. Anton came running through the living room. He had been playing next door with Filip, the neighbor's grandson, who was also visiting during the midterm vacation.

"Mom!"

Nina got up a little too quickly, but a discreet hand on the doorjamb allowed her to retain her balance.

"Come here, you rascal you . . ."

He had grown so big during the past six months. Everything downy and babyish had been whittled away. He was a boy now, with knobby knees and broad hands and an apparently bottomless reservoir of energy. He was still happy to give and get hugs, but he had begun to protest if she tried to kiss him.

Right now he dug in his heels and put on the brakes so you could hear an almost cartoon-like shriek of boy feet against the lacquered wood floor.

"What happened to your eyes?" he asked.

"It's just a mask to hide my secret identity," she said. The swelling from the raccoon-eye hematoma was mostly gone, thank God, but traces of the bruising still lingered.

He gave a single awkward croak-like laugh, but she could see that he was startled and uneasy.

"It's okay, sweetie," she said. "It'll fade soon."

"Someone hit you," he said as if he was only now realizing it.

"Not here," she said and touched one cheek. "It's because I got bonked on the back of the head."

"But someone did that," he insisted. "Hit you on the head, I mean." His face was serious, and she could see a deep, glittering fear in his eyes.

"What's wrong, sweetie?"

He bit his lower lip for so long that she could see the mark of his teeth remain for a brief moment when he opened his mouth.

"What if he does it again?"

"He won't."

"Yes . . . but what if?"

"If he tries, the police will come and arrest him," she said firmly. "They are already searching for him."

She pulled Anton close, and he clung to her in a highly uncharacteristic way. She could feel his shoulders shaking and knew he was crying but trying to suppress it.

"It's okay," she said. "Nothing is going to happen. It's okay."

Her reassurances only made it worse. A heartbreaking sob emerged from the boy.

Ida passed by with the cake tray and punched him in the shoulder.

"Come on, Anton. Only losers cry."

"Ida!"

But Ida got it right. Anton took a deep, uncertain breath and freed himself from Nina's arms.

"Yep," he said. "The rest of us get up and go for the gold."

"Precisely, maggot!"

"Maggot yourself. You . . . booger!"

"Fart!"

"Earwax."

"Tapeworm!"

They grinned more and more broadly with every disgusting word.

"Same to you . . . dog turd!" Anton concluded, apparently completely restored to his boyish composure.

"Yes, all right," said Nina. "I think we get the general idea."

But later, when the cake platter had been vacuumed for the last crumbs and Anton sat in his favorite corner in the living room, absorbed in a PlayStation game, Ida stood staring out the kitchen window with her hands stuck as deep in pockets of her hoodie as they could possibly get.

"What's wrong, sweetie?"

"Nothing." But then she turned around anyway, and Nina could see how tense her face was. "You're not going to leave us, are you?"

"Ida. No! Of course I won't. Where would I go?"

"I don't know. One of those places where people die."

Nina put her hand on her daughter's cheek and for once was not pushed away.

"People die everywhere, sweet pea. But Grandma is going to get well."

In the course of the afternoon coffee ritual, Nina had finally realized what all those pink hearts were all about. Ida had discovered the existence of death. Not as an abstract concept or as a symbol you could flirt with to be hip and Goth and a little different. Dead as in "gone." It was clearly visible in the desperate care her normally slightly distanced daughter lavished on her grandmother. Smiles. Small pats. Hugs for no reason—or at least, hugs that weren't part of the usual rituals of arrival or departure. It was heartbreaking to watch.

Nina's mother had spotted what was going on long ago, but just returned smiles with smiles and hugs with hugs and pretended that everything was as usual. That was almost as heartbreaking. Nina felt the urge to yell at them both that the prognosis was decent and there was no reason to bury anyone yet.

But it was apparently not just the cancer that had shaken Ida out of her teenage worldweariness

"It's not Grandma so much," she said and looked at Nina with an angry and vulnerable gaze. "It's more you."

The expression in Ida's eyes hit her like a sucker punch. *You have two children who are afraid to lose you*. Her mother had been right.

"I have no plans to leave here anytime soon," she said lightly and stuffed her own fear of death back into the cave where it belonged.

• • •

IT WAS ONLY later, when the rest of the household slumbered sweetly, that the terror came creeping out of its hiding place again. Sleep seemed to her to be a healthy and normal but completely unattainable state—something other people did. It only helped a little that Søren lay next to her in the spare room's less than king-sized double bed. His body created a landscape both alien and familiar underneath the comforter, a shoulder mountain and the curve of a back, a ridge of sloping fabric covering a leg. His breathing was calm and only slightly obstructed, and she was pretty sure he was sleeping . . . no, peacefully was probably an exaggeration, he had his own nightmares . . . but deeply at least.

His unconscious presence was somehow provoking, but, she admitted to herself, probably not the only reason why her brain seemed to have reached a state of permanent wakefulness. Her sleep rhythms, unstable at the best of times, had been shattered completely during her hospital stay, and when she stayed with her mother she never slept very well anyway—neither peacefully *nor* deeply.

Ida's fear continued to haunt her. *You're not leaving us, are you?* The thick oozing black substance of it mixed with the memory of her dream father, spilled oil and brackish water, a dull, evil-smelling upwelling from the depths of her unconscious.

"Most of us show clinical symptoms of depression if we are woken between three and four in the morning," her new therapist had explained when Nina finally admitted that she often woke up after just a few hours of sleep. "You are vulnerable, all defenses are down, and you have zero control. Remember that it doesn't last. Morning comes; the light returns."

It was her old boss Magnus who had recommended Marianna, who, apart from being highly trained in crisis psychology, was also calm, classically beautiful, and fond of hand-woven shirts and sandalwood perfumes. Without either of them acknowledging it, Nina had the sense that she and Magnus were childhood friends, maybe even childhood sweethearts. But where Magnus's Swedish accent was thick enough to grease a Volvo, Marianna's had almost disappeared. Nina *liked* her, which was probably a good start. In the daylight, when she was herself, and held distance as a shield in front of her more vulnerable parts, she could smile ironically at Marianna's metaphors. Now, in the dark, they weren't just images.

"Didn't you think I'd come back?" her father had asked in the dream, while he held her, alive, physical and palpable, an attempt, she supposed, on the part of her subconscious to lay to rest that ancient, hopeless horror. In Ida's eyes, she had recognized the same fear. *You're not leaving us, are you?*

She wished that she had been able to give a better answer. She wished that her self-image wasn't as cracked as her all too vulnerable skull.

She cursed quietly. The worst and most insufficient oaths she knew.

Luckily it would soon be morning.

There were no clocks in Hanne Borg's spare room. Marianna had taught her to take off her wristwatch before she went to sleep, as a part of her battle against her somewhat obsessive time checking. "Time will look after itself while you sleep," was the way she put it. But there was no sleep right now . . . Nina fumbled for the damned watch but couldn't find it. Had she actually put it in the drawer?

In the end, she found her cell phone instead. 3:27. As soon as the screen darkened, she touched it again, not because she thought the time it showed would have changed, but simply to keep alive the cold digital glow a little longer.

Yet another Facebook message had arrived. Yet another Bible quote.

> "*Weeping may endure for a night, but joy cometh in the morning.*" Psalms 30:5. I'll be in Denmark soon. Can we meet? Very important! God bless, Victor.

THE PHILIPPINES, THREE YEARS EARLIER

"COFFEE?"

His mother didn't wait for an answer, but resolutely placed the jar with instant coffee and creamer on the table in front of him and poured boiling water into his glass. From the patio of his parents' house they had a view of his uncle's yard and his ten long-legged fighting cocks, each tied by the leg to its stake. The heat made the air billow and shimmer above the pocked asphalt of the driveway. Vincent had arrived half an hour ago, but had gotten no further than the plastic chairs and cracked paving of the patio, where he was served sweet, ripe mangos, bananas, and *kutsinta* rice cakes by his mother and his aunt. His father was still at work.

San Marcelino.

His home. And his hometown. It all looked exactly as it did when he had left it. The dogs barking on their chains behind the house, the white cats slinking around the table on the patio, and a small army of barefooted grandnephews and grandnieces fiddling with their bikes in the shade by grandma's house. Two puppies were bounding about underfoot, snapping at the tires and the children's flip-flops with sharp baby teeth, and at regular intervals the children tipped them onto their backs and rubbed their bellies in a distracted fashion.

"Did you bring me a present?"

His little sister Mimi landed on the white plastic chair next to him and stretched out her long brown legs. She had grown tall since he had last visited, and there was a pair of small, pointy girl's breasts under her T-shirt. It didn't look as if she had much interest in either bikes or puppies any longer.

"Of course I didn't bring a present," he said and laughed. "Only good girls get presents, you know that."

Mimi laughed with her big white teeth and gave him a soft punch. She was wearing lip gloss, he noticed. Pink with glitter.

"Where is it?"

Vincent sighed, searched around in his backpack and pulled out the bag with Mimi's present. Two T-shirts and a pair of Calvin Klein shorts, which he hoped would fit her new, slightly rounder bottom. He had bought it all at the market, no doubt copies, but neither he nor Mimi cared.

She got up and kissed him fleetingly on the cheek. She smelled of strawberries and pineapple and the scented rinse that their mother usually used in the wash. Still very much a child.

"I'll try them on right away," she said and disappeared on fleet feet across the sun-warmed paving stones of the patio.

"And it's going well?"

His mother was observing him with anxious eyes.

Here it came. He had been waiting for it. "Why don't you ever visit us?" "Why didn't you go see Uncle Alfredo when he invited you?" "Cousin Maria says you've only been by once, and she hasn't seen you in church either."

He had already had the full barrage over the phone. His mother thought he was letting the family down. She was especially annoyed about Cousin Maria and church. Maria didn't live far from him on Antonio Vasquez Street, and when he moved into his dorm room, she had brought him to church at once and introduced him to the priest and a couple of even more distant relatives. Try as he might, he could not remember their names or how he was related to them, but there was no doubt that they carried on a busy correspondence with his mother. All the old people had learned how to text in record time and this was one of the reasons why his mother was so well informed about his skipping church. His mother was deeply religious, but it was probably Cousin Maria's jibes that bothered her the most. His mother might call her "a sanctimonious busybody," but the taunts stung.

"I'm studying, Mom," he said. "Do you have any idea how massive the first year curriculum is?"

His mother picked up a paper plate from the table and fanned herself with it. The heat was oppressive today.

"You've always had lots to study," she said. "But it never stopped you from attending church before. I worry about you. We never hear from you."

"I'm fine. I'm just . . . busy."

He hoped she couldn't hear the lie.

It was almost six months since he had last been home. It took three hours each way in a crowded and hellishly hot jeepney, which was not a very tempting way to spend your weekend. Vincent hated the trip, and he always got carsick and had to bring about a million bags he could vomit in and then toss out the back of the jeepney.

But that wasn't the main reason. He just didn't want to go home.

There were the weekends with Vadim and Victor, the nights out on the town with a few bottles of San Miguel and girls who slinked softly through the dark. He didn't touch them; he had Bea. He just loved the slight buzz, Vadim's laughter, and Victor's calm and slightly crooked smile, which followed on the heels of the first five San Miguels. Victor normally didn't say much, and seemed to have the same unflappable nature as the water buffaloes he had bossed around in the rice paddies. But when he got drunk, he sang Britney Spears on the bar's karaoke system.

Vincent couldn't explain that to Bea and his family at home in San Marcelino. Plus, there was that other pang of conscience that jabbed him every time he thought of them.

His grades on the year-end exams had been catastrophic. Nothing less. He had no proper grasp of the material, didn't understand the professors during the lectures, and was behind with his reading both of the textbooks and of the compendiums of notes which were placed in his pigeonhole once a week. The others did not seem to suffer the same agonies. Victor appeared to have everything under control, and Vadim did too. And Vadim had reassured him again and again

"Weren't you top of your year in high school? What the hell are *you* afraid of?"

So he had suppressed his initial anxieties and had calmed his nerves with more San Miguels and more Vadim. Evenings under the open sky on Vadim's balcony with endless and exalted conversations about life and death. Vadim borrowed a motorcycle from a dealer and kept it for almost two months. At night they drove through Manila's humid darkness, in shorts and without lights. The wind blew coolly against his gleaming sweaty skin, and it felt as if they were headed directly for the future. As if the future was an actual place, shiny and unused, waiting for them just around the corner. It had felt so right and so secure. As if nothing could go wrong. Which was of course a lie. He knew that now.

He knew it the same moment he sat down in his seat in the meltingly hot examination room. The papers with the many questions and far-too-multiple choices flickered in front of his eyes, and he knew, knew, knew right there and then that he was in trouble. The realization was a black hole, a sucking vacuum that it had taken him a frantic half an hour to escape, and after that there was nothing to do but try to patch up the damage. He crossed off the answers blindly or based on vague notions and then waited with fear and loathing for the grade lists to be posted on the wall in front of the director's office.

He had passed, but only just. He, who had always been at the top of every class at every point in his life, had barely made it through first-year anatomy and had been stumblingly close to failing three other tests in the laboratory. With such low grades, he would not get his scholarship renewed. That much was certain.

The fee for the third semester would be an unimaginable fifty thousand pesos. A dizzying and impossible amount. And then there was his rent, and food, too. He did not need a detailed knowledge of his parents' finances to know that this was beyond them. Unless they broke into the money they had saved for Mimi. She wanted to be a nurse and work in Europe, like all other sensible girls. He did not want his future to come at the cost of his sister's.

"What do you think?"

Mimi was back from their parents' bedroom in the new jean shorts and T-shirt. The shorts were a bit of a tight fit, but she looked happy, and their mother smiled too.

"You look nice, sweetie. She's getting big, isn't she? High school next year and she's already begun looking at colleges."

He fiddled with his coffee cup. Suddenly felt as if it was much too hot here. One of the cockerels stretched its neck and began to crow like mad, and as if on command, all the others did the same.

The noise was deafening, and his mother sighed, got up and walked with stiff, uneven strides down the patio steps and across to the wooden bin that contained food for the raucous creatures.

She was getting old. He could see that her back was bothering her. Arthritis. There wasn't much to be done, but she got pills from the pharmacy to help with the pain. The back problem was the result of her three years as a maid in Saudi Arabia. Washing by hand for a family of nine. The heavy *niqabs* that had to be dragged in and out of the laundry tub, rinsed and wrung out. His mother still spoke about it with dread in her voice. But that was how she had saved up for his schooling, from when Vincent was seven until he was ten. She had been like a stranger when she finally came home. His father had been working in Germany.

She scattered a handful of corn for each of Uncle's cockerels, and they immediately calmed down, settled their wings, and started to eat.

"Would you like another mango?" she asked on her way into the kitchen.

"No, thank you. Later." He smiled and got up. "I think I'll drop by Bea's."

"Young love." His mother smiled, and the worry in her gaze melted away for a short, grateful moment.

He cringed, slipped into his flip-flops and headed for Bea's house.

"VINCENT! YOU'RE HERE already? So the traffic from Manila wasn't so bad?"

Bea's mom, Tia Merlita, was outside on the family's bit of land, weeding around a few young coconut palms. She lit up when she saw him. She was a tall, thin woman with light skin and high cheekbones. Her late father had been Chinese, a relatively wealthy entrepreneur who had founded the family business, a cultured pearl farm that lay a few kilometers further south. It was a good business; Bea's family was wealthier than Vincent's.

He walked over to Bea's mother and raised the back of her hand to his forehead as a sign of respect.

"No, it wasn't so bad," he said. "It only took three hours."

She nodded and sighed with all signs of sympathy. If you were unlucky, the trip from Manila could sometimes last up to six hours. Endless roadwork, rush hour congestion, accidents . . . or you might simply get stuck behind one of the pig transports. Big open trucks with sweating and exhausted sows who had to be doused regularly with water by the equally sweaty farmers balancing on the truck beds. Journeying on the foul-smelling rivers of Manila's traffic was no pleasure trip for anyone.

"Bea is inside," said Tia Merlita, giving a quick toss of her head in the general direction of the house. "She's not well."

A faint uneasiness coursed through Vincent.

"What's wrong?"

"Upset stomach. She must have eaten something that didn't agree with her." She shrugged. "She'll be feeling better now, I think. Probably just needed something to drink and a bit of a lie-down. Her exam went well, but you probably know that."

He continued up the driveway and opened the door to the small living room. It was cool and dark inside. The air conditioning hummed loudly above the worn plush sofa where Bea lay slumped. The television was on, but Bea had her eyes closed. He hadn't seen her since that weekend at the resort with Vadim and Victor and Diana. Her face seemed pale in the gloom and the blue flickering light from the TV, and her forehead was covered in sweat. She was wearing a thin, sleeveless black-and-red checked dress that made her look like a serious and intense little girl.

Everything in him grew tender.

"Hey . . ." he whispered, raising her hand to his lips and kissing it gently.

"Hey." She didn't open her eyes but smiled. It struck him that she had the most beautiful teeth in the world. And the most beautiful lips.

"I've been waiting for you," she said. She stretched and finally opened her big dark eyes. "I thought we could go for a walk down to the river. If you feel like it?"

He didn't feel like it. It was almost noon, and the heat outside was a hostile and consuming force. But he knew that it was important to her. They had kissed for the first time on the suspension bridge by the river, and when they were younger, they had bathed together and had splashed water at the washerwomen and at people picking *bayabas* by the shore. The river was their place.

Vincent's mother liked to say that God had brought them together, long before it occurred to the families that it would be a good idea. That his mother had mentioned quite early on that Vincent was planning to become a doctor, and that Bea's parents had ambitions on their daughter's behalf, may have eased the Lord's work considerably, thought Vincent.

They walked hand in hand down the road, and Vincent bought a couple of bottles of water in the little shop selling gum, rice, cola, and canned food. The lady behind the counter smiled and revealed a couple of black gaps in her teeth. She was the mother of Georgio from his old class. He had left school after high school and traveled to Norway to work in the oil industry. Now his mother had bought the shop and the little brick house behind it.

"You haven't written to me since we saw each other last," said Bea and gave his hand a small, firm squeeze. "You haven't forgotten me, have you?"

"Are you kidding?" He gave her a crooked smile. "I haven't thought about anything but you and . . . it."

It was a bit of a lie, but not much.

The two nights with Bea had been impossible to shake off, and he took pleasure in replaying them when he went to bed at night. He missed her more than ever. But it took up too much space to fit in one of the usual letters. He wasn't good at putting feelings into writing.

"I did call," he defended himself.

"Yes." She laughed. "But it's not very easy to say what you are thinking with a mother or an aunt constantly hanging over your shoulder. They are *so* curious. One day it'll kill them."

She became serious.

"I envy you, Vincent, because you moved away. Because you're in Manila doing new things. And I'm afraid of losing you; I'm afraid you'll find another girl—some bright and pretty medical student with as much money as Vadim and expensive black underwear and sky-high stilettos."

She pointed down at her flip-flops, and they both couldn't help laughing. Bea's slender brown legs and narrow ankles were covered by a thin layer of dust from the road. It was the dry season.

"You don't need to be afraid of that, Bea. Really," said Vincent, putting his arm around her hips and pinching her teasingly in the side. "The girls studying medicine are small and fat and boring. All of them. There's no one like you in all the world, my flower. No one."

They had reached the bridge. It was a narrow affair with wooden slats and worn netting along the sides, and reassuringly thick ropes for those who were afraid of heights to cling to. The river slid by lazily far beneath them, murky and dark green in its seasonal low.

Bea pulled herself free of his arm and danced out onto the bridge, playful and light on her feet. He suddenly had the urge to tell her about his final exams and the money he didn't have for the next semester. He had no one to talk to about it, even though he had a feeling Victor might know how bad things were. Thanks to his uncle, Victor didn't need a scholarship, but he was poor enough to know what things cost. Ironically, Victor had achieved top grades in every damn subject that had been put up on the bulletin board this year.

And he must have noticed Vincent's miserable results. He must have.

Bea skipped over a few holes in the bridge where boards were missing. That was always the way of it, ever since they were children. The bridge was under constant repair and in just as constant decay. As soon as the rotten parts had been replaced at one end, the boards in the middle began to sway and sink under your feet. They turned grey and black and fell from the row, like the teeth of an old woman, and the peasants who crossed the bridge every day to reach their rice paddies on the other side of the bridge were used to hopping it, tools balanced in their hands.

Bea jumped again, and he set off after her and caught her in the middle. She stood with her hands tightly clutching the thick rope, staring upriver. The warm wind tugged at her smooth, black hair and the red checked dress.

"Vincent," she said. "I'm pregnant."

"HOW MUCH DO you need?"

Vadim calmly lit a cigarette, narrowing his eyes. It was afternoon, and the bar was only half-full. Vincent sipped his whiskey carefully. He felt like getting drunk, but he had to take care of this before he could sink into a longed-for dizzying and necessary darkness.

"Fifty thousand now and fifty thousand more in six months. At least."

"No more? It's expensive to have a baby. Diapers and private school and college. It all adds up."

Vadim's face was unmoving, and Vincent couldn't quite tell if his friend was making fun of him, mocking him. The child was barely a child yet, and the thought of diapers had in fact crossed Vincent's mind, but beyond that, the fact that he was going to be a father was mostly an abstract, swirling hole somewhere on the horizon. Private school and college . . . He didn't want to think about it. Had to look at what was right in front of him, which was next semester and a hole in his budget of a hundred thousand pesos.

"It's just to pay for the next two semesters," he said. "Bea and I were going to get married in six months anyway, and she and the baby will live with her parents in the beginning so she can continue her studies. I'll pay you back when I can. I promise."

He would have liked to say something more. Give Vadim some form of assurance, something that definitively proved that the loan was temporary and therefore had nothing to do with their friendship. But first of all, he had nothing to give Vadim but his word, and second of all, it was already too late.

Something had changed between them.

He had seen it in Vadim's eyes when he told him about Bea and the lost scholarship. Vadim had looked like someone who had just been given an unexpected slap. The gaze was naked and vulnerable. But only for a moment. Then the hurt look had slipped from his face and he had become cool and to the point.

"So I'm your rich uncle now." He smiled faintly. His cigarette hung in his mouth, in the style of an American gangster. If

Vadim had been an actor, he would have been Leonardo DiCaprio. No, he would have been better—and more beautiful.

Vincent shrugged. Tried to make it all look like nothing.

"You're not my father. Or my uncle. And I don't like to owe you anything. We're friends, right? The V-Team and all that?"

"But," said Vadim thoughtfully, "my father's pockets are, as we all know, deeper than the Philippine Trench, and I can bury my hands in them as long as I behave. That much money is hard to ignore when the shit hits the fan, right? Oh, I understand. That's how I feel about my father, and you feel that way about me. It's natural. And what else are friends for?"

The last was said with a lash of sarcasm, which made Vincent even more uncertain.

The music coming from the diminutive stage at the end of the room was turned up higher. A three-man live band was playing eighties pop and old ABBA songs.

"I've been expelled from St. Francis," said Vadim calmly. "I won't be allowed to start next semester, no matter how much money I throw at them. I haven't told Diana yet."

He considered Vincent over the rim of his whiskey glass with a gotcha sort of look.

"Why?"

Vincent didn't understand. Vadim had done all right at his exams. Not brilliantly so, but definitely acceptable, and as he said himself, money wasn't exactly a problem.

"Because I cheated, Vincent. What else? I'm no good at the book stuff. My father is right about that much. He was against me studying medicine."

Something fell into place inside Vincent.

Vadim hadn't shown up at a single morning lecture the entire spring, and he usually spent his evenings down at Joye's or Cabana Bar—with or without Vincent, but usually with. And Vincent *had* wondered when Vadim actually had time to study. The answer had of course been obvious. Vadim was one of the rich students who paid others to write their papers and sit their exams.

"How did they catch you?"

Vadim pulled his hand through his smooth hair.

"It was stupid," he said. "I got Bryan to write my name on his paper for the final. He needs the money because his father is sick. Cancer. It costs an arm and a leg. And he can retake his own exam in the fall. Or so I hope. So far, I'm the only one they've thrown out. Bryan is a genuine scholarship boy from the slums, and the director has chosen to show understanding for his difficult family situation. Being lazy and drunk is apparently not enough of an excuse. They have professional standards and the school's reputation to consider, or so the director assured me. I don't think I've ever met a more unbribable man. Pretty unsettling."

"So what will you do?"

Vadim shrugged.

"I've told my father that I don't want to be a doctor after all. He wants to put me in charge of a part of his construction business. You know, concrete and steel and the bribing of officials and politicians. He's busy with his election campaign, you know? It's perfect for me." He smiled palely.

Vincent shook his head. How could he have been stupid enough to believe that Vadim was doing the work himself? Him and all his carpe diem shit. All those lost hours. The cigarettes, the booze, the wild nighttime rides through Manila's streets on that damn motorcycle . . .

He suddenly felt terribly alone. Bea was still pregnant, and he hadn't done any of the things his mother and father had expected of him. Their money was lost if he couldn't stay in Manila. What would there be for him to return to in San Marcelino? A newspaper stand by the main road? Showing the tourists the sights for a few pesos a day? Bea, who would get up every morning and go to a badly paid job at the public hospital and smile bravely when the neighbors bought a new car and built a new house? The families would grow to hate him—both Bea's and his own

"The money, Vadim . . ." He tried to smile. "Can I borrow the money?"

He couldn't think of anything else right now.

Vadim turned back to Vincent with a look that had taken on a new hardness.

"The money. Right." Vadim whistled quietly. "It's a lot of cash, Vincent, my man. Haven't you heard of condoms?"

"Please don't jerk me around. It's just a loan," said Vincent. "I can work it off, can't I? Just say yes or no. Do you have a job for me? In your father's business maybe? Something . . ." He fumbled for the words. Didn't really know exactly what he imagined. "Some kind of office work or . . . anything at all, damn it. I can study during the day and work at night. It's just these two semesters. Just until I get another scholarship."

Vadim laughed.

"Fuck it, Vincent, you don't earn fifty thousand pesos working in an office. Come on! What world do you live in? We're on the third rock from the sun, just so you know."

Vincent slumped over his whiskey, and it struck him that Vadim was like a miserably sad little boy dangling a hunk of meat just out of reach of a chained dog. He, of course, was the dog. Snap, snap. Teeth closing on empty air.

"Does it feel good?"

Vincent could hear the anger in his own voice.

"What?"

"To have so much money that you can act like an asshole twenty-four hours a day? I said I would pay the money back. It's a loan. I'll find a way to get it."

Vadim lifted his hand with a tired gesture.

"Yes, Vincent. It feels great. Really. You should try it." He dropped the irony. "It doesn't matter about the money, Vincent. You can have it. Believe me, it means nothing. I don't even want it back. Five hundred pesos at a time or whatever you can manage? Forget it. I've got better things to do with my time."

"Thank you." The relief was so enormous that Vincent's anger evaporated in a split second, and he felt a ridiculous impulse to lift Vadim's hand to his forehead, as if Vadim was an uncle or grandfather he felt compelled to respect. He barely managed to stop himself. Instead he emptied his whiskey glass and stood up on weak legs.

"If you don't want the money back," said Vincent, looking at Vadim, "then what do you want me to do?"

Vadim searched the pockets of his jeans and pulled out five crumpled ten-thousand-peso bills, which he threw on the table in front of Vincent. A sad smile flickered in his dark eyes.

"You work for me now," he said calmly. "Simon says. You'll do whatever I ask you to do."

"WHO DID YOU say he was?" asked Søren sleepily.

"Victor Galang. I met him some months ago in Manila. A medical student . . . There was this terrible accident, several thousand people were hurt, and they needed people with my kind of training . . ."

Nina could hear how defensive she sounded, as if Søren had become Morten and she needed to justify herself. Søren merely looked at her with his calm Paul Newman–blue gaze and waited for her to finish explaining.

The spare room had once belonged to one of her younger brothers, and its dimensions were rather modest. When the double bed was pulled out as it was now there was just a minimal passage along one wall. The only lights apart from the pendant in the ceiling were two small, ball-shaped bedside lamps at either end of the window ledge. The sheets were white with blue pinstripes, and Nina's mother had painted the pine wall panels a shiny white to brighten the narrow space, but with two people in it, it remained a bit of a den. They had left the window slightly ajar, and the blinds slapped against the windowframe with every gust of wind. Yet Nina still felt as if the air was too thick for her lungs.

"What were you doing in Manila in the first place?" asked Søren. She glanced at him, but his expression was, like his tone, neutral and calmly receptive. No blame, no accusations. But why would there be? He wasn't the father of her children. It wasn't *his* vacation that . . .

"Morten was making a presentation at a conference . . . He asked if . . . if we might not at least try a vacation together. For the sake of the children." She glanced at him because in a way it also concerned him. Nina and Søren had already gone out together before the Philippine trip, but only a few times. That was in fact partly why she had agreed to Morten's invitation. Because *if* . . . if there really was a way back, she had no intention of messing it up by starting a relationship with Søren.

The airplane tickets had cost a fortune, but accommodation, at least, had been cheap: a surprisingly inexpensive week at a resort to begin with—pristine white sands and turquoise waters right on their doorstep, too—and later those days as the guests of Morten's colleague. At first it had gone pretty well. Civilized conversations, mini golf and splashing in the pool with the kids, even a certain bodily chemistry what with all the swim suits, tans and so on. She still found Morten . . . attractive. When he wasn't biting her head off, that is, or making her feel guilty enough to provide material for an entire conference of psychologists. The first evening in Manila they had gone out together for the first time in about six hundred years. As she remembered it, they both tried like mad to look as if they were having fun for each other's sake, until they almost simultaneously had broken down and confessed that they would rather be home. In the taxi, an out-on-the-town mood had somehow still surfaced.

Morten had suggested a midnight swim in the pool, and they had made love, otter-like and slightly absurd, in the warm, chlorine-filled water. Afterward, lying next to him in bed, she had cried noiselessly for almost an hour. Over wasted efforts. Over good intentions. And the fact that it just wasn't enough.

When the accident happened a few days later, she had known exactly how he would react if she went out there. And if she had to be brutally honest with herself, it hadn't been necessity alone that made her volunteer her services.

Their marriage was over and could not be resuscitated. The sense of defeat had filled her with a panicky anxiety that did not go away until she found herself once more in the midst of real disaster, cool and competent, completely capable of saving *other* people's lives.

"It didn't work?" Søren asked carefully.

"No. The accident . . . that's exactly what he can't stand about me. That I help other people but not . . . not us. Not him." *Not our own children*, she confessed silently to herself, but couldn't quite say it out loud.

"And this Victor was . . . what? A kind of colleague? A friend?"

"Victor? No. A fellow volunteer. But . . . something happens when you work together under conditions like that. Even if it's just for a few days. You never quite forget."

Her heart pounded so hard and so quickly that her thin undershirt vibrated with every beat. The familiar dry, metallic taste of the adrenaline rush appeared in her mouth, as if Victor's name alone and the memory of Manila were enough to evoke it. She didn't understand it. That wasn't the way it was when she thought of the camps at Dadaab, for instance, and she had been there for much longer and under much riskier circumstances.

"What was he like?"

"He was good. He knew what he was doing, but it was more than that. He exuded calm, and people trusted him. He was extraordinarily tall and broad for a Filipino, and I think that helped."

"Was he very religious?"

"You're thinking of the Bible quotations?" She had told him about the flowers and the cards they came with. "Not like that . . . not very. But almost everyone there is to some degree. They were everywhere, those Bible quotations—on T-shirts and caps, on buses, even as neon signs outside churches. Some of the nurses subscribed to a text service that sent them one a day, and they usually showed them to each other and compared. I think for them, it's about as normal as sending Christmas cards or something similar."

She didn't tell him how effectively the last one had gotten to her. "Weeping may endure for a night, but joy cometh in the morning." She wasn't sure she expected *joy* from the light of dawn—a certain relief would do. But as for the weeping bit . . . at least she wasn't alone in the dark now. She scrupulously admitted to herself that it was not only objective, clue-gathering motives that had made her wake up Søren to show him Victor's message.

He sat with his shoulders against the pine-clad wall, one leg stretched, one bent. His scarred chest was covered by a white T-shirt, his legs by the comforter and a pair of loose, striped boxer shorts. A lock of greying dark hair hung down over his forehead in a slightly post-rebellious way. She thought he resembled someone—some aging rock singer maybe—one of those men like Leonard Cohen and David Bowie who managed to make age, experience and reading glasses seem sexy.

"And you think he was the one who sent you those lilies?"

She shook her head.

"I don't know what to think. The Bible quotations . . . there can't actually be two people in the world sending me that kind of thing at the same time?"

"No. That would be stretching coincidence to the breaking point."

"But the flowers were from a florist in Viborg."

"Did you save the card?"

"No." After the scare with the man who may or may not have been following her mother, she'd searched for it in the bin in her hospital room, but this had, of course, long since been emptied. Hospitals had to have efficient cleaning services. "But I'm sure. They were bought locally and delivered by a messenger."

"Then we'll have to assume that the person who sent you these messages may be somewhere in the vicinity of Viborg."

"But he wrote that he was on his way to Denmark—not that he was here already."

"Nina. Don't be naïve. Anyone can write anything on Facebook—doesn't make it true. Can I borrow that?" He stretched his hand in the direction of her phone.

She handed it to him. He typed for a while with fierce concentration and swore when his broad fingertips slipped on the undersized keypad, or the spell check inserted especially useless suggestions.

"What are you doing?" she asked.

"Seeing if I can lure him further out of hiding."

"Søren! That's my phone. And my profile!"

He looked up at her with something resembling real wonder.

"Surely you don't actually believe what he wrote?" he asked.

"Does it matter? You can't just . . . pretend to be me!"

He drew his glasses down on his nose and observed her over the top of them.

"Right now he knows quite bit about you," he said dryly. "Your real name, your whereabouts—can't you at least turn off that function?—what your family looks like, how you're feeling, and what you think about everything under the sun. If we assume the flowers were from him, then he figured out what hospital you had been admitted to. We don't know if he is alone or part of a team. *If* he was the one who photographed your mother, it might have been to give his colleagues the ability to recognize her. He's got you and your life at his fingertips. Whereas you only know that he *might* live in Manila, *might* have been educated at the St. Francis College of Medicine, and that he likes the International Red Cross, a couple of Filipino pop groups and something called Young Christian Diamond. But have you seen his list of friends? He has one—and that's you."

She wrestled the phone away from him. First to read the message he had written in her name—"Where are you? What is so important?"—and then to conclude that he was right. In the Facebook universe, she was apparently Victor's only friend.

"That profile was created solely to contact you," said Søren with an irritatingly professional expression. "Victor may not even have been the one who did it. But the person looking for information can sometimes end up giving away more than he gets. He wants something from you. That's a weakness we can exploit."

She glared at him.

"We aren't all terrorists," she pointed out. "Some of us are who we say we are—with or without a thousand friends on Facebook."

"Okay," he said. "Let's wait and see how he answers."

"You don't understand," she said angrily. "The people you meet under conditions like that . . . you go through hell together. You hardly sleep, you don't get enough to eat and drink, all of that is pushed aside because . . . because it's life or death, literally. People are dying right here, right then. Every mistake, every break can cost some poor wretch their life. Under those circumstances, the masks drop. You see who people are—and what they are not. You see what they are capable of, what they can take, and what they find unbearable. And the Victor I got to know in that way—he was a good man. A good person. He wouldn't hurt a fly."

He nodded very faintly—she barely caught the movement. There was something disarming about it, even though she wasn't sure exactly what he was agreeing with.

"You've just been attacked by an unknown assailant," he then said, calmly and neutrally.

"That Westmann woman says it's some kind of eastern European gang."

"No. That Westmann woman would like to know *if* it's them—or not."

"I *have* thought about it," she said. "And I just can't see how it can have anything at all to do with Victor and Manila."

"I'm not saying it does. Not yet—we don't know enough. That's why I'm fishing for more information."

"By abusing my profile!"

"Yes."

He didn't even say he was sorry. And he didn't look the least apologetic. What were you supposed to do with the man?

She kept glaring at him for quite a long time, but he was one of the few people you simply *couldn't* stare down. A faint smile had appeared on one side of his mouth, and he returned her look in a way that was entirely devoid of confrontation.

"What are you doing?" she asked.

"Looking at you."

She couldn't remember the last time someone had made her blush, but the warmth in her cheeks—and a few other places—could not be ignored. She could hardly be a sight for sore eyes right now, but his gaze followed everything, took it all in: the fading bruises, the hematoma, the hollows below her cheekbones and the swelling under her eyes.

"You're crazy," she whispered and meant it. "Are you sure you want to do this?"

"This?"

"Us. Me." Her voice broke a bit. "A lot of people would think you're out of your mind."

His smile grew noticably broader.

"A few people have said something of the kind," he agreed.

She deliberately placed her hand on his chest precisely where the scar was hidden under his T-shirt. He let her do it without breaking eye contact. Then she felt his hands on the small of her back and let herself fall into him. The cell phone slid out of her hand and disappeared somewhere under the covers. She didn't care about the headache that buzzed constantly in the background or the faint smell of hospital that still clung to her skin. His lips tasted like sleep and a little of toothpaste, and she suddenly began to shake all over—long, shuddering jolts that she couldn't control.

"Are you okay?" he asked.

"Yes. No." She pulled herself out of his embrace. "I don't know . . ."

It felt ridiculously dangerous to relax her wariness and allow someone else to be on guard. Like stepping out in front of a bus and hoping the driver would have time to put on the brakes. Dangerous, but at the same time unbelievably tempting.

"Come here."

He held her for a while, calm and silent. Then she felt the cell phone vibrate against her right thigh. Victor had answered.

"I'll be in Denmark tomorrow. I must speak to you. My life is in danger—and so is yours."

"MOMMY . . . CAN WE go to the Swim Center? Please? Pretty please?"

Anton was old enough now to have complete control over his powers of persuasion. He knew it irritated her when he whined and begged in that pathetic way, so he opened his eyes extra wide, batted his eyelashes, and offered her a smile that made Shirley Temple look like an amateur. All of it with just enough ironic exaggeration that she couldn't help laughing.

"We'll have to ask Søren first." What was she supposed to say if he asked why? *Because Søren has to determine if it's safe.* "And it won't be today, Anton. Maybe tomorrow."

"Why not?"

Luckily, he reacted to the limit she could more easily defend.

"Because . . . because I'm not completely well," she said.

The smile disappeared as if someone had erased it with a wet cloth. He tugged at his blue Man of Steel hoodie ("*I'm not saying I'm Superman. I'm just saying nobody has ever seen me and Superman in the same room.*") and looked both more grown-up and more afraid.

"Tomorrow is fine," he said quickly. "Filip and me can play at Filip's if you want."

You have two children who are afraid of losing you. Oh, Christ.

"Ask Filip if he wants to come here instead," she said and tried to look perky in spite of the stubborn headache. "Then we can make apple fritters and watch *The Lord of the Rings.*"

"All three of them?" he asked.

"If Filip is allowed." She quickly calculated what that promise entailed. Damn it. Nine solid hours of orcs and elves and epic battle scenes. So much for that day.

They were only halfway through the Mines of Moria, however, when the doorbell rang. Caroline Westmann, of the Mid-West Jutland Police.

"I hope I'm not interrupting," she said. "But there's something I'd like to show you. Is there someplace we can talk?"

Nina quickly evaluated the possibilities. The living room was occupied by fantasy fans and echoed with clashing swords and monstrous roars; in the conservatory her mother was teaching

Ida to knit (Ida? Knit? It was so unlike her that it almost defied belief). The three bedrooms, Nina felt, were all just too small and intimate for police interviews.

The kitchen. It would have to be the kitchen.

"Coffee? Would you like an apple fritter?" she asked.

Caroline Westmann declined politely but allowed herself to accept a cup of tea.

"I have to be a little careful about how much coffee I drink," she said apologetically, then immediately became professional and business-like again.

"I'd like to show you some photos," she said. "Please tell me if anyone seems familiar."

She looked around—it wasn't easy to find a ready surface that wasn't covered in grease and fritter batter. Nina quickly cleared the small dining table by dumping two bowls into the kitchen sink and wiping the vinyl tablecloth with a damp cloth, not entirely clean.

"Sorry. Half-term break."

"That's okay. My sister has children; I know what it's like."

Westmann placed the photographs on the table as if dealing a game of solitaire. There were a dozen or so, all men, all between about twenty and thirty-five, all more or less "European" looking—whatever that meant these days. Nina studied them, one at a time.

"No," she said. "They don't ring any bells. Who are they?"

"Try again," said Westmann. "Take as long as you need."

Søren emerged casually from the fantasy marathon and exchanged polite greetings. He loaded the coffee machine with water and freshly ground beans, but Nina didn't think it was a desperate craving for caffeine that had brought him here, and she suspected that Caroline Westmann was equally unconvinced.

He kept silent while Nina took another tour through the photo archive. Not until she repeated her negative—"I'm sorry, but I don't remember ever seeing any of them"—did he get involved.

"Did you find them? Your eastern Europeans?"

Caroline Westmann hesitated. Then she nodded.

"They were caught red-handed," she said. "Breaking and entering a holiday home on the coast. Two of the victims have already identified them, and so we were hoping . . ."

Nina shook her head again.

"No," she said. "I'm sorry."

"What about the DNA?" asked Søren. "From the jacket. Does it match?"

"We've only just sent the samples to be analyzed. That is, the new samples from our three bandits."

"And they were all eastern European?"

"Yes. From Bulgaria."

"Do you have anything that leads in a more Southeast Asian direction?"

"Where are you thinking of?"

"The Philippines?"

"No. That's not something we see every day here. Why?"

Søren held out his hand.

"Nina, may we see your phone?"

She became irrationally angry. Felt yet again that he was flattening the picket fences around her private life and stepping in the flower beds with very big feet. Still, she handed him her cell phone.

"I suspect that Nina has a kind of stalker," said Søren. "Look at this."

He showed Caroline the messages from Victor. Or she assumed that's what he was doing. She couldn't see the display.

"My life is in danger, and so is yours," the detective sergeant read. "It's a bit vague, but I'll make a note."

"And follow up?" asked Søren. "I could help you obtain a bit of info on this Victor Galang. If that's his real name."

"Through the PET?"

"Yes. We have excellent international connections."

"I was under the impression that you were on sick leave," said Caroline Westmann pointedly.

Søren looked as if she had just thrown the contents of her teacup into his face. It was only a second—a glimpse so brief that Nina afterward began to doubt it—then he smiled disarmingly and smoothed things over.

"That's correct," he said. "But that doesn't mean I can't ask a friend for a favor."

Caroline Westmann looked as if she regretted the jab.

"Well then, thank you. But as I said—we've not previously had problems with people from that part of the world."

She got up, put on her blue duffel coat and left, in a flurry of wind and autumn leaves.

Nina turned to Søren.

"Sick leave?"

There it was again—and this time she was more certain.

Shame. But why?

"Torben's idea," he said. "Completely unnecessary, but right now it means I can be here."

She bit her lip.

"And why is that so important?" she asked. She tried not to sound too cold, too dismissive.

"Don't you want me here?" he asked and suddenly looked like Anton when he was most uncertain.

"It was nice that you were there," she admitted. "At the hospital. It was nice for someone to be there. And that it was you. And . . . it was also nice that you were there last night."

That elicited a smile at least. But she had to go on.

"I was just a little surprised that you had moved into my mother's house."

"She invited me."

"She is perfectly entitled to."

"That didn't sound very heartfelt," he said and straightened to his full height. He was very nearly Morten's height, she realized. Her shoulder fit under his in almost the same way. Without warning, a jolt of desire shot from her belly button downward and made her legs rather wobbly.

He noticed. She could see him noticing, and that did not improve matters.

He pulled her close and kissed her thoroughly.

"Is it okay?" he asked. "That I'm here? Is it okay with you?"

"Yes," she answered hoarsely.

He let go of her. The house was full of kids. It was the half-term break. And they weren't teenagers who could go sit in the car and let their hormones take over.

"Good," he said, fairly hoarse himself. "That makes body-guarding you much easier."

He said it lightly, with the suggestion of a smile. But she was pretty sure he meant it seriously.

THE PHILIPPINES, SIX MONTHS EARLIER

"MY HOUSES."

Vadim pointed across the steering wheel at something that at this distance was merely a group of shimmering dark smears in the heat haze across the rice paddies. "Four blocks, six stories each, altogether eight hundred apartments and homes for almost four thousand people. My work is done."

"You do realize, don't you, that the people who are going to live in those fancy buildings of yours are being forced to move out here because the city council in Manila would like the city to look at bit more appealing to tourists?" Diana considered Vadim across the edge of her Gucci sunglasses, and it was as if her gaze punctured his smugness.

"And do you realize that every teenage girl you treat for pneumonia in the slums will have ten undernourished kids who'll also get pneumonia and live a shitty life? Stuck in the mud—quite literally. Filthy, sewage-contaminated mud. Here at least there's some sort of future. Indoor plumbing. Flushing toilets. No more crapping in the river," he said.

Vincent took a sip of his cola and glanced in the rearview mirror. The mood in the car had been oppressive since they left Manila in the early morning. At first Diana had not wanted to go at all, and it was Victor, not Vadim, who had at last convinced her.

Now she sat looking out at the landscape with a dark and sombre gaze. White T-shirt, dark blue shorts and a pair of worn flip-flops. She had become a resident just a month ago and was now working for starvation wages in a minor hospital only ten kilometers from "Vadim's phallic constructions," as she called them. In pediatrics. She wanted to become a pediatrician.

"Have all the apartments been let?" asked Victor. His enormous body occupied so much of the backseat that his hair grazed the roof, and Diana was perched against the door on her side to give him a little more room.

"Yes, most people moved out here a month ago. All the units went pretty quickly. People like it."

Diana snorted.

"It wasn't as if they had much choice. The police bulldozed a half-kilometer strip along Pasig River and burned the rest."

Vadim ran his hand through his hair with an irritated gesture. It had been like this since he and Diana broke up about six months ago. A constant battle. It would, of course, have been easier if they had stopped spending time with each other, but that had apparently not occurred to either as a possibility. They met as usual at the Cabana Bar when Diana was in town, and presumably also at home in their respective laps of luxury. Vadim and Diana's families saw each other socially, lived in the same gated community and attended the same cocktail parties. Vincent also knew that Vadim and Diana still occasionally slept together. It seemed to be a kind of withdrawal symptom sex, and when it happened Vadim would be whistling, cheerful and full of hope, and Diana dark and shuttered. Like now.

"Sometimes people don't know what's best for them," said Vadim. "In fact, I'd think that most people, myself included, would do better to have others make the decisions about their lives."

"I'm not surprised that you think so," said Diana. "After all you've always had your father to do precisely that."

Vadim slapped a flat hand against the steering wheel but didn't answer.

They were slowly approaching Vadim's apartment complex. The road was newly paved and bordered by long, brown grass, skinny palm trees, and flat, vividly green rice paddies. Here and there were small clusters of old-fashioned huts with woven bamboo walls and tin roofs, but the teeming multitude of roadside booths and advertising signs that had edged Paradise Road closer to the Manila suburb of Lungsod had dwindled to nothing, and the four buildings towered like lonely human silos in the flat landscape. A few discarded trucks and cement mixers from the construction were still parked in the yellow dust in front of the first building. The remains of cement sacks and plastic tarps flapped in the faint breeze, and a group of kids who had been playing among the building materials ran away screeching when Vadim stopped the car.

Vincent opened his door and was instantly hit by the oppressively hot air. He knew the buildings already. Had been here several times with Vadim during their construction to keep an eye on the work force and the suppliers. Vadim had gradually become a kind of job to him. They were together almost twenty-four hours a day. Lived in the penthouse apartment Vadim's father had bought—cool and spacious, with white tiles on the floors and a room for each of them, including Victor, a huge living room, and a state-of-the-art kitchen. Not to mention the roof deck that had its own swimming pool. Everything was neatly cleaned by a housekeeper who came every afternoon and removed the empty, greasy glasses, the ashtrays, and the pizza cartons. That was the kind of service you got used to when you were with Vadim.

Vincent had dragged himself through the third and fourth semesters, but by the fifth it was over. He had failed spectacularly. Both subjects. Finished and done for.

It hadn't come as a surprise. It felt inevitable, as if the numbers posted outside the director's office were predetermined.

Father Abuel used to speak of the inexorable will of God. Death was unavoidable, and man's fate lay in the hands of God. You could try to fight against it, but it would be like attempting to stop an earthquake with your bare hands. Impossible. God's will was, after all, stronger than that of Vincent's parents and infinitely stronger than his own.

It must have been the episode at the hospital that had been the final straw. Officially they weren't graded on it; it was just a study visit to give them a chance to observe some orthopedic surgical procedures. A knee operation came first. Vincent had had a nervous sensation in his body, a kind of tremor in his chest—it felt as if some alien creature in there was throwing itself against his ribs to get out. He could barely think of anything else, but had managed to put on the green operation gown with slow, stiff movements and to pull the mask over his mouth. The chemical smell of the plastic made his abdomen contract, and he tried to think about something good. About Bea and the boy. Carlito. This tiny, perfectly formed person who had clung to his hand with chubby fingers when he visited them two weeks earlier. But all that kept coming back to him was the two hundred thousand pesos he had gradually received from Vadim, and all the money his parents had paid for his dorm room the first year, for the food he had eaten and the beer he had drunk. Money that had been set aside with great effort over twenty years, paycheck by paycheck, bill by bill. His mother drawing the heavy, black *niquabs* out of the steaming laundry tub. His father smoothing boiling asphalt in some distant land. Vincent pictured the money torn fluttering from their hands, as if they were caught in a hurricane.

The patient was already lying on the operating table with strips of sticky tape on his closed eyelids. An elderly man, somewhat obese. No doubt rich. Cruciate ligament ruptured on the tennis court, the surgeon said. The room stank of rubbing alcohol and metal, and the instruments for the operation were being laid out. Victor was already bending eagerly forward to take it all in. Something that looked like a compass saw, a hammer, and a chisel. Tools to break bones and sinews. A panicked sweat broke out under Vincent's T-shirt, and he suddenly felt certain that he was going to die. Right now and right here on the tiled hospital floor. It was only with the utmost effort that he managed to obey the lecturer's order to come closer.

At the first cut the skin parted willingly, like it did when his father cut up a pig in the kitchen at home. The fat, the sinews, and the patella itself gleamed whitely through the brilliant red flow of the blood. Perhaps it would have been better if he hadn't eaten, but he had. Rice cooked with garlic and *daing*, dried fish.

When the nausea finally overpowered him, the lumpy breakfast shot out of both nose and mouth with great power and hit the tiles with a splash. He was escorted out by nurses with tight smiles, and the surgeon's gaze above the edge of his mask said it all.

He would never become a doctor. All his parents' plans, all the carefully stacked bills . . . in vain.

Now he did the things Vadim asked him to do, and in return Vadim handed him the occasional handful of cash. Or paid for his drinks. Once in a while Vincent sent Bea a picture of himself standing outside the director's office at the university, making a victory sign in front of the grade board.

He still hadn't figured out what would happen next year when he was supposed to be a resident earning a little money. He tried not to think too much about it, just as he tried to avoid thinking about little Mimi, who had finished high school and gotten a temporary job as a clerk at the pharmacy back home. The plan was for him to start saving money toward a software-programming course for Mimi as soon as he was being paid, because unfortunately she had not distinguished herself with good grades or especially moral behavior. At least, Father Abuel had not recommended her for the church's scholarship. She was a good girl, said their mother, but the boys liked her and it seemed to be mutual. Father Abuel did not look kindly on that kind of behavior.

Vincent kicked one of the empty concrete sacks so the cement dust rose around him in a white cloud. They were covered with

Chinese characters, and Vincent was taken aback. The engineer who had originally been responsible for the construction had insisted they stay away from the Chinese supplier. He and Vadim had had a long and heated discussion about it back when the enormous pits for the foundations were being dug.

"Eden Towers," Vadim announced with a "Ta-da!" voice worthy of a circus ringmaster. "Well, what do you think?"

He jumped familiarly over a couple of abandoned plastic basins and strode to the front of the massive grey building.

"The rent is cheap, and there's running water, electricity and gas. A public school in that direction . . ." He pointed out across the fields toward something in the distance that looked townlike. Tin and tile roofs that glittered in the sun.

Even Diana couldn't help smiling at his enthusiasm.

"Very nice," she said in the same exaggerated tone that she might use to praise a child and its sand castle. "Did you build it yourself?"

"Yes, damn it, I did." Vadim leaned his head back and looked up toward the top floors. Skinny, half-naked children played on the covered walkways, and a couple of teenagers perched on the railing with no apparent qualms about the drop.

"But you know, of course, that there's nowhere for them to earn money for the rent," said Diana. "The men are probably already back in Manila, in the process of building a shack along the railroad tracks or in one of the cemeteries. And as soon as they've knocked together a few pieces of tin, the whole family will be back where they started."

Vadim took out a cigarette, lit it, and followed the smoke with narrow eyes.

"That's all politics, Diana. Can't you just be pleased that things are going well for me, and I've built some pretty decent buildings? Those kids have never tried sitting on a proper toilet before."

Diana nodded and flashed a rare, sweet smile.

"Okay," she said. "The buildings are nice, but the politics are rotten. Can we agree on that?"

Vadim turned his palms upward as a sign of his total capitulation, climbed into one of the old trucks, and hammered the horn in as deep as it would go.

"She smiled!" he shouted. "Vincent and Victor, break out the champagne."

THEY DRANK CHILLED champagne and ate longan fruit in the sizzling heat of the truck's battered cab. Flocks of kids had already scavenged just about everything that could be scavenged, but there was still a bit of cushion foam left to sit on.

Afterward Victor and Diana took their bags and started on the first stairwell, looking for infected wounds, undernourished children, and pregnant women. Their favorite Sunday pastime.

Vadim's narrowed gaze followed them.

"How are Bea and the boy doing?"

"Fine." Vincent didn't feel like talking about it. "Did you get the cement from the Chinese after all?"

Vadim took a few longans, peeled them and threw the juicy, grape-like fruits into his mouth.

"It was too expensive with the other supplier. I wouldn't have been able to stay on budget. I think that engineer had been bought by the others, so I fired him. I'm actually a good businessman, Vincent. It's in my genes. And . . . speaking of business . . ."

Vincent's muscles clenched automatically. There was something about Vadim's look that made him think of free diving. Of being under nine meters of water with no air in his lungs.

"You owe me a favor, my man."

"Yes," whispered Vincent. "I do." He hadn't intended to whisper; it kind of happened on its own.

"That engineer. The one I fired."

"Yes."

"He is blackmailing me. Or trying to."

"How?"

"It's the thing about the cement. It's completely legal and up to standard, but he's pissed off about the firing. Said he would report me for swindling the World Bank. It's a lie, but he knows that a report could harm both me and my father. He's just an envious little asshole. And this is where you come in, Vincent my man."

"How?"

"You have to make him stop. Teach him to behave."

"Me?"

"Yes. Why not? Those biceps you've so carefully developed should be used for something."

"I don't want to beat anyone up!"

Vadim furrowed his brow.

"And you won't. You just need to . . . look threatening. I know his type of asshole; they fall apart as soon as they come up against opposition. So? Can I count on you?"

It wasn't a real question. Vincent could see the chill in Vadim's eyes, the costs of saying no.

"Fucking hell, Vadim. You want me to be your gorilla?"

"No. I want you to be my friend. And friends help each other when things get tough. Right? *I helped you.*"

Vincent sank a small sharp lump in his throat.

"Okay, okay," he said. "Of course . . . I'll help you."

Vincent thumped him on the shoulder—so hard and loud that it resounded.

"I knew it," he said. "You and me. And Victor too, of course. The V-Team forever!"

"The V-Team forever," mumbled Vincent, momentarily bedazzled. Vadim's approval washed across him like a warm Pacific wave.

He got out his cell and put some music on. Ella Fitzgerald and "Blue Moon."

"You should start smoking," said Vadim, glancing over at him with a half smile. "It would suit you now that you are a grown man with a dirty secret."

Vincent nodded and drank the last of his champagne. The heat and Ella made him sleepy. He was no longer a student, no longer the best in any class, and no longer a boy who behaved well in the eyes of God . . . But what was he then?

One day before too long he would have to ask Father Abuel. You could crouch by the toilet bowl and hold back your vomit for only so long. At some point the deluge would come.

"But what if it's true?" asked Nina. "What if his life really *is* in danger?"

Søren would have preferred to have this conversation in a less exposed place—at home in the house on Cherry Lane, for example. True, Viborg's new Swim Center and Water Park was so full of shrieking, splashing, shrilly screaming children and attendant grown-ups that an attacker would need to be unusually cold-blooded to act here, and the first assault had hardly seemed professional—but as Torben often said, "Only fools do not fear the amateur." The lone madman, that invisible and ordinary man with his hidden insanity, was one of the worst nightmares of any intelligence service. Unpredictable and almost impossible to trace because he didn't communicate with anyone, but cultivated his murderous fantasies alone. Until the day he attempted to carry them out in reality . . .

It was Anton's careful begging—oddly defeated and without expectations—that had made him give in. It was the boy's half-term break, after all, it was a public place, and they couldn't shut themselves in indefinitely. He had sent off a couple of emails to Gitte in the hope of getting something on Victor even before he had so assiduously offered Caroline Westmann his assistance, but as he had pointed out himself, there was absolutely no guarantee that Facebook-Victor really *was* Victor. And the line the man had used—"My life is in danger—and so is yours"—was apparently quite effective because Nina was, as far as he could judge, deeply disturbed.

"Mommy!" shouted Anton from the one-meter board. "Mommy, look now. BOOOOOMB!"

The board gave a metallic *sproooiiing*, and Anton threw himself into the air, bent his legs up against his body and let himself drop toward the water's surface like a small, boy-shaped missile. The splash was impressive, considering his skinny nine-year-old frame.

"Nice!" shouted Nina when Anton's head appeared again like a seal's in a hole in the ice. He grinned proudly and exuberantly, swam with only slightly awkward breaststrokes to the ladder and raced back to rejoin the line by the diving board. Water ran down his torso and legs and collected in a small puddle at his feet. The Swim Center was buzzing with the holiday crowd—the worst bottleneck was the long water slide where several children had begun to shiver with cold while they waited for their turn. Anton had sensibly thrown his affection onto one of the less populated attractions, and Ida was drifting contentedly in the warm-water pool next door.

Anton undertook a number of small jumps in place to stay warm.

"Aren't you coming in?" he shouted to Nina.

"Not today, sweetie."

Søren cleared his throat carefully to prevent a cough—the swimming pool's chlorine vapors were not exactly what his annoyingly delicate lungs needed. *What a pair*, he thought. Nina with her fading blue-black "raccoon eyes" and the shaved, bandaged spot at the back of her head, he with his bronchial weakness. Quite pathetic, really.

He hadn't yet revealed the actual reason for his enforced medical leave, and she hadn't asked. Maybe the fractured skull had shaken her more than was first apparent.

His physical weaknesses were only half the truth, although there were plenty of them by now. It was as if his bed rest had made everything fall apart. His dodgy knee had grown worse instead of better from the break in training, go figure; infections seemed to be lining up in order to invade his compromised chest; and the doctors had begun to talk about chronic bronchitis—bronchitis, he had never had bronchitis, damnit, not even the almost obligatory pollen allergy. Colleagues had sniffled and coughed their way through the birch while he had remained unfazed. Not so anymore. To add insult to injury, something that felt like repeated stabs in his left hip turned out to be arthritis, caused by many years of favoring the dodgy knee, and as if that wasn't enough, he had begun to suffer from headaches and attacks of dizziness for the first time in his life. They had pulled out all the stops to make sure that he hadn't quietly suffered "a minor stroke" or an aneurysm—"It happens occasionally at your age, Søren, when we are forced to stay in bed for a while," explained the surgeon, not a day over thirty-five and annoyingly chipper in spite of his twelve-hour-long workday.

Being a group leader in PET was no walk in the park. You couldn't just go home at four in the afternoon or "take a break when you need to," as his physical therapist had recommended.

He didn't damn well have the *time* to have a headache. Pinex and Tylenol became standard inventory in his briefcase and glove compartment. He wasn't stupid; he didn't exceed the maximum dosage; the problem was that *every* day was a hard day, and that the pills only took the edge off the headache and, as time passed, barely that.

His attempt to return to work had ended in the most embarrassing form of collapse. In the middle of a meeting with the fraud squad, or the Department for Special Economic Crime as it was properly called, about the flow of money in a minor but fairly complicated anti-terror case, he had begun to have tunnel vision. He tried to sit completely still, eyes deliberately unfocused, which sometimes worked, but you can't really direct a meeting without looking at the person who is speaking. He had had to suggest a break, even though he could see that the others thought they had barely started. He had planned to go and lie down on the floor in the bathroom, another occasionally successful trick, especially with the application of a wet paper towel to the forehead, if he could find a bathroom that had not yet had those noisy, energy-consuming air dryers installed instead.

Instead, he collapsed the moment he got up. Bang. No further warnings, the light just went out and returned several minutes later as he lay on his side—Recovery Position, of course, he was surrounded by people who knew their first aid—on the woodblock floor of the conference room.

He was brought to Herlev Hospital, sirens and blue lights ablaze—it seemed no humiliation was to be spared. He had, of course, also crapped in his pants—that was unavoidable when you were deeply unconscious, he knew that, but that didn't make it any damn less embarrassing. And after almost a week of observation and tests, someone mentioned the S-word for the first time:

"There is also the possibility, Søren, that this is your body's reaction to stress."

No way. He wasn't the kind who got stressed out. It didn't matter how many times he had advised others on his staff that it could happen to anyone, and that you shouldn't consider it a weakness, but rather a sign that you had been much too strong for much too long. This was not a logic he thought could in any way apply to him.

Now he was on leave. Three months at least, "and then we'll have to see," Torben had said.

But the writing on the wall blinked neon bright. The PET could not afford to have a group leader who was incapacitated by stress. Stress resistance was a part of the job description. It damn near *was* the job description. He knew without having seen it what Torben had written in his private notes: "Transfer to other work?" That's probably what it would have said in his own notebook had the roles been reversed, but that didn't make it any better. The question mark might even be optimistic; it might be an exclamation point.

Søren felt betrayed. By his friend, by his boss, by life in general, but first and foremost by his own body. How could it trick him in this way?

He knew, of course, that it was only in the world of fiction that the hero groaned, "It's only a scratch," got up with a bullet in his body, and went on as if nothing much had happened. He also knew that a body with nearly fifty years on the clock healed more slowly than one with twenty-five. He had been prepared for a certain convalescence. But that he might not get better, that this might not be just a question of time—that he would have to sit here and twiddle his thumbs to avoid "physical and psychological stress"—this, he would never have believed. He was one of the tough guys. That had always been taken completely for granted as part of his identity, not something he needed to announce or pay attention to, it was just *there*—the knowledge that he could take more than most people.

That was probably why he hadn't told Nina. Because he was ashamed.

He hauled his focus back to the present and to the matter of Nina's Filipino Facebook friend and possible stalker.

"He's just trying to manipulate you," he said. "Classic technique. If he can get you to suspend your normal judgment, he is on a roll. It's pretty much the same principal as Nigerian prince scams."

"Nigerian prince scams?" said Nina, raising a sarcastic eyebrow. "You think he's just out to get my banking details? Aren't we short a dramatic story about an unclaimed inheritance, or something?"

"There's plenty of drama," he said dryly. "The lure here is just fear and compassion instead of greed."

"Mommy! Look!"

It was once again Anton's turn on the diving board.

"Yes, sweetie."

Anton began to bounce up and down on the board to build maximum power for the jump. Then he launched himself into the air, curling up into his usual bombing style. But Søren saw in a chilling second, and Nina apparently also, that the jump was *too* vertical. He hit the board on the way down, gave a cry of pain and rotated so he hit the water's surface sideways instead of with his bottom first. The impact was so loud that Søren cringed in pure reflex. Nina had kicked her shoes off even before Anton hit the water. She dived in fully dressed—head first, Søren noted—and had hold of her son before the professional lifeguard at the end of the pool had a chance to react. Søren could hear her speaking quietly and soothingly to him.

"Lie still for a moment. I've got you. Just relax."

She lay on her back and held him close to her chest with one arm while she kept them both afloat with powerful kicks and paddling strokes of her free arm. The other bathers made room so she could cross to the ladder, but when one of them moved to take hold of his legs, she sharply told him not to.

"It's okay," she said. "I have him."

The lifeguard had reached the edge of the pool.

"Is he okay?" he asked.

"We need a board or a stretcher," said Nina. "I want to have his back and neck supported before we try to get him out."

The lifeguard nodded briefly and professionally and sent a short signal on his walkie-talkie. Then he let himself slip into the water next to Nina. He didn't try to take Anton from her.

"I'm just here if you get tired," he said.

Nina nodded.

"Mom, I . . . it's not that bad," said Anton, but you could see in his pale face and trembling shoulders that he was both battered and scared.

"Good," said Nina.

More lifeguards appeared, and Anton was carefully lifted out of the water on a stretcher. Nina climbed out, soaked and with water streaming from her T-shirt and jeans, and knelt down next to Anton.

More and more of an audience gathered around them, and the swimming pool's personnel were having a hard time keeping them at a distance.

"What happened?"

"Did he drown?"

"Did someone die?"

Søren slid routinely in front of some of the pushiest onlookers and forced them back with a mixture of brawn and authority. Most moved willingly; a pair of loud young teenagers were the only ones with whom he had to seriously use his "police" glare.

"Please give the staff room to work." The words were polite, but the words didn't mean anything. It was the hard, completely unsmiling look and a certain steeliness in his posture that made the incipient teenage rebellion fold.

"Okay, okay. We're going . . ."

"Søren!" A hand hooked on to his sleeve. "Where's Anton? Where's Mom?" Ida's eyes were pitch-black with fearful foreboding.

"Nothing serious happened," he said. "Ida, it's okay."

She didn't listen. She slid under his arm and snaked her way past a couple of broad lifeguard backs.

"Anton!"

Søren could hear Nina speak calmingly to both her children, but he could no longer see them properly. What exactly it was that made him look up then, he didn't know. Maybe just the hyperawareness that his fear for Nina's safety had equipped him with.

Up on the balcony, a figure stood leaning on the railing. Or rather, several people, following the drama. But there was only one who was eagerly photographing the scene.

It could be an overzealous local journalist or some random person with enough carrion instincts to figure that there might be money to be made, especially if a death was involved. Søren had caught the glint of a lens, recognized the stance, but other details were difficult to determine. Was the coat greenish brown, as Nina had described it? He couldn't tell. It was too high up, the balcony group was backlit, and his glasses had a tendency to mist up in the steamy atmosphere.

He had to try to get closer. He looked back. The Center staff looked as if they had the situation well in hand. Anton had not been allowed to get up, but he was moving. Two lifeguards hoisted the stretcher and carried it in the direction of the changing rooms, and Nina and Ida followed them, Nina with her arm around her daughter's shoulder. Søren glanced again in the direction of the balcony. The photographer had stopped shooting and was on his way out. It was now or never if Søren was to get a better look at him.

Søren hurried toward the exit to the parking lot. It was a gamble, because there were other routes that were just as likely—the Swim Center was right next to the train station and therefore central to just about every kind of public transportation, or a taxi for that matter. But he knew he wouldn't be able to get up the stairs fast enough to maintain visual contact, so this was the only option. He was lucky. Shortly after he reached one of the tall glass doors, a man came racing down the stairs still with a camera in his left hand. Søren automatically noted certain basic details—Southeast Asian–looking, young and fairly fit, sunglasses, baseball cap and the overly large military green parka that to a certain degree blurred the outline of his shoulders and upper body and made the rest look thin and twiggy, like the legs on a stick figure. Søren fished his own car keys out of his pocket and followed him, calm and relaxed, just a man who happened to be getting his car.

The parking lot was full, and there was even some unauthorized parking where drivers had pulled their cars halfway onto the sidewalk outside the delineated spaces. The photographer headed for a white Toyota Land Cruiser that was clearly equipped as a camping van, with heightened ceiling, a mini satellite dish, a rolled-up sun shield along one side, curtains in the windows, even a rubber raft on the roof—it looked like something that should be driven around the Australian outback rather than Viborg's smooth asphalt streets. Søren was still too far away to see the license plate and much too far to plant a tracer. If he had had one, that was . . . damn. He was as civilian as you could be. He riffled through his pockets, but knew that a microtransmitter wouldn't miraculously appear no matter how many times he turned them out.

On the other hand . . . one of the Land Cruiser's back windows was open a crack. Another possibility popped into Søren's head and he felt a wide, self-satisfied grin pull at the corners of his mouth. He sped up. The photographer had already gotten in and was starting the engine. Søren had to run a few steps to make the timing work, but just as the Toyota backed out of the row, he slapped his hands hard against the side of the car and shouted at the top of his lungs.

"Hey! Watch out. Look where you're going, asshole!"

He didn't think the man would be able to understand the words, but road rage was an international phenomenon, and the anger ought to shock and frighten him sufficiently that the driver wouldn't notice Søren's real mission. His iPhone slid in through the open window and landed someplace in the camper's interior with a barely audible thump.

The man behind the wheel looked suitably shocked. His mouth was a dark distorted hole, his shades gleamed in startled blindness, and he hit the brakes so hard the ABS came on with an uneven shudder.

But what happened next took Søren entirely by surprise. As the door flew open, a fist shot out, and something else, something hard, hit him in the chest. His entire nervous system sizzled and shut down. He collapsed like an ox in an abattoir, and his head hit the asphalt with an ominous crunch.

A Taser, he thought before the lights faded completely. *The guy has a fucking Taser.*

THE PHILIPPINES, SIX MONTHS EARLIER

"COME ON. GET it over with."

Vincent had to say it out loud to himself before he could do it.

He had to be strong now. Had to nerve himself up like he had done when he was little and what he had been told to do scared him. Do it. Be a good, obedient boy. Darkness had just fallen, and the car, still parked in front of the engineer's office, would not be there much longer.

The man who owned the silver Toyota would appear and drive it home, and then it would be too late for today. And it was important, Vadim had said. It was urgent.

Vincent took one of Victor's chef's knives from his backpack and squatted down next to the car. There were still people in the street, men in suits, and street vendors, and teenage girls in brief shorts who reminded him of Mimi. It stressed him out, but he doubted that anyone would notice or make any move to stop him as long as he was quick and effective. He jabbed the knife into the first tire. It was surprisingly hard and tough to cut through—he had to push with all his weight against the knife handle and wriggle it back and forth to create even a crack in the rubber. He made as long and deep a cut as he was able to.

The result was not impressive, and the tire didn't even seem punctured.

"What are you doing?"

A man, dressed in jeans and a shirt and wearing a pair of off-center spectacles, had stopped and was staring angrily down at Vincent's kneeling figure. Three large warts jutted from his chin. He looked like a toad, thought Vincent. It helped to think ugly thoughts about other people, he had discovered. It produced an anger he needed. Still, he had to pull himself together in order not to get up and walk away.

"I work for the guy with the car," said Vincent in as hard a tone as he could muster. "Mind you own business."

The guy shrugged his shoulders and walked on, while Vincent prodded the tire. The sweat was already pouring off him, and he hadn't done any significant damage yet. He had to give up on the tires and think of something else. He let the knife's point slide along the silver-grey side of the car. A deep scratch appeared, and in a few places the paintwork cracked and fell off in small flakes. Much better.

He repeated the procedure on the other side of the car. The man needed to be able to tell that the damage was deliberate. A punishment. People like him weren't afraid of the police, said Vadim. They could buy their way out of anything.

A few pedestrians were slowing down to look at him before passing by. He had a knife, he reminded himself. They were more afraid of him than he was of them. He took a step backward and considered his work with narrowed eyes. That would have to do, but the most important element was still missing. He put the knife back in his bag, walked away from the car and went to stand at the entrance to the small run-down park on the other side of the road. The man had to see him.

A little more than half an hour passed before the engineer appeared. Vincent recognized him from the construction site and many heated arguments with Vadim. He was around forty and a good-looking guy. Muscular and well built in a nonshowy way and with a youthful energy. He usually wore jeans and a T-shirt and had an attentive dark gaze.

But that didn't mean he couldn't be an asshole.

He had started blackmailing Vadim some months ago, just after he was fired as chief engineer on the rehousing project. Vincent didn't know the details, but some men from the building crew outside the city had seen him several times out at the construction site, where he stood smoking and staring at the workers. He had also started sending letters to Vadim. Vincent had seen them lying on Vadim's desk.

The guy produced a cigarette and went into one of the narrow shops a bit further down the sidewalk. A little later he came out with a steaming carton, which he poked at with a plastic fork. Rice and some kind of meat and sauce. Dinner already. He rested his back against the wall of the nearest house while he ate and was clearly in no hurry. Music reached the street from a window above him, house remix with a psychotic pounding rhythm. Vincent wanted it all to be over, just as he wanted Vadim not to have given him the task in the first place. There were definitely others whom Vadim could have hired and who would have been better qualified than Vincent.

But it wasn't a question of qualifications. Vincent knew that. It was about something else. This was Vadim's punishment because he had asked him for money and received it. It was the thumb ring and the lead belt all over again—"How far would you go for me? Friends do anything for each other. Come on, Vincent, my man. Show me that I can trust you . . ."

The engineer caught sight of him from the other side of the street and stopped mid-movement. The fork hung suspended in front of his mouth for a long second before he finally shoveled in the last bit of rice, threw the carton away and headed for his car. He let a hand run along the scratch all the way around the car before he shot Vincent another fast look, got in and drove off with shrieking tires. The car sideswiped one of the horse-drawn *kalesaes* and made the skinny horse jump on the pocked asphalt.

Vincent dried his forehead and headed in the same direction. He didn't know how long he would have to keep this up. Hunting the asshole twenty-four hours a day. Until he had had enough, Vadim had said, but only Vadim knew when that was.

He caught a taxi at the corner of San Pablo and J. P. Rizal. He had enough money at the moment; Vadim had been generous when he assigned the task and the means to carry it out.

"You don't have to hurt him, just frighten him," Vadim had said. "I don't care how you do it, as long as it is effective and he stops sending me those damned letters. He sent my father one last week. To his home address. Jesus Christ. It was only because I happened to be there that weekend that I had time to snatch it before my father read it. The man is crazy."

Vincent looked at the piece of paper with the address that Vadim had given him. It wasn't a fancy neighborhood. Apartments for the lower middle class, no swimming pools or lush gardens. The engineer's scratched car was parked outside already. Vincent paid the taxi and looked around quickly for his backup, as Vadim had called him. Vadim had insisted he bring an extra man when he went to see the engineer.

"I don't trust him," Vadim had said. "Some of the things he has written are clearly threatening. You can bring Martinez. He looks the part."

Martinez was a security guard at the company's construction sites, employed to ensure they weren't completely cleaned out of construction materials. He was half a head shorter than Vincent but broad in all the right places, had several gold teeth and a tattoo of a skull on his calf. Vincent had never spoken with him before. Now he appeared from the opposite side of the parking lot, waving with a complicit grin. He had a loose, relaxed gait and was showing off his round, beefed-up arms in a snow-white tank top.

Amateurs, thought Vincent. *What the hell are we doing?*

"You know what we're here for?"

"Yes, man. I've spoken with the boss." Martinez flashed all his gold teeth in an idiotic grin. Vincent didn't like him and didn't feel like chatting. Instead he turned around and rang the lobby bell.

The reception cubicle was manned by a uniformed doorman with a pistol, but that shouldn't be a problem, as long as they spoke politely.

"Lorenz Robles?"

The doorman, who wasn't much older than Vincent, sent them a haughty look through the no-doubt bulletproof glass door. Then he walked over to the intercom with his hand on his pistol.

"And who should I say is here?"

"We have a message for him from Vadim."

"Who?"

Either the guy liked to take his time or he was unusually slow.

"You don't need to worry about that," said Vincent and smiled as nicely as possible. He held a one-hundred peso bill up against the window. "Just tell him what I said."

The guy turned around and carried on a short, inaudible conversation with someone else on the other side of the glass door. Then he nodded, opened the door for Vincent, and had his reward pressed into one palm.

"You can take the elevator to the fourth floor. It's apartment 4B."

Vincent walked past him to the elevator. He was nervous now, and his heart was beating much too fast, as if his body was preparing for something terrible. He had never liked direct confrontation. Martinez was bouncing about next to him like a boxer on speed.

"He's an asshole," Vincent repeated to himself. "He wants to destroy everything."

"YES?"

The man who opened the door looked surprisingly calm. He was wearing glasses now, the modern kind that you saw in American commercials, and he had changed into knee-length shorts. He crossed his arms and regarded them with a neutral gaze. He was a couple of inches taller than Vincent. From behind him came the sounds of a couple of teenage boys arguing mildly in front of the television.

Vincent cleared his throat.

"Vadim asked me to tell you that you're to keep your mouth shut and stay away from his buildings."

The man shifted his stance. Made himself broader. He had a wide jaw and was chewing on something. Gum, maybe. His eyes narrowed as he considered Vincent through his specially made high-index lenses.

"You're a couple of tough guys, you and your pal. Am I supposed to be scared now?"

Vincent felt like saying no. He didn't like this. His heart was pounding so hard he could feel it in his throat.

"Tell your boss that I'll keep this up as long as it is necessary," said the engineer. "He asked for it." He took a step backward and prepared to close the door.

Vincent's shoulders slumped. If he was supposed to scare this man, he clearly wasn't doing a very good job. He had thought it would be different. A quick exchange during which the man would reveal himself as a first-rate asshole, would bluster a bit, and then cower in terror. Vadim, after all, was not just anybody. Most particularly, his *father* was not just anybody in this city.

"Don't count on getting any work again," he shouted through the closing door. The engineer paused to bare his teeth with a haughty snarl.

"You're a dog. A mangy, cowardly dog," he said. The voice was cold and steady, and for a brief moment Vincent felt as if the man had X-ray vision and could see right through him. Could see all the dirt and dishonesty. The boys in the living room had turned up the volume on an Elvis song they'd found someplace out there in the crackling electronic universe. "I'll remember you." Soft voice, slow calypso. Vincent's grandmother loved Elvis.

He closed his eyes and wanted to turn away. Disappear. Then he felt a movement next to him. Martinez, who shot forward and kicked the door open the second before the lock clicked.

"I'll kill you," he shouted. "I'll fucking kill you, you big asshole." The engineer tumbled backward into the hallway, cradling one hand. Martinez grabbed him by the neck and hammered his knee into the engineer's face.

There was a faint crunch, of spectacles or cartilage or both, and the engineer sank to his knees with a long sigh.

Elvis crooned on.

"Did you have trouble understanding anything my friend just told you?"

Martinez kicked him in the face again, so the crumpled glasses flew to one side and slid along the tiled floor.

The engineer remained on his knees, curled over to protect his body and face. He didn't look up at them. Blood and saliva dribbled between his fingers.

"What are the names of your boys in there? And your wife? Is she good in bed? A sweet little *pinay* with a shaved pussy? Cameltoe? Make sure it's shaved. That's how I like it, even when it's an older lady. If you have a daughter, that's fine too."

Martinez was still bouncing on the balls of his feet, raring to go, like a boxer waiting for his opponent to get up after a knockout. When the engineer showed no sign of answering or rising to his feet, Martinez concluded his display by firing off a large spitball into the man's sweaty hair.

The living room had gone quiet. It was as if the entire world was holding its breath along with Vincent, paralyzed by Martinez's insane dance.

Then Martinez turned away, shot a crooked smile at Vincent and pounded him on the shoulder, before striding off toward the elevator, beefy arms swinging.

"Come on. We're out of here."

Vincent didn't move. He couldn't take his eyes off the engineer on the hallway floor. He was stirring now. Wiped one hand across his face, and looked up. Two teenage boys had appeared behind him and stood staring at Vincent and their father. Their mother shouted something from another room, but no one answered her.

The engineer's bloodshot eyes rested on Vincent.

"I'm actually trying to help your boss," he said. "It's important for you to understand that. There's still time. Tell Vadim that."

And then, as if this was the signal he had been waiting for, Vincent could suddenly move again. He turned and ran toward the waiting elevator without looking back.

"That took you long enough," said Martinez.

He pressed the button for the lobby and pounded some kind of idiotic drum rhythm on his thigh all the way down. He was clearly in a good mood and was feeling generous enough to leave twenty pesos for the guard in the lobby. Outside in the parking lot he threw a shiny, glass-like look at Vincent and put a hand on his shoulder.

"Do you want to grab a beer? The night is young."

Vincent took an involuntary step back and fervently wished the warm darkness would swallow him. Let him disappear out of the world as easily and unconsciously as he had entered it.

"No, thank you," he mumbled.

"Need a lift?"

Martinez gestured toward a beat-up red Mazda that had clearly seen some heavy infighting in Manila's traffic. The license plate was crooked, like the mouth of someone partially paralyzed by a stroke.

"I'll walk," said Vincent, but that was a lie. He ran.

"COME ON. BREATHE. Don't die!"

Die. Søren wasn't planning to. Hands took hold of his face, tipped his head back, then pinched his nostrils closed, which didn't seem to gel with the command to breathe. Seconds later, he felt a wet, onion-smelling mouth close on his own while the mouth's owner blew a lungful of recycled air into him.

Mouth-to-mouth resuscitation? Why was someone trying to resuscitate him? A cramped cough loosened something tight and strange in his abdomen, and the first-aid fanatic mercifully retreated. Søren opened his eyes and saw the bulky camouflage-colored parka above him, with a person inside, presumably, but the enormous fur-lined hood covered most of the face.

The hood and face disappeared out of his field of vision.

"Don't move. Don't scream. If you do, I have to kill you."

A few minutes after giving me mouth-to-mouth? Make up your mind. Søren had received several much more convincing death threats in his career, but there was a buzzing, singing lack of response in his body when his brain tried to send instructions to his muscles. The Taser. The man had shot him with a stun gun. He could see the thin cables and feel a sharp soreness in his chest where those fiendish little metal darts had entered. He tried to lift one hand to feel if they were still there, but produced only a single, random movement of his arm. He had a long way to go before motor control could be said to be reestablished.

Instead, he concentrated on his senses. His vision was a bit cloudy, probably because he lacked the muscular control to focus properly, but he was able to open his eyes, and that had to be a good sign. He was lying, he realized, in the back of the Land Cruiser, in a narrow passage between the galley and the dining nook, made narrower still by various boxes of equipment.

Why had the man given him mouth-to-mouth? Had he really stopped breathing? Was his heart . . . had his heart stopped? Taser shocks were normally designed to affect the striated skeletal musculature more than the heart, but as one of the department's more legendary action types had once said—after experimenting on himself, naturally—"being shot in the chest really sucked." The closer to the heart, the greater the risk.

The man in the parka grabbed his wrist. For a brief moment, Søren thought it was to check his pulse, but then he felt the sharp contours of a cable strip. He attempted to free his arm, sit up, and try a bit of self-defense, all to no avail. His arm was pulled over his head and his wrist attached to something fixed and metallic—perhaps the front seat's frame. The maneuver was repeated with his left arm. His already sore abdomen tightened unpleasantly, and he hoped the parka-man didn't plan on making this a permanent arrangement.

"Hey . . ." he tried to say, but he only managed a wheezing

exhalation that was totally drowned by the roar from the Land Cruiser's powerful diesel engine. The car moved, and Søren had to acknowledge that he hadn't just been disabled and tied up, but was now officially abducted as well.

He couldn't help wondering what Torben would say if he knew what was happening to his anti-terrorist group leader. Anti-terrorist group leader on sick leave, but still.

Nothing nice, probably. And almost definitely something that involved an international array of expletives. Søren's own reaction was somewhat less varied.

Fuck. Fuck. Fuck.

HE OBVIOUSLY COULDN'T see his wristwatch, and his sense of time and place was still a bit distorted. As the Taser paralysis faded, a splitting headache joined his collection of symptoms, and he remembered the unpleasant crunching sound caused by his collision with the parking lot asphalt. Did he have a fractured skull to match Nina's? It was, of course, an alternative to matching jogging outfits, but still . . .

Pull yourself together. With a huge effort, Søren dragged his chaotic thoughts back to the starting point. How long had passed since the Land Cruiser had left the parking lot by the Swim Center? In which direction were they headed? Where on his mental map of Denmark should he place the little red pin?

Half an hour? More? Less? His sense of direction was normally well tuned, but today it failed him. They had stayed on asphalt for the first twenty minutes, he thought, but now it was gravel and forest tracks, and maybe not even that—the Land Cruiser rocked from side to side, and its four-wheel drive was working overtime. Branches and twigs slapped against the car's sides and roof, and the engine's sound was erratic—light and even one moment, strained and shrill the next.

The rocking sensation nauseated him, but to throw up now would be potentially life threatening. He swallowed. And swallowed again. There had to be a limit to how long one could drive through the woods of Viborg? This wasn't exactly the Black Forest, or northern Sweden's vast expanses of dark pine.

His cell phone rang somewhere on the floor behind his head. He didn't know if the parka-man could hear it—he hoped not. The longer it remained undiscovered, the better. His original, relatively low-tech plan had simply been to use the "Find my iPhone" app to trace the parka-man, but the police in general—and the PET in particular—had more advanced tracking options, as long as the phone remained on and traceable.

That, of course, required that they knew they should begin searching. How long would it take for Nina to miss him?

Perhaps he needed to rephrase the question, because he wasn't sure whether Nina would *miss* him. Once the worst of the crisis had passed, it had clearly been awkward for them both that he was already installed at her mother's and had presented himself to her children as her "friend." All of it didn't matter; he was prepared to eat a substantial portion of awkwardness as long as he felt certain that his being there was helpful. But that certainty had crumbled after she had come home from the hospital. It was as if she vacillated between intimacy and . . . and a place that was colder than outer space, and just as remote. It disturbed him deeply. Was that why he had felt so driven to play the bodyguard? Was that why he felt such a need to tackle the enemy that threatened her? To justify his own presence?

My God. How pathetic was that?

But even if she didn't exactly miss him, there would still come a point where she would wonder where he had gone. Would she raise an alarm? Contact the local police? Caroline Westmann, maybe? And how would they react?

He was neither a minor nor an aging family member suffering from dementia. The alarm bells wouldn't sound right away. And because of the stupid sick leave his absence wouldn't be noticed at the office either.

The depressing truth was that several days could easily pass before anyone reported him missing. Unless of course the kidnapper himself called attention to the situation, and he would probably only do that if he thought Søren had some value.

Did he?

It had seemed so random. The parka-man had reacted to something he might justifiably consider an attack. He could have driven off without Søren and have left him in the parking lot, with or without a heart attack—Søren still had a hard time believing that all that first-aid nonsense had really been necessary, just for a Taser. Instead he had hauled Søren into the Land Cruiser and had revived him. Only then had he driven off. It could hardly be called a well-planned, well-executed abduction. The man must realize that Søren had some kind of relationship with Nina—he had, after all, been up there on the balcony photographing them together. But other than that, did he know who and what Søren was? And how should Søren try to present himself if he didn't?

Two parameters were relevant: His connection to Nina and his connection to the police. The first increased his value and might keep him alive—perhaps it would be a good idea to exaggerate it a bit; the latter, on the other hand, would probably be seen as a threat and should either go unmentioned or at least be minimized . . .

His attempt at analysis seemed to have eased the nausea, or maybe the tracks were smoother. They were going downhill now, and this to some extent relieved the cramps in his arms and abdomen. Instead, an ominous thumping had begun at the back of his head, and the vehicle was now lurching back and forth in a way that revealed that they were completely off-road.

Finally the lurching stopped. The engine was turned off, and the front door opened. Shortly afterward the back door opened, too. Fresh, moist forest air streamed in and the nausea dissipated entirely.

"I'll cut you loose now," said the parka-man in his slightly singing English. "But stay lying down until I say you can move. I've shot you once, and I'll do it again if necessary."

"Okay," said Søren, somewhat more hoarsely than he had planned.

The parka-man crawled halfway across him to get the Taser, which he apparently had just thrown into the car on top of Søren. Then he disappeared out the back door again.

"No moving until I say so," he reminded Søren. Then a little snip sounded and Søren's left wrist was free. The right one followed.

Søren remained where he was, as he had been told to, but bent his arms so the pressure on his abdomen was relieved. Air, oh, air. He had once read that what killed a crucified human being was neither the nails nor hunger and thirst, but but the simple fact that one could not continue to draw sufficient breath in that position. Lying flat on a floor did not put anything like the same amount of pressure on the respiratory musculature, but still he had had to fight more and more to catch his breath. Shocking how little it took—it had probably not been the parka-man's intention to do anything more than keep him immobilized.

"Sit up."

That was easier said than done. Even though he hadn't been tied for very long—an hour, maybe?—his hands were numb, and his first attempt to grab hold of the edge of the containers that surrounded him failed miserably. Just eight months ago it would have been easy to raise himself using only his stomach muscles—sit-ups were an unmissable part of his training routine. He had been in good shape his entire life and had taken it for granted, as he progressed smoothly from the gymnastics team in the small Jutland town he came from to the military service of his youth, then on to the rigors of his training as a language officer in military intelligence, and after that the police academy. He was not quite like Torben, to whom every bench press was a competition that gave some kind of testosterone charge to the training, but he liked the solitude of the long runs, liked the way his body functioned, smoothly and naturally, letting his thoughts flow free.

He hadn't been on a run since February. Visits to the gym under PET's headquarters in Søborg had been sporadic and unsatisfying. And now he couldn't even sit up without using his arms.

He managed to plant an elbow on the seat to the right and made it to a sitting position. The parka-man stood watching him through the open back door, armed with that damned Taser. He tipped it in an awkward come-hither gesture.

"Get out of the car. Nice and slow, please."

Nice and slow was pretty much the only possibility right now. The connection between brain and muscles still felt oddly woolly, and even the modest movement toward the door made him uncomfortably dizzy. He touched the back of his head and felt, not surprisingly, the sticky sensation of partially dried blood. A lot of blood, it seemed. Four fingers and most of his palm were stained with it after the brief touch. He looked at them glumly. Yet another step toward total physical decrepitude. Lovely.

Out of the corner of his eye he noticed that the parka-man had taken a step back.

"Wipe it off," he said hoarsely.

"What?" asked Søren. "This?" He deliberately extended his hand, and the man retreated yet another step.

"Yes," he said. "Wipe it off. I don't want you to leave blood stains everywhere. Here!" He searched his pocket and threw an unopened pack of paper napkins to Søren. "Get rid of it."

Aha, thought Søren. *A kidnapper who doesn't like the sight of blood. Interesting*. He managed to open the package and rub off most of the blood. Then he threw the bloody napkin into a bush.

"Pick it up."

"Why?"

"Just do it!" The Taser tipped again, this time threateningly.

"Okay."

"Put it in your pocket."

"Okay."

Søren wasn't quite sure what to conclude from this small experiment. He hoped it meant that the man was not planning to make this particular clearing the site of a murder—if he was planning to leave a body, then a single bloody paper napkin didn't mean much. If, on the other hand, they were moving on . . .

On the other hand, it might just be that he didn't like littering. Or hadn't decided yet.

"Go to that tree." The Taser pointed at a young birch tree nine or ten meters from the car. "Lie down. No, on your stomach. Hands over your head."

Søren estimated distances and options. The Taser's range was probably about thirty meters at the most, depending on the model, but it required a clear line of sight. Both the little harpoon-like darts had to hit their target in order for the cables that connected them to the gun to send the charge through him. If just one of the darts snagged on a branch, it would take time to get the pistol ready to shoot again. He didn't think much of his chances of outrunning the parka-man, who seemed a good deal younger and hadn't just sustained a lengthy electric shock with attendant injuries from the fall, but might Søren be able to overpower him while he was trying to get the Taser ready? It was clear that the man felt he needed the weapon, that it was this that gave him the upper hand. Consequently, he would feel at a disadvantage if he lost it . . .

He walked toward the birch tree, but continued on.

"No. Stop. That tree!"

"Which one?" he said without turning around. "That one?" He pointed pretty randomly solely to win time.

"Stop! Turn around!"

Søren skidded sideways instead and zigzagged through the trees. He heard the Taser crackle and turned around. As he had hoped, the darts had hit the tree instead of him. Unfortunately they hadn't embedded themselves. One cable, though, had snagged in the shrubbery, and that would have to be enough. He charged at the parka-man while still mentally rehearsing the kick to the solar plexus, the follow-up to the back of the neck, the sleeper hold that would stop the blood flow to the brain . . .

The parka-man wasted several split seconds on shock. His mouth gaped; the eyes glinted whitely under the hood. Then he took a step backward and with a hard tug jerked the Taser cables free of the shrubbery. Søren leaped, kicked, connected . . . not well enough; he knew that at once, but there was no way back now; he went for the strike just as the Taser crackled one more time.

The darts hit him in the thigh this time, not the chest, but the effect was almost as overwhelming. Intense pain, paralysis, helplessness . . . He was on the forest floor with his face half-buried in the fall leaves, and though he didn't lose consciousness this time, movement was again impossible.

"Aouuuhhhh, aouhhhhh, aouhhhhhh . . ."

The half-choked moaning sound didn't come from him; it came from the parka-man. He had fallen over as well. He had dropped the Taser and was on his back rolling from side to side, his knees pulled up to his stomach.

Pull the darts out, Søren silently ordered his hands, but they just trembled in unhelpful spasms.

The parka-man managed to get up on his knees. The moaning continued, but he looked around until he spotted the Taser and began to crawl toward it.

Get those fucking darts out! snarled Søren to himself, and this time he managed to make his left hand close around one of the cables.

The parka-man picked up the gun and fired. The pain was just as bad as the first time, and it went on for longer.

WHEN SØREN COULD sense anything again, he was lying at the foot of the birch tree. A long thin metal chain was attached to the tree with a padlock. The other end of the chain was fastened snugly around Søren's right wrist with yet another padlock.

The parka-man was sitting in a camping chair under a sun sail that was attached to one side of the camper. In one hand he held a Coke bottle. In the other the damned Taser.

"Tell me who you are," he said. "And who you work for."

THE PHILIPPINES, FIVE MONTHS EARLIER

THE EXPLOSION THAT leveled the first housing block could be felt all the way to nearest bit of urban development three kilometers away.

In the grainy video on the news one could see a brief flare off to the right, and then the building went down on its knees like an old man. Left side first, where the explosion had been, then the right side followed. The five upper stories remained standing for a moment, balancing in a cloud of dust and flying debris, then they too subsided. They disintegrated from the bottom to the top as they melted into the ground.

Vincent glanced at Vadim, grabbed the remote, and shut off the television. The only sound was the enervating hum of the air conditioner. Manila had been hit by a historic heat wave with asphalt melting in the streets and a smog level that had led the authorities to warn the population not to go outdoors for any length of time.

Vincent and Vadim had sought refuge in the apartment with a good supply of beer and PlayStation games when the call came from Vadim's office in Makati City. Then they had seen the news.

"Who do you think it is? Muslims?"

Vadim hid his face in his hands. His hair was an unruly sweaty mess.

"I don't know," he said. "Muslims, enemies of the project, enemies of the government, enemies of my father . . ."

"How many people were in the building?"

"I don't know," he repeated. "Eight hundred, maybe a thousand, it happened in the middle of the night, so everyone was sleeping. Damn it . . . I should go out there."

He got up and began to frantically collect his cigarettes, wallet, and cell phone from the coffee table.

"Are you coming?"

It wasn't a question that called for an answer. Vadim was his job. He armed himself with four water bottles and a pack of crackers and followed Vadim out to the elevator onto the diesel-stinking parking deck.

It felt oddly apocalyptic, sitting here in Manila's traffic on their way to a catastrophe. The sky over the bay was yellow with smog, and the hot caustic sunbeams that did burn their way through formed a shimmering white veil against the murky background. Vincent had been drunk yesterday for the first time in a long time, and he could still feel the alcohol as an intense discomfort in his entire body. His brain felt white and blank. He had been unfaithful to Bea.

The girl had been a pretty, gentle-looking first-year law student. Not one of those self-confident stiletto girls. Just sweet and young, with fine, round breasts under a thin, blue dress. She was a lot like Bea, before Carlito and all the lies. He had presented himself as a medical student, as he always did, and she had placed a hand on the back of his neck and told him he had sad eyes.

The sex part had been awkward, in a hotel room on Juan Luna Street. She hadn't been sure, he could tell, but he had not managed to stop, and she hadn't said no. Afterward she held him and said she was in love. Mary Jane. He had thrown her phone number out in order not to be tempted to call and fuck everything up even further.

It wasn't because he didn't love Bea anymore, but because they were no longer in the same place. Even when he was on one of the rare visits, all the things he couldn't talk about came between them. Bea had finished her nurse's training last year and had prepared to move to Manila. He had postponed it, evaded the subject, and fooled around until she stopped asking and became glum and silent. Now she worked at the public hospital in San Marcelino.

Vadim and Vincent sat silently in the car for most of the way out of the city.

Vadim distractedly maneuvered the beautiful royal-blue Porsche through the mass of men and children selling water and flowers and dried mango. On the sidewalk in front of a narrow shop that sold spare parts and car scrap metal, a woman stood washing a fat, naked boy of six or seven. She held a water hose over his head, and the water ran in a soft, lazy arc over the boy's black hair and dark-brown body. The rest of the family slouched on plastic chairs and clapped-out couches, under frayed canopies. Vincent looked out at the crumbling plasterwork and the mess of telephone wires, faded advertising posters, washing lines, and beat-up bikes. And children, children, children. He saw Carlito's face everywhere. After a while he had to lower his gaze and began to scroll through the music selections on his phone instead.

The slums retreated, and they entered the no-man's-land at the outskirts of the city—the enormous billboards shouting about "new luxury accommodation," perfume, furniture, Armani suits . . . and behind them the fields and the peasants trudging along the hard-stomped paths through the rice paddies.

Vadim had turned on the radio and listened with clenched teeth to the most recent updates.

The first estimates said two hundred dead, but neither Vadim nor Vincent dared believe that number. It was always that way when a typhoon or an earthquake or a flood hit. The authorities began by saying ten killed, and it ended up being ten thousand. They were digging in the ruins, the radio said. All available medical personnel were on their way to the area, and the remaining slum dwellers along Pasig River had begun to stir. There was insurrection in the air. The police had turned out with batons and guns.

"It'll be bad," said Vincent.

Vadim didn't answer.

VADIM'S CONSTRUCTION SITE was unrecognizable when they finally reached it.

They had had to leave the car almost three kilometers away because of the roadblocks. Only ambulances, police cars, trucks and diggers were allowed past the barrier, but Vadim managed to talk his way in by showing his ID and giving the guard five hundred pesos.

"Those are my houses," said Vadim. "I have important information for the rescue workers."

The guard shrugged. He had gotten his money and didn't need any further information.

"But you'll have to walk," he said sourly. "There's barely enough room for our own vehicles."

Walking three kilometers in the smog and glaring sun was exhausting, but it was the sight of the collapsed building that really finished Vincent. It was like a mountain, and the rescue workers who climbed around the rubble and the bristling steel supports looked like ghosts. The red, green, and yellow helmets, safety equipment and gloves were white from dust. There were also ordinary people, men and women digging with their bare hands among the cables and the distorted steel. Sweat and tears drew dark lines in the dust on their faces, necks and naked backs.

All these people worked silently and with concentration, only interrupted by scattered shouts when something emerged from the mountain's interior. The first bodies had already been placed in neat straight rows, covered with white sheets.

"Who's in charge here?"

Vadim walked over to a helmeted man holding a walkie-talkie.

The man shook his head.

"I just brought the dogs," he said. "The police are over there."

Vadim narrowed his eyes and looked in the direction the man was pointing. A couple of uniformed policemen had placed themselves at a safe distance from the actual digging and dragging and had spread some official-looking maps over the hood of a civilian car. With them stood a man in plain clothes, but his light-blue shirt and blue pants made Vincent guess that he had been promoted out of uniform and was either lacking in imagination or missed the visible signs of his rank.

They walked over, Vadim in front with his cell phone in his hand. Vincent tried to shut it all out. A casualty had been found somewhere in the ruins. He could hear the rescuers bark short instructions to each other. Lift. Careful. Stop. A little more. A moaning scream from a child or a woman who was being lifted free of the rubble. Vincent couldn't help looking after all. The limp figure being carefully maneuvered on to a stretcher was covered in blood and dirt. One leg dangled loosely before it too was also lifted up and arranged on the stretcher. A thin European woman in shorts and a T-shirt looking as if she was responsible for this part of the operation gave short and precise orders on the way down to the waiting ambulances.

Then she turned around and directed her attention to the next victim being carried out of the ruin. She stuck out, thought Vincent, and not just because she was European. People calmed down around her and followed her lead. Whoever she was, she had clearly done this before.

Chaos.

She knew it and went with the flow. And as if she could feel his eyes on her, she turned her head and met his gaze for a brief moment. Her eyes shone intensely under the too-large red helmet she was wearing. Then she moved on.

So did Vadim.

"Do you know what happened?"

He was standing in front of the two policemen with all the authority his twenty-four-year-old persona could muster. "My company built these buildings, so I would appreciate being informed."

The plainclothes guy nodded; he was a middle-aged man who

clearly had some kind of rank here. He had an enormous birthmark over his right eyelid which Vincent found it hard not to stare at.

"If you can provide us with plans of the building, we can talk," he said. "But so far we know nothing besides what's already on the news. There's been some kind of explosion. The ones we have dug out so far are mostly women and children. Hellish work. We think there must have been about a thousand people in the building."

"I'll call my office and ask them to send the building plans out here at once," said Vadim. "Thank you for your trouble."

The officer sent him a sharp look. Then he scrawled something down on a slip of paper and handed it to Vadim.

"Commissioner Roberto Abiog, Philippine National Police, counterterrorism. Here's my number. I'll try to keep you informed to the best of my ability," he said, rubbing his meaty fingers together in a telling gesture. Vadim nodded.

"Thank you," he said shortly. "I'll be in the area for the rest of the day."

THE WOUNDED WERE divided among several nearby hospitals, and still there was a crush and chaos everywhere. When they finally managed to find Diana in an overcrowded hallway at Christ the King General Hospital, she barely had time to look at them. She stood bent over a man who had clearly broken a leg, but otherwise appeared more or less unharmed.

"He wasn't in the building," said Diana shortly. "A piece of wall fell on him while he was digging for his wife. It's a complete mess out there; no one knows what the hell they're doing."

Vadim spread his arms.

"Is there anything we can do here?"

Diana glanced up at him, surprised. Then she smiled crookedly.

"You can give me a cigarette," she said. "And then you can find Victor for me. I need some help for this guy, and we've got several seriously wounded coming in any minute."

Vadim produced a cigarette, lit it and took a couple of drags himself before he placed it between Diana's lips.

"Victor? Is he here too?"

Sighing, Diana pushed back a drifting lock of black hair with one wrist "I don't want to discuss this now, Vadim. Victor came yesterday to visit me and see the hospital. He's thinking of doing some volunteer work here."

"Okay," said Vadim. "Fine, we'll find him."

They left. Vincent nearly had to jog to keep up with Vadim's long, rapid strides. There was quite a bit of activity along the external gallery. Nurses and doctors had to force their way through a constantly growing group of confused and despairing relatives clustered in front of the battered reception desk.

Vincent tried to shut it out. The shouting and the weeping that emerged as high-pitched moans and screams. The clutching hands, and the figures on the gurneys just emerging from three ambulances in the bumpy parking lot in front of the hospital.

The first two were children. Vincent couldn't help looking as they were rushed past him. A glimpse of a bloodied faces. One completely without signs of life, the other drawn in a silent scream of pain. Delicate white teeth exposed in something that looked like a snarl. He tried to catch sight of Victor in the tumult. The nausea and chills that had lurked inside him ever since he got out of the car in front of the collapsed ruin had begun to overwhelm him.

He had to get away from this. He had to find a place where he could throw up without anyone noticing, where he could get something to drink, but the mass of people around him kept growing and made it difficult to move.

"Come on." Ahead of him, Vadim gestured impatiently with his chin. Forward. Onward. Vincent made a halfhearted attempt to fight his way through the chaos, but his progress was blocked by the third gurney being ushered past him, so close that his hand brushed the nearly severed arm of the victim. Astonishingly enough, the man's face was untouched except for a narrow cut above his right eyebrow. He was conscious but clearly submerged in an ocean of pain that made his gaze distant, dull and wandering. Vincent recognized him with a few seconds' delay. The engineer. Lorenz Robles.

It was Victor who was accompanying the stretcher. And the European woman Vincent had noticed earlier in the rubble.

"Diana is looking for you," said Vincent, but Victor didn't hear him. He was too busy with his mutilated patient. He didn't even react when Vadim caught his arm, except to absently shrug himself free. His huge body was intensely focused on the wounded man. His right hand was buried somewhere in the bloody mess under the man's gaping shoulder.

The engineer turned his head and for a brief moment focused on Vadim behind Victor, and something happened in his face. A brief moment of *presence* and a jerk of the body, as if he was attempting to reach out to Vadim with the damaged arm.

"Not a bomb," he said. "It wasn't . . . a bomb."

Someone pulled on the gurney and it rolled on past them. Vincent stumbled in the sudden emptiness in front of him, and Vadim hauled him back to his feet and out into the blazing heat, where he threw up behind a huge acacia tree. When he was done, Vadim settled him into the car's front seat, turned on the air conditioning and found a bottle of water in the trunk.

They sat silently and stared at the growing tumult outside. More ambulances, more cars sardine packed with families, children and adults stumbling into the hospital or settling down in resignation in the shade of the trees in front of it. Vadim had once again turned on the radio and hunched forward, listening intensely when there was news of his collapsed building. Under the sunburn, his skin was pale.

Eventually, he got out his cell phone and punched a number.

"Abiog?"

He waited for a moment.

"I should have told you this before, but I wasn't sure how much to make of it. It's just that we have in fact received a number of bomb threats at the office lately. Against the project and against me. I thought it was just a bit of harassment from a disgruntled ex-employee, and I didn't really take it very seriously. But it popped back into my mind a minute ago . . ."

Vadim's voice was calm and modulated, but Vincent noticed the fine beads of sweat trickling from his hairline. When he finally ended the conversation, he leaned forward and sat for a long time with his head resting on the steering wheel. The cold air from the air conditioning took hold of his T-shirt and sweaty hair.

"The engineer?" asked Vincent.

"I didn't think it meant anything. I thought you had him under control," said Vadim. "You and Martinez. I had forgotten all about it."

Vincent emptied his water bottle and crushed it with a practiced movement of his hand.

THEY SAT IN the car for a few hours, interrupted only by a pee break behind the acacia tree that Vincent had already soiled, and a trip for a burger at the local Jollibee. Vincent didn't know what they were waiting for. Vadim just sat there, chain-smoking and staring at the people who came and went in the parking lot. As if he were searching for someone or something.

The stream of ambulances and stretchers was petering out. Altogether they hadn't seen more than about forty living survivors. Vincent hoped it was because they were also sending the wounded to other hospitals, but the sheer number of desperate relatives was heartbreaking.

Then Diana finally came out. She walked with Victor, holding a fresh cigarette between her fingers. She looked exhausted, thought Vincent. She tipped her head back and rolled her shoulders in limbering circles while she said something to Victor.

They weren't even touching, but there was something about the way they were standing. Relaxed and intimate, bodies that were familiar with each other. Victor answered her. Smiled faintly. The peasant boy and the rich man's daughter. Why hadn't Vincent noticed it before?

He glanced over at Vadim and could tell that Vadim saw the same thing he did. Neither of them said anything.

Then Vadim opened the car door, a little too abruptly, and walked across the parking lot with a large, welcoming smile. It was probably only Vincent who noticed the tension in his normally relaxed gait, but he followed hesitantly and saw how Diana and Victor stiffened at the sight of them.

"Finished for today?" Vadim smiled and smiled and placed his arm around Victor. "We thought you might be in need of some food. My treat."

Diana shook her head.

"You go on," she said. "I'm done for the day."

Vadim nodded.

"But you'll come, right, Victor?"

A sigh expanded through Victor's massive chest; then he smiled, almost as broadly as Vadim, and nodded.

"Yes. I just have to get my things."

"The guy with the arm," said Vadim. "The one we saw on the stretcher. Is he okay?"

Victor, already moving away, stopped without turning around.

"No," he said. "He was one of the first to die."

SØREN WAS GONE. It took a while before Nina missed him, since she had been one hundred percent focused on Anton and Ida. At first she was just annoyed that he wasn't there to drive them to the emergency room. She took a taxi instead, and after a fairly reasonable wait she managed to confirm that Anton had been let off with a scare and a sore, bruised shoulder, with no broken collarbone or other fractures and no damage to the spine, neck, or throat. She considered calling Morten but didn't have the energy. No doubt it would somehow be her fault that Anton had had an accident in the swimming pool. You would think nothing like that ever happened when Morten was with the kids, she thought darkly. Every bike crash, every scraped knee or sunburn, every wasp sting—these days all such mishaps, too, could be attributed to Nina's irresponsibility.

And her head hurt. At the emergency room, they had been kind enough to change her chlorine-stinking, soaked bandage, but once the first hideous fears for Anton's safety had been put to rest, her body let her know in no uncertain terms that her lifeguard stunt was not what the doctors had in mind when they told her to "take it easy for the next two weeks."

It wasn't until she and the children were waiting outside

Viborg Hospital's emergency room for yet another taxi that Nina started to seriously wonder what had become of Søren. It wasn't like him to just disappear. Especially not in the middle of a potential emergency.

She told the driver to take them back to Cherry Lane. Her mother came out and stood waiting for them on the front path, surrounded by wet shrubs, wet paving, and wet grass, and Anton ran over and threw himself into her arms while Nina paid the taxi.

"I've been to the emergency room," he told her with poorly hidden pride. "I got X-rayed."

"So I hear," said Hanne Borg. "It was a good thing that nothing was broken." Ida got a half hug in passing. "Were you afraid, Ida?"

"A little," admitted tough-as-nails, only-losers-cry Ida, carefully rubbing the mascara by one eye. "The maggot is, after all, my little brother."

Nina noticed that Søren's Hyundai wasn't parked at the curb.

"Have you heard anything from Søren?" she asked.

Hanne looked up with an arm around each grandchild.

"Søren?" she said. "Wasn't he with you?"

"Yes, until he . . . disappeared or whatever he did. I couldn't find him when we were going to the emergency room, and he had the car keys. That's why we had to take a taxi."

"It must have been crowded at the pool. It's easy to lose track of each other. Call him."

Nina called Søren's number but he didn't answer. After several rings, it went to voice mail. Søren's message was cool, unsexy, and devoid of frills. "I can't answer the phone right now. Call back later or leave a message."

Nina let herself dwell for a second on the things she felt like telling him, but limited herself to an "It's Nina. Call me." She hadn't yet adjusted to the fact that identifying yourself nowadays was a superfluous gesture. It seemed impolite not to.

Darkness was falling. She called a few more times, with the same depressing lack of response. She and her mother helped each other make dinner—spaghetti with meatballs for Anton's benefit, and Ida didn't say anything about being a vegetarian. It came and went a bit, the vegetarian thing, and Nina sensed that Ida was annoyed at herself for not being more persistent and uncompromising. Nina didn't interfere. She just made sure there was always hummus or tofu or some other form of non-animal protein available.

Finally the phone rang, but it wasn't Søren.

"Caroline Westmann from the Mid-West Jutland's Police. I wonder if you could come in tomorrow morning?"

"Where?"

"At the station. I've got permission to arrange a witness lineup."

"Involving whom?"

"Um. I'd just like you to have a look at our detainees in real life, so to speak. They won't be able to see you."

"I didn't see anyone or anything."

"There's a pretty big difference between seeing someone in a picture and in person. Who knows? Maybe you might have noticed one of them sometime before the assault. While you were shopping, for example? Or when you parked?"

Nina sighed.

"Just a minute. Let me just check if my mother can take care of the kids . . ."

Hanne Borg merely nodded, depriving Nina of her best excuse for not showing up at the station.

"Okay," she said reluctantly. "Can you give me the address?

She wrote it down on the note pad attached to the refrigerator door. It was a pink-and-green affair framed by jolly pigs. The entire door was decorated with postcards and photographs and school calendars—Nina dryly noted that her mother basically had more mastery of the kids' daily life than she did. Hanne Borg had lived alone for more than twenty years now, and still the house remained a family home full of litle details that revealed relationships, feelings, friendships, and warmth. Despite the rooms carefully set aside for Ida and Anton, Nina's new post-divorce apartment could not muster a fraction of such signs of belonging.

"So, see you tomorrow," said Caroline Westmann.

"Yes," said Nina hesitantly. "Oh . . . I . . . You've met Søren Kirkegaard."

"Yes?"

"He . . . It seems as if he's disappeared."

"What do you mean?"

"We were at the Swim Center with the kids, and there was a small accident—fortunately nothing serious. And then he was suddenly gone. Without a word. It's not like him."

"Did you try calling him?"

"Yes. He isn't answering. Hasn't even sent a text."

"Could he have been called back to Copenhagen?"

"Do you mean by the PET?"

"Maybe there was some kind of emergency. They mave have urgently needed his expert knowledge."

So urgently he couldn't even text? thought Nina with a pang of irritation. But at the same time she wanted to believe Westmann's explanation, because it eased the raw anxiety that had been creeping up on her. *He's driving, she told herself. That's why he can't answer the phone.*

"Yes," she said quickly. "That's probably it. No doubt he'll call me when he can. Sorry. Perhaps I'm still not as clearheaded as I'd like to be."

"That's completely understandable. See you."

But after she had tucked in Anton with a Children's Tylenol to dull the worst of the pain in his shoulder, there was still no answer when she called Søren's cell.

THE PHILIPPINES, TWO MONTHS EARLIER

"BEA CALLED."

Victor was sitting on the couch with the phone in his hand when Vincent let himself into the apartment.

"Thanks. What did she want?"

Vincent reached for his cell with a resentful gesture. He knew he should have had it with him, or at least only turned it off while he was actually on the pier. There was an amusement park there, with colored lamps and lots of students who hung out on the edge of Manila Bay. The atmosphere was light. Like candy floss and Bacardi Breezers.

He had needed it. The mountain of rubble still lurked right behind his eyelids when he tried to sleep. Almost three months had passed, and in that time he hadn't seen much of Vadim, who had been working like a madman in his office and only called to check if Vincent was awake and, of course, to get him to pick up things. Idiotic things. Lunch, which *had* to be brought to the office, bread that *absolutely* had to be bought at the Manila Hotel on the other side of town. Porn videos that could be inserted directly into the big screen in the living room to run all night with the sound off.

There had been close to a thousand people in the collapsed

building. Little more than half had still been alive when they were dug free of the rubble. It was a hopeless disaster.

"Carlito has a sore throat, but that's probably not why she called," said Victor seriously. "What are you doing with your life?"

The lightness leaked out of Vincent. No more candy floss and Breezers. He got himself a beer from the refrigerator, and paused in the open door to his room. Victor certainly knew how to hit the sore spots. He never deliberately tried to cast blame or prod Vincent's conscience, but that actually made it worse: the knowledge that his big friend only wished the best for him even when he so clearly didn't deserve it.

"I'm not in the mood for this," said Vincent. "I'm tired."

"But what are you going to do?" Victor had gotten up. "You can't live off Vadim for the rest of your life. He's . . . not good for you. You aren't good for each other."

Vincent blew across the neck of the beer bottle and produced a delicate, soft note. He didn't know what to say. He did have a vague sort of plan. A job abroad. Something that paid well and made him look successful. And then he would tell Bea the truth, how it had all gone wrong, but that he was past that now and had made something of himself after all. That everything would turn out all right in the end.

Vadim could get him that job if he wanted to. Vadim could do anything.

"What about yourself?" said Vincent. "Isn't there something bothering you too?"

"Yes," said Victor. "But I'm not going to make it worse by lying. Not anymore. Bea wants you to call her back."

"Okay." The phone felt leaden in Vincent's hand. "I'll do it later. Do you want to watch a movie?"

Victor shook his head but remained sitting on the couch.

"Think about it, Vincent. It's not too late to come clean. You've got to talk to the people who really matter to you. Life is long, but it's also very, very short."

"Victor. Not now, all right?"

Vincent finished his beer and blew a final deep note in the direction of his friend. Then he turned around and went into his room. He had mounted a flat-screen on the wall, and a small basketball hoop on the door of the closet. With the matching miniature basketballs, he could make ten perfect baskets in a row from his bed. He turned on the television without turning up the volume, closed his eyes and felt the faint inebriation from the evening's Breezers charge around his body while he imagined that his bed was floating through the universe. The freedom of empty space.

His cell beeped. Bea had sent a text. He turned the phone facedown, trying to hang on to the sense of freedom a little longer.

SOMETHING SHATTERED ON the living room floor.

He must have drifted off. The light and television were still on, but that's not what had woken him up. It was the voices from the living room. Victor's and Vadim's.

"We're friends . . . We live together . . . How the hell could you do this?"

Vadim raged with the fury of a drunkard or a child. Something else was thrown and shattered, this time against the wall.

Victor said something, but it was impossible to hear what it was. His voice was softer and more measured. Calming.

"Have you fucked her? Have you? I want to know if you've fucked her . . . I can't . . ." Vadim's voice slid over into an indecipherable mumbling. Then it was silent.

Vincent slipped silently across to the door so that he could hear what they were saying. His heart was pounding wildly, as if he himself was a part of the battle on the other side.

"There was something else I wanted to talk with you about," said Victor. His voice was calm and controlled. Vadim remained silent. Waiting.

"A patient was brought to the hospital after the collapse. A man who kept mentioning your name. An engineer. Lorenz Robles . . ."

Silence.

"I know him, and he's a damned liar who hates me and my firm. What did he say . . . ? Did he say something about me?"

"Vadim . . . what if he is right? There are three more buildings out there. What if they come down in the same way?"

"It's a lie. Nothing more than a damned, jealous lie! Did anyone else hear what he said?"

"Why do you want to know?" asked Victor.

"What about the nurse? Did she hear it? Victor, you don't know what people are like when someone has money. They'll say anything, do anything, to get at you. It doesn't matter if it's pure fiction, the mere suspicion can harm us—me and my father. Ruin everything. Do you understand?"

"Okay . . ." Victor's voice was flat. "I had to see your face when I told you this. You don't need to say anything. Vadim, I hope for your own sake that you take the proper steps. Quickly. Because . . . it's not possible to live with the alternative. Neither for you nor for me."

"Victor. You're my *friend*, damn it!"

Silence.

And then steps and the sound of the front door being opened and closed.

Vincent turned off the light in the ceiling, went back to bed and shut off the television. The red numbers on his alarm clock showed 4:23 and from the living room he could hear someone, probably Vadim, move around, picking up the shards from whatever it was that had been shattered.

Once in a while he could hear someone moan faintly. Crying, thought Vincent. Vadim is crying.

"WHAT ARE YOU doing out here?"

Vincent looked over his shoulder and saw Vadim in the doorway. Then he turned his gaze to his bare feet on the diving board. Bounced slightly on his legs and jumped, and let the cold water close around his body. He drifted, feeling the slight pressure, watching the shadows from the artificial palm trees flicker across the bottom of the pool. He stayed under for as long as he could. Had in fact learned to conquer his panic. How to turn it off. He shot across the tiles to the opposite end. His fingertips looked so white they were nearly fluorescent.

"It's twelve o'clock," said Vadim when Vincent, out of breath, hauled himself up onto the edge. "You'll get fried out here."

Vincent shrugged. He needed to do something. Anything.

For the third week in a row, the smog hung like a black curtain over Manila and had long since driven the city's more affluent classes up into the mountains or out to the coast. Vincent and Vadim were practically the only ones left in the thirty-story apartment house. Or that was how it felt.

"Have you heard from Victor?"

Vadim pushed off his flip-flops and sat on the edge with his feet dangling in the water.

Vincent hesitated.

Victor had come home that same morning after Vadim had gone to the office, had gathered some books and T-shirts and left again. He had some work to do outside the city, and it was more convenient to sleep at the clinic in Las Pinas City, he had said. Besides, he and Vadim needed to get away from each other a bit. He hadn't needed to explain why to Vincent.

"I don't know where he is," said Vincent honestly. "He must have gone on vacation or something."

"He lives in *my* damn apartment." Vadim kicked at a lonely beach ball floating on the water. "He might at least tell me where he's going."

"I don't know where he is," Vincent repeated.

With a certain relief he heard the housekeeper let someone into the apartment. Moments later a stocky figure appeared in the doorway facing the pool area. Roberto Abiog of the Philippine Natinal Police.

"Gentlemen."

The commissioner didn't look as if he was enjoying the weather anymore than the rest of Manila. Two huge, dark sweat stains spread from his armpits down across his rounded belly. The shirt was the same as the last time they had seen him, or one identical to it—light blue and official looking, like the long pants. Even his sneakers managed to look more formal than other people's.

"I wanted to follow up on our conversations about the threat against your firm," he said and nodded at Vadim. The heavy birthmark on his eyelid had almost closed one eye, Vincent noticed, but by contrast the other was knife sharp.

"To make a long story short, it appears that the engineer who threatened you was among those killed in the collapsed building. He had no legitimate reason to be there at four in the morning, since you had fired him several months earlier, and he had both the motive and the technical know-how to set off an explosive device. We will, of course, continue our investigation of the case, but between you and me, the official feeling is that the case has been solved, and a press release to that effect will be issued presently, which should also help settle unrest in the slums. The faster we get their insane conspiracy theories laid to rest, the better. Don't you think?"

"I'm glad to hear it," said Vadim calmly. "I'll sleep better at night knowing that the guilty party has been found and has in a way been punished."

"God's punishment," said Abiog solemnly. "But the case is not yet officially closed."

Vadim squinted against the sunlight and rose from the edge of the pool.

"May I offer you a beer, Mr. Commissioner?"

Abiog nodded, and Vadim turned to Vincent.

"Please go buy us something to drink," he said. "I think we're out of anything decent."

Vincent obeyed his orders. The sun had already dried his body, and he pulled on his shirt and shorts without a word, took the elevator down to the ground floor, and walked through the building's spotless lobby. The heat radiating off the asphalt made him think for some reason of Father Abuel and Hellfire. Father Abuel was no fire-and-brimstone fanatic dwelling endlessly on the torments of eternal damnation, but he made no bones about the existence of Hell.

"Everyone gets their time in the fire," he would say. "And it will be like standing on glowing hot coals. Cleansing your soul is painful."

Vincent cut across the street in front of a screeching tricycle and some angrily shouting boys with a horse cart. He had never got around to asking Father Abuel exactly when you reached the point of eternal damnation.

When Vincent returned, Vadim was alone. He had taken off his shirt and had jumped in the pool in his Hawaiian shorts. His slender, muscular body broke the surface in an aggressive butterfly stroke. Then he caught sight of Vincent and swam to the side, smiling.

"He was in a hurry," he said. "But hand me one of those beers. The investigation is over; everything has been solved. Let's celebrate a little, for God's sake."

Vincent handed a bottle down to Vadim and opened one for himself. He suddenly wished with burning intensity that Victor was there. And Diana. And Bea and Carlito. Bea was pregnant again. Incredible, really, when in the past six months, they had only been together one single rushed and fumbling time. She hadn't told him as soon as she found out. In fact, she had waited a month to deliver the happy news because, as she said, she wasn't sure it would interest him.

"Cheers, my man."

Vincent returned the salute with his own bottle and felt the beer go down like an icy trickle all the way into his stomach.

Being with Vadim felt like loneliest party in the world.

"WHO ARE YOU?" asked the parka-man.

Søren leaned back against the birch tree in an attempt to signal that he was calm, relaxed, and sincere. The chain around his wrist was too tight for him to wriggle out of it, he had discreetly determined.

"My name is Søren," he said readily. "I'm Nina's husband. And I'd really like to know why you're following her."

The answer appeared to surprise the parka-man.

"Her husband?" he repeated.

Søren nodded. It was always easier to lie convincingly if you didn't need to say anything out loud.

"But she . . . are they your children?" He spoke rapid, fluent English, but with a singsong accent that made it necessary for Søren to concentrate.

"No," he said. "She's been married before. Do you know her from Manila?"

It seemed as if the man was about to answer but stopped himself. The rain was pouring down through the meager cover provided by such leaves as were left on the birch. Søren's windbreaker was what the manufacturers euphemistically called "shower-proof," which in real life translated into "insufficient in proper rain." He was getting wetter by the minute, and that could be a problem for his long-term survival—provided that was relevant at all, of course. He found it hard to read the man. There was a vagueness, an uncertainty in most of what he did, but in the parking lot he had used the Taser without a second's hesitation.

"Why are you following her?" he asked again. "Are you the one who contacted her on Facebook?"

The man didn't answer. He sat about ten yards away from Søren, out of his physical reach, which was probably not accidental. The Taser rested loosely against one thigh, and Søren tried not to think about the fact that one of Amnesty International's reasons for campaigning against stun guns was that it was far, far too easy to use them as instruments of torture.

"Are you a policeman?"

The question came more quickly than Søren had expected, but perhaps his few pathetic combat moves, despite their limited success, had been enough to arouse suspicion.

"No," he said. "Not any longer." It was the right answer according to the strategy he was tentatively developing, but it was also depressingly close to being the simple truth.

"Why not?" The man leaned forward, and the camping chair's canvas creaked under his weight.

"They didn't want me anymore."

"They threw you out?"

"You could call it that."

"Why?"

Søren shrugged. "There are so many rules," he said. "You can't always follow them all."

That ought to be a perspective that would resonate with the parka-man. Søren wasn't sure how much he could deduce about the values and normal operational limits of the guy from the abduction itself, haphazard and unplanned as it was. But possession of a Taser was illegal, and acquiring it must have been premeditated and deliberate.

Create solidarity. A shared humanity. Build up a relationship that made violence or killing more difficult. Page one in the manual for hostage negotiations, and who was to say that the hostage couldn't take the preliminary steps himself?

If that was what he was—a hostage. Right now it seemed that even his abductor wasn't completely sure.

He studied the man's expression as keenly as possible given that ridiculous parka hood. He had the sense that his first attempt at a common identification—*we both break rules*—had fallen completely flat. What had flashed across his captor's face had looked like a combination of fear and distaste. He had clearly reacted more strongly to "corrupt policeman" than to "former policeman."

Søren revised his strategy. His abductor did not consider himself a criminal; he identified with law-abiding morality, not with lawlessness.

"Could I have something to drink?" he asked. "I'm terribly thirsty."

"Yes, of course," said the parka-man and promptly got up. "Just a minute."

Curiouser and curiouser, as Alice said when she began to explore Wonderland. Most kidnappers felt a need to dominate their captives and rarely responded to requests without at least deliberating or demonstrating that they *could* have said no. The parka-man was acting more like a waiter who had been informed that the breadbasket was empty.

"Water?" he said and help up a plastic bottle. "Or would you prefer a beer?"

"Beer sounds good," said Søren in a friendly tone even though he would actually have preferred water. "What do you have?"

"Um, let me see. Stella Artois? Or . . ." He turned the can in order to read the name. "Warsteiner?"

A selection hinting more at German autobahn than Danish gas station kiosk. And the Land Cruiser had German license plates. Did the man have an actual base in Germany, or was that just the route he had chosen? There were far more long distance connections from a hub like Frankfurt.

"Stella is fine," he said. "Thanks, pal."

"You're welcome."

The parka-man was still careful not to get too close. He threw the can to Søren.

Søren caught it, opened it, and snatched it to his lips to catch the foam that bubbled up. He took a couple of consciously loud gulps and wiped his mouth with the back of his hand.

"That hit the spot," he said. "Aren't you having one?"

The parka-man looked at the cola he was drinking. Then he shrugged.

"Why not?" he mumbled and opened a Stella as well.

Søren gave himself a mental high five. The man might still have a Taser, and Søren was still chained to a tree. But the balance of power was shifting. In a few minutes—much too easily in fact—he had managed to change the relationship between them from interrogator and victim to drinking buddies, and best of all: the man had allowed himself to be directed to do something he hadn't actually planned on doing. He no longer controlled everything about the situation.

Søren couldn't help wondering why it was so easy. Especially since the man seemed to be alone. To carry out a crime single-handed and in a foreign country normally required a certain amount of initiative, independence, and willpower. Not characteristics that seemed immediately obvious here . . .

"Cheers," said Søren and raised the beer can one more time. "What's your name? I can't continue to think of you as 'the parka-man,' can I?" He said it with a grin, and the other man unconsciously smiled back.

"The parka-man," he said. "No, that . . . doesn't work, I guess." Then the smile disappeared abruptly. "You can call me V," he said.

"V . . . as in Victor?" Søren tried.

The man's eyes and jaw muscles twitched. His eyebrows contracted in a spasm of emotion. Grief? Or at least . . . sadness? He abruptly put his beer down and turned away.

"No," he said.

"Weren't you the one who sent the flowers?"

The man gave another shrug.

"It was nice of you. She was pleased," lied Søren.

"When people are in the hospital, you send them flowers," said the parka-man slowly. "That is common courtesy."

"Yes, but why did you choose those exact Bible quotes?" They had been about peace and life after death, he thought. On the surface innocuous enough, but . . .

At first, it seemed the man would ignore the question.

"I wanted her to think of heaven," he finally said. "People . . . think too little about that kind of thing while they are still alive."

Søren felt a chill along his spine. *While they are still alive* . . . did that mean that he had wanted Nina to prepare herself for death? As when you send a priest to a condemned man and allow him a last prayer before his execution?

"If you sent the card and the messages," said Søren, "then you must be Victor."

"No," the man said again, more explosively. "I am . . . not like him." He climbed into the car and slammed the door shut.

That particular probe had exposed a nerve ending, Søren noted. He leaned back against the tree trunk and stared into the rain and the oncoming darkness. The beer bubbled sourly in his stomach, and he was not at all sure whether the probe was progress or a fatal mistake.

His clothes were clinging wetly to his skin, and he felt it more now that his abductor had put himself out of reach of Søren's mind games. The man stayed stubbornly inside the Land Cruiser. Was he waiting for something, or was it just to avoid further conversation?

Then Søren's cell phone rang inside the car, so loud and penetrating that he could hear it easily in spite of the distance and the closed car door. The light inside the camper was turned on, and he could see the parka-man—V—rummage frantically between the seats.

He felt a kick of adrenaline throughout his body. He didn't know how the man would react, but he had no doubt that the game had just entered a new phase.

The car door slammed open. V came toward him with rapid steps, holding the Taser in his outstretched arms. Søren jumped up and backed as far as the chain permitted, holding his hands up defensively.

"No," he begged, at the moment not caring how many points it cost him in the power struggle. His body shrank in remembered pain, and all he could think was that he didn't want to experience that pain one more time. "Don't. I'll do whatever you say."

"Lie down. On your stomach, please."

It was now too dark for him to be able to read anything on V's face. His voice was hoarse with some kind of excitement, but also so decisive that Søren was convinced that the man would fire if he encountered the tiniest opposition. He lay down.

"Hands on your back."

He obeyed. The chain was slapped twice around both wrists, and the lock clicked. He tried to keep his hands apart to have a bit of room to maneuver, but the yank that tightened the chain was too powerful.

"Thank you. Now I must ask you to walk to the car."

The polite phrasing was all that was left of the accommodating pleaser type with the beer cans. It was bizarre. Would the man kill in the same servile manner? *I'm terribly sorry, but I have to ask you step into this mass grave?* Did he have an actual personality disorder, or . . . no, Søren didn't believe he was a psychopath.

"I'd like you to lie down in the center aisle like before."

In a way it was easier to say what he *wasn't* than what he was. Not a rule breaker. Not a soloist, even though he was alone.

Not a dominating alpha male. And, no, not a callous psychopath either.

Would he kill?

Søren remembered the onion smell and the peculiar sensation of his mouth-to-mouth "resuscitation." He still wasn't sure if it had been necessary, but in any case the man had thought so, and there had been real desperation in his voice. He didn't *want* to kill, that much was clear. But in spite of the risk he had used the Taser again without hesitation.

Søren crouched on the camper's floor and rolled over on his stomach with difficulty when he was instructed to do so. More rattling, more clicks. He wasn't sure where the chain was attached this time, but in the short interval between V's slamming the back door and getting into the front seat to start the Land Cruiser's engine, Søren's attempt to sit up or roll onto his side failed completely. At least he didn't have his arms over his head this time. No long battle to get enough air into his lungs.

The Land Cruiser lurched through the dark forest. There was a thump that shuddered through the entire body of the car, and something slid along the side of the car with a metallic screech. V cursed, hit the gas pedal, and turned the steering wheel frantically. Not exactly a candidate for Paris-Dakar, Søren thought dryly. His level of alarm had fallen a bit again, really for no other reason than that he was still conscious, still alive, and hadn't been shot with the Taser.

About forty minutes later, the Land Cruiser pulled off the road and crunched onto the gravel of a rest stop surrounded by a windbreak of dark pine trees. Søren's vision was severely limited—only by craning his neck could he glimpse a bit of his surroundings through a side window—and his sense of direction had been through yet another carousel trip, but a short while ago an airplane had passed so near to the treetops that he was convinced that it had to be in the process of landing. Tirstrup Airport? Or Karup? He decided Karup was more likely.

V shut off the engine. In the silence, Søren could hear the man's quick, superficial breathing, and the regurgitated air from the Land Cruiser's ventilation system had a sour and sweaty smell of fear that wasn't just Søren's own.

During the drive the man had had two brief phone conversations, both in a language completely inpenetrable to Søren—Tagalog, maybe, if the man was from the Philippines—but sprinkled with occasional English expressions and words. "Highway" and "gas station" and "cell phone" swam like small recognizable islands in an ocean of incomprehensibility. Now he got out of the car and began a jerky pacing, back and forth, like an expectant father in a maternity ward.

It had stopped raining, and the moonlight fell with photo flash–like clarity across treetops, gravel, graffiti-decorated picnic tables, and garbage cans. V had left the front door open, and cold, damp night air seeped into the Land Cruiser's stuffy cabin. Søren was grateful—not only for the change of air, but also because he could now see a substantial part of the rest stop without overtaxing his vertebrae. They were here to meet someone—or so Søren concluded. If he was right, it took V out of the category of "lone madman," but opened a new can of unanswered questions. If there were more of them, why was V driving around alone in the absurdly well-equipped Land Cruiser? Who were the others, if there was more than one? What was the setup? International organized crime? Terrorism? There was a Muslim minority in the Philippines, and the country had been a significant base for Al-Qaeda since the nineties. Still, very few so-called "ordinary people" associated Filipinos with terror. Or with organized crime, for that matter. Filipinos were so ubiquitous. There were over one hundred million in the world, and sometimes it seemed as if most of them worked abroad—as sailors, truck drivers, construction workers, cleaners, nannies, and so on. From a conference he had attended in the fall, Søren seemed to remember that the Filipino international workforce actually numbered about ten million, a quite considerable population base for any illegal network to hide in and recruit from, whether the goal was terror or more "conventional" crime.

But who would recruit a man like V? No training, as far as Søren could judge. Not especially cold-blooded. Not especially callous or psychologically disturbed. Not especially dedicated or fanatic or certainly not a radical Muslim, or that beer would never have gone down so easily, nor would he have quoted the Bible. Once again, it was the inverse descriptions that came to you first. As if you could only see his outline when you had peeled away everything he *wasn't*.

But his nervousness was palpable. He couldn't stand still out there; if he wasn't marching up and down, he stood rocking on the balls of his feet like an anxious diver on the high board.

The traffic on the Jutland country road was sparse but speedy—the drivers around here clearly saw no reason to take the eighty-kilometer limit seriously. However, the little red Triumph convertible that overshot the rest stop, braked schreechingly, and then reversed fifty meters in a few seconds made the local infringements fade into insignificance. Søren put an imaginary minus in the "international terrorism" box. No terrorist in his right mind would choose such a flashy mean of transportation, and then use it in such an attention-grabbing way. The roof was up, but even so, Søren's eardrums were assaulted by a blast of synthetic pop that must have put the car's speakers under considerable strain. Steel guitar, synthesizer and slightly asynchronous choir, like a Hawaiian orchestra on acid.

The figure that leaped jack-in-the-box-like from the little car was not very tall. There was something odd about his physique. Broad shoulders and a shaved head as round as a bowling ball; slim, almost delicate-looking hips; and thighs as disproportionate as those of a prize turkey. He clapped his hands three or four times with obvious enthusiasm, gave V a chummy knuckle punch on the shoulder, and began to speak quickly and incomprehensibly. Tagalog again, Søren assumed.

V handed his partner Søren's cell phone—or that's how it looked from Søren's perspective; strictly speaking he couldn't actually be sure that the little black thing was his. The man studied it for several minutes, patted V on the shoulder again, this time with a flat hand, and nonchalantly threw the telephone into the Triumph's passenger seat. Then he headed for the Land Cruiser. V exclaimed in protest, but ended up rushing after him like a child afraid to be left behind.

His partner pulled the front door wide open and bent his upper body at a right angle so his face was level with Søren's. His eyes glinted with an odd oily shine.

"You police?" he asked and revealed a set of gold teeth worthy of a James Bond villain.

"I was," said Søren.

"Danish police?"

"Yes."

For some reason the man apparently found that statement hysterically funny. He laughed heartily but more or less soundlessly—though his face cracked from ear to ear and his upper body rocked back and forth in good humor, a short chortling sound was all that came out at the end of each of his silent roars of laughter.

"Danish police," he repeated, with a new cascade of laughter. Then he grabbed Søren's face with both hands and pinched his cheeks in much the same way Søren's grandfather had done when he was a child. Søren didn't like it then, and he didn't like it now. One of the man's thumbnails was less than a centimeter from Søren's left eye, long and thickened and bone colored, and a fine spray of laughter-borne saliva hit him in the face.

"Danish police," the man with the gold teeth said a third time, jerking Søren's head up and down a few times in time with the laughter eruptions before letting go with a final amiable pat to the cheek.

"Leave him alone," said V, with a timing that precisely aligned with the moment when the man was straightening up anyway.

"Okay, boss," said Goldtooth, and that was apparently even funnier than "Danish police" because he laughed all the way back to the convertible.

"Okay," he shouted again over his shoulder. "Let's go find this guy's wife."

Was he speaking English to be certain that Søren understood him? Deliberate or not, it worked.

THE PHILIPPINES, A MONTH AND A HALF EARLIER

VINCENT WAS WOKEN by someone shaking him and shouting.

The room was dark because he had pulled the blinds down so only a small sliver of light could get in. He had no idea what time of day it was.

"Vincent. Come on, you little pussy. Wake up."

This time he recognized the voice as Vadim's, but there was a new ring to it. Something shrill.

Vincent sat up and tried to orient himself in the almost total darkness. The air conditioner was humming at him from its usual position, with one green and two shining red eyes. Grey light was seeping in through the door from the apartment's living room.

"What time is it?"

"Eight-thirty. Come on, damn it!" Vadim pulled the blanket off him in a short angry tug and turned on the overhead lights.

Vincent blinked. It was Sunday. It had to be Sunday, and it wasn't more than four hours since he had gone to bed. He had played World of Warcraft on Vadim's computer most of the night while Vadim was out looking for a girl. He did that from time to time now that he and Diana no longer saw each other regularly.

A man has needs, as he usually said, and then he was gone all night. Vincent had no idea when Vadim had gotten home, but here he was, physically dragging Vincent from his bed.

"What?"

Vincent had slept without boxer shorts and frantically tried to cover his dick and pubic hair, but Vadim didn't seem to notice.

"Victor is dead," he said. "Abiog called me half an hour ago. Come on, you have to come with me."

The world froze.

How could so large a human being die? Vincent wondered. He had seen Victor a week ago, and he had been fine. His enormous body was warm and calm. His heart beat. His lungs took in oxygen and exhaled CO_2. He had hoisted Vincent up in an effortless fireman's lift to swing him around a few times before putting him down again, just like he usually did when they hadn't seen each other for a while. Hugging was such a girly thing, he said.

Vincent's mouth was dry, and all he could think about was water.

"You're fucking with me," he said, edging past Vadim. Into the living room and on to the kitchen and the refrigerator. He found a bottle of water and emptied it without looking at Vadim. He didn't dare.

"Put on some clothes," said Vadim. "We're leaving now."

LAS PINAS LOOKED the same. And the smell was the same too.

A violent shower had washed the smog from the sky in the course of the night and the slum was steaming in the morning sun. A bunch of children were playing in the puddles between the shacks, half-naked and with dirty feet. Lines of dirt on the round, smiling faces. White shining baby teeth amidst all the grime.

Vincent tried to look straight ahead as he threaded his way through the narrow, tunnellike passages following Commissioner Abiog, Vadim, and a uniformed policeman who clearly knew the area. The heat and the dimness of the light created a flicker before his eyes. He ducked under low-hanging laundry and stumbled over plastic tubs and cackling hens that ran straight across the path. He tried to catch snatches of the conversation between Vadim and Abiog up ahead.

"We don't know precisely when . . . was dead when we got there . . . your friend . . . everything is gone . . ."

They passed a couple of uniformed policemen who had fastened an inadequate length of red-and-white plastic tape across the small walkway. Abiog bent under the tape, puffing slightly with the effort. Sweat was pouring off him; he pulled a well-used handkerchief out of his pocket and wiped his face and neck. Then he continued toward the corrugated hut that housed Victor and Diana's clinic.

There were more uniforms guarding the doorway, but from the outside there was nothing dramatic to see. A dog had darted through the makeshift police line and was sniffing around at the corner of the house. It cocked a leg and pissed against the white wall. People were hanging out of window openings and doors, staring curiously.

"I called you when I saw the address he had listed. He lives in your apartment?"

Abiog tilted his head back and observed Vadim under half-closed eyelids. He looked like a fish, thought Vincent. A big dopey one. His face was completely expressionless.

"Victor is a close friend," said Vadim. "We've known each other for years. We studied together."

"So you'd be able to identify him?"

Vadim cleared his throat and for once seemed physically unwell. His face was grey and the corners of his mouth stiff, as if he was fighting off tears or nausea.

"Yes . . . unless he's in very bad shape?"

"We'd appreciate it if you'd try," said Abiog, without answering Vadim's question. "We've contacted his mother, but she lives outside Angeles, and that's a drive of at least eight hours. It's better if we take care of it now and send him north to his parents when the autopsy is finished."

He waved them on through the door. The clinic seemed smaller than the last time Vincent had been there. Claustrophobically small. Shelves and cabinets had been toppled across the floor, together with the little camping table with the electric kettle. Victor was lying on the examination couch. He was partially covered by a sheet of thick clear plastic, which reminded Vincent most of all of a trash bag. One long and muscular leg dangled over the edge, the foot still wearing its size fourteen flip-flop.

There was blood on the walls. Large, explosive blotches like paint hurled against a canvas.

It smelled like the meat market at home in San Marcelino. Meat and blood simmering in the tropical heat. Vincent held a hand up in front of his mouth and nose and remained standing in the door while he tried to make sense of what he was looking at. He had seen dead people in medical school, but they had been freed from a history. They lay naked in a white room, covered by a white cloth, and did not have names. Regardless of what they had suffered and experienced in their last moments, it was invisible there on the table. Their lives were completely erased.

But Victor . . .

His fight for survival was on the walls and in the coffee which dripped from the shattered cup on the floor. His light blue backpack still slouched against the wall where he must have dropped it when he came in. There was a crumpled up blanket in the corner and a toothbrush by the tiny sink.

Vincent took in every detail. The story of Victor's last moments. Vadim had to steady himself on the doorframe.

Abiog didn't say anything. Possibly he was attempting to be tactful, but his professional impatience was revealed in the rapid tapping of one foot and the way he kept wiping his forehead and cheeks. He produced a cigarette and lit it, taking long, demonstrative inhalations. After half a cigarette they had apparently had all the time for reflection that he could spare.

"So . . ."

He went over the table and pulled the thick plastic away from the dead man's face.

It really was Victor. A part of his face was missing, leaving a gap through which skull and jaw cavity and vertebrae were visible. But what was left was sufficient. The powerful jaw and the characteristic gap between the front teeth. The guy was built with extra room for everything, as Vadim used to say. Like a house where there was still plenty of space between the furniture.

His white Manila Mustangs T-shirt was soaked through with blood, and his right arm had been all but ripped off at the shoulder. He must have fought, thought Vincent. Victor was a big man. He must have thrown things. And yelled. Maybe he had been afraid, even though that was hard to imagine. Vincent had never heard Victor express unease or fear of anything at all, and he would prefer to think it had been that way until the end.

"It's Victor," he said calmly to Abiog.

He felt cold and oddly distant. As if he wasn't quite there. *Strange*, he thought, *that it's only warm and living blood that I can't handle*. He looked over at Vadim, who still stood leaning against the blood-spattered doorframe. He was pale as a corpse.

"Did he suffer much?"

Abiog looked at Vadim with surprise. Then he pulled the plastic sheeting over the corpse again and signaled one of the policemen outside.

"He put up resistance, as you can see, but I doubt that it was a long struggle. Some of the neighbors heard a commotion from inside at about four in the morning and a shot shortly thereafter. Altogether we're talking about a few hectic moments. I have no idea how it felt."

Vadim's jaw muscles were so strained now that the sinews stood out under the skin like cables. His teeth ground against each other. Two EMTs made their way past him with a stretcher so he had to retreat backward out of the clinic.

"When did you last see him?"

Vincent hesitated.

"About a week ago. But I thought he had gone to work at a hospital up north."

Abiog sucked the last vestiges from his cigarette and threw it in a puddle.

"He had, but the old kook who takes care of the clinic when the young idealists aren't here called to tell him there was some disturbance. People sneaking around and trying to break open the lock. We assume Victor Galang slept here for some days to prevent a break-in. The world is full of murdering thieves. Junkies maybe . . . Witnesses saw a couple of young guys drive away in a red Mazda."

Abiog looked as if he had dropped both the thread and his interest in the conversation. Instead he thoughtfully observed Vadim, who was squatting with his eyes closed, with his back and head leaned back against the white corrugated wall.

"You'd better get our rich kid out of here. He doesn't have the stomach for this."

He winked at Vincent.

"Our rich kid?"

Abiog smiled faintly.

"Don't pretend that the two of us are that different," he said. "We both live off of his kind. He is what keeps our heads above water, isn't that so? Mine *and* yours. What would your sorry ass be worth without him? I don't know how it was with your third musketeer, but it might be worth finding out."

Vincent retreated, got Vadim on his feet.

"Come on," he said. "We can go now."

"NINA-GIRL."

Her father was floating in the pool with both arms spread wide. The water flickered blue green around him, and the light in the Swim Center had been turned off. Only the underwater lamps were still on, so it was hard to see his face, hard to see him. But the voice, the deep, soft Dad voice, was unmistakable.

"What do you want?" she asked.

"Want? I don't want anything. Just want to talk to you a little. Come on in. The water is nice and warm."

She took a hesitant step down the ladder. He was right. The water *was* warm, much too warm. It felt more like bathwater than pool water. The steam rose in misty spirals, and her breath felt wet, as if she was drowning a little bit every time she breathed.

She was wearing all her clothes. He was too. And from his wrist spread dark, swirling streams of blood.

"Help!" she yelled. "Help! He's dying!"

Her shout echoed in the empty hall.

"There's no one here but you and me," he said. Totally calm, as if his life's blood wasn't leaving his body.

She didn't understand why she hadn't seen it before. It was a spreading stain around him, dark like octopus ink, and there was so much of it—much more than a single human body ought to contain. If she wanted to reach him, she would have to swim through it. The thought was almost unbearable.

Still she did it. With her head raised so her face wouldn't touch the bloody water, stroke by stroke, closer and closer . . .

"I'll help you," she said. "Dad, I'll help you."

She made it to his side. Grabbed hold of his wrist, found the artery and pressed down as hard as she could. She kicked her legs wildly to stay above water and with her free hand tried to pull the string from her hoodie so she could use it as a tourniquet.

He flopped onto his side and rose half out of the water. His face was lit from below, but . . . but it wasn't his.

"Sorry," he said. "It won't take long, I promise."

It wasn't her father. The shock paralyzed her stiff fingers, her kicking legs. It wasn't him. The face was oddly smeared, as if it had been painted with watercolors that ran, but she knew it wasn't his.

He placed both hands around her throat and pulled her down into the bloody water. She didn't even have time to scream.

NO. OH NO. Shock, fear and abhorrence clung to her body long after she had turned on the light and seized hold of waking reality as best she could. Her breath hissed from her lungs, troubled and uneasy, and she was soaked in sweat. She grabbed the watch she had dutifully taken off before bed.

4:21.

Not that that meant anything in itself. Still, she felt better anchored in time and place, better able to tell the difference between nightmare and normality.

As she sat staring at the black display with the large, pale, easy-to-read numbers, she realized that it hadn't just been a nightmare.

Sorry. It won't take long, I promise.

She had heard the words before, in real life. As she had been lying on the concrete deck of the Mathias Mall's parking garage with a crack in her skull. And he had said the Lord's Prayer. In Tagalog.

That's why his face had looked like something Anton had painted with his watercolor set. She hadn't seen it clearly, hadn't been able to focus. And then he had placed his jacket over her face, as if she were already dead.

4:22. Caroline Westmann probably wasn't at work—and if she was, it would be because she had more urgent things to do than to listen to vague flashbacks of something they still thought was a violent robbery that had been interrupted.

It wasn't a robbery. She knew that now, with the certainty that comes with *remembering*. The odd apology, the prayer, the engine that she could hear being revved up . . . if he hadn't hit the other car, would he have hit her? Victor's warning had been completely justified. *My life is in danger—and so is yours.* Someone had tried to kill her.

She didn't feel like trying to go to sleep again. She pulled on a shirt and stuck her feet into the worn canvas shoes she used for slippers here. Her mother had an entire box of them in various sizes so every guest could find a pair that fit.

Many of the neighbors had gone open plan long since, but her mother had kept the little kitchen and its breakfast nook. Even the cabinets were the originals, now painted a lavender blue with white frames. About the only bit of redecorating had been a new solid beech work top and the narrow dishwasher next to the sink. Nina turned on the electric kettle and made a cup of instant coffee.

Someone had tried to kill her.

After the fear, her most prominent emotion was a violated sense of justice. It wasn't fair, protested a small voice some place in her mental universe. Not now, not when she had actually tried so hard, done therapy and everything, and fought her save-the-world complex, the time checking, and the old demons. Even if Morten didn't believe her, she really *was* trying to get out of the war zone and live a normal, quiet life. She hadn't done anything that would give anyone reason to murder her. She thought of Ida's new fear of death, of the loss of illusion that had eliminated her teenage sense of invulnerability.

"If I die, she'll never get over it."

The thought hit her with such intensity that she said it out loud. The words sounded flat and out of place in the cosy fifties kitchen, designed for the cereal-eating, drip-coffee drinking middle class. On the bulletin board above the little foldout table—room for five with a bit of goodwill—still hung the school planner whose predictable fortnightly rhythm had been interrupted by the cancer diagnosis. Colorful, homemade *Get Better!* cards from four of Hanne Borg's classes now hung side by side with "Nutrition Hints" from the Cancer Society, the recipe for the disgusting devil's claw tea, and brochures and appointment slips for the Oncology Department.

Her mother was sixty-two. As far as Nina knew, she had had no plans for early retirement, but even though the chances of survival looked good, the illness, the treatment, and its aftermath might well put an undesired end to her working life.

"Nina?" Her mother stood in the doorway, in the old blue velvet robe she had had for at least fifteen years. Her bald head was covered by a soft cotton hat. "I thought I heard someone rummaging around."

"I'm sorry I woke you."

"Well, you didn't exactly wake me . . . I was mostly just lying there thinking."

"About what?"

Her mother just smiled, a crooked and tired smile.

"What a scare with Anton today," she said. "Lucky it wasn't worse. Was that why you couldn't sleep?"

"I don't know. I did dream something about a pool though." Just that small revelation made her heart rate increase. The blood, her father who wasn't actually her father, the apologetic phrases from a man who was planning to kill her . . . She didn't say any more. She couldn't lay that worry on her mother.

"Were you afraid?" she suddenly asked, almost against her will. "When you got the diagnosis, I mean."

"That's a stupid question, Nina."

It probably was.

"What about now? How do you feel now?"

Hanne Borg looked at her for a while, and the gaze was not particularly friendly.

"It must be a relief," she said.

"What?"

"That I have a clinically diagnosable illness that you can approach professionally."

"Mom! That's not fair!"

"Isn't it? I'm sorry then. Maybe I misunderstood something. It's just that this is the first time in more than twenty years that you are voluntarily spending time in my proximity, but maybe that's just a coincidence."

"That's not true. I've been here plenty of times . . ."

"For the sake of the children, yes. Or because Morten insisted."

"Mom!"

Hanne Borg sighed. The animosity in her gaze flickered and was extinguished, and she seemed merely tired.

"I'm sorry," she said. "Maybe you get a little . . . impatient. When life punches you in the face with a new perspective."

"Impatient?"

"With all the formalities. Everything we just *pretend* to do. Is it because you think it was my fault?"

"What?"

Yet another sigh.

"You know very well, Nina. That he killed himself. You've been so angry at me ever since."

"Stop it. That's not true." Oh, fuck. She was about to cry. What the hell was wrong with her? *You're not falling apart*, she told herself. *It's the fractured skull.* Head trauma can lead to a certain instability.

"No one could have stopped him, Nina. He was ill. He didn't do it to hurt us; he just couldn't . . . take any more."

"I. Know. That." She managed to force the words out between tightly pressed lips.

"You do? It doesn't seem like it."

"Mom, I can't. Do this. Right now."

"Well, when?" asked her mother in a hard tone. "When I'm dead? It'll be too late, then, sweetie."

Nina poured the practically untouched coffee into the sink and fled back to the guest room.

When her phone began to ring, about an hour later, she answered it with gratitude, even before she saw the number and noted that it was Søren. She had been lying with the light on, catnapping in an attempt to get some rest without actually falling fully asleep. She still had the sense that the nightmare was just waiting to sink its claws into her and pull her down if she lost her grip.

"Where have you been?" she said sharply and with no preamble. "You could have left a message!"

No one answered.

"Søren?"

Still no reaction.

"Heavy breathing went out of fashion in the eighties," she said. "Now all the freaks live in cyberspace."

But it couldn't be a random stalker. This was Søren's number. She listened intently but couldn't hear anything but a bit of wind. Rustling leaves? She wasn't sure. Then even that bit of life disappeared, and the connection died. She pressed the "redial" with an angry index finger.

No one answered. She could hear it ringing and ringing. And suddenly she realized that she wasn't just hearing it over the phone. There was Søren's ring tone, *riiing*, *riing*, like an old-fashioned analog phone.

The sound came from the front yard—the small strip of grass and privet hedge that shielded the house from the street. She tore the blinds to one side, too impatient to jiggle the tricky rolling mechanism.

She couldn't see anything or anyone, but she could still hear the phone until voice mail took over. She hung up and redialed. *Riing, riiing*.

She edged by the bed and in passing grabbed the fairly hideous jogging pants the Swim Center's lost and found had loaned her to replace her own soaked, chlorine-stinking jeans—they were an unusually aggressive pink that made her think of Miss Piggy from *The Muppet Show*. In the laundry room, she stuck her feet into her mother's old gardening shoes and clattered out onto the back steps. It was freezing; she really should have given herself time to find a jacket, but her brain kept throwing adrenaline-charged scenarios in her face. Søren unconscious. Søren paralyzed, Søren in spasms, having an attack, Søren dead . . . What might cause a man to call but not speak? Not say anything, not as much as a half-choked moan?

"Søren?" she called, with no great expectations. The wind rustled through the hedge, white petals from her mother's favorite roses clung wetly to the grass, and Søren was nowhere to be seen. She dialed again.

This time she got a better sense of the call signal's direction. It came from the carport, from the white-painted wooden shed at the end that housed the trash cans and her mother's bicycle. She crossed the lawn. The grass was so high that her bare ankles got wet, but the sensation was distant and irrelevant. She opened the shed door and fumbled with the light switch. Nothing happened. But in the light from her own cell phone, she could see him. He was lying on the dirty cement floor, in a pile of dried leaves that had drifted in under the edge of the door. He lay in a bizarrely awkward position—on his side, with hands and feet gathered together—but it wasn't until she was kneeling next to him and that she realized why.

Wide black strips of duct tape covered both eyes and mouth. Hands and feet were similarly stuck together. Her heart gave a shocked leap in her chest, and she reflexively began dialing 112.

She only made it as far as the first digit.

"Sorry," a voice whispered behind her. Something hit her at the nape of the neck, just above the webbed collar of her T-shirt, and an overwhelming, painful paralysis put her body out of commission.

IT TOOK ALMOST eight hours to drive to Angeles and an additional half-hour before Vincent, Vadim, and Diana reached the village Victor came from.

His mother and father grew rice on rented land, and their house lay in a field with flooded paddies on all sides and just a few packed paths connecting them to the rest of the world. Vincent and the others had to leave the car in the village and walk out to the house in the evening heat, with mosquitoes swarming in a dense cloud around them.

Diana hadn't said a word on the entire trip; had merely stared straight ahead between the two front seats. As the tiny house came in sight, with its weathered grey plank walls, it was as if she woke up and began to see for the first time.

"I don't get it," she said, mostly addressing herself.

"What?"

Vadim had an almost defiant expression on his face, as if he had decided not to speak to her, but still couldn't help it.

"That he came from this," said Diana. "That a boy raised on rice and eggplant and a few strips of chicken could become a man like Victor. He grew out of nothing. How could they kill him? He was just like them."

She began to cry, in the quiet introverted way of someone who does not want comforting. Vadim placed an arm around her shoulder all the same, and pulled her close. They walked like an old married couple tottering in mutual sorrow.

A couple of men were playing the guitar outside the dilapidated house, their song grating and melancholy. Mostly about unhappy love. Another group had settled down with dice and cards.

A woman whom Vincent instinctively knew was Victor's mother was cooking rice in an enormous pot hanging on a tripod over an open fire. Bare feet on the ground. She was tiny. No more than five feet tall and skinny like a plucked bird. The dark face was furrowed and streaked by tears, but to Vincent's great relief, it looked as if she had come past the first furious storm of feeling. He sensed that she had been a cheerful woman not long ago, because the wrinkles around her eyes looked as if they came from smiling.

Victor had been their only child, Vincent knew, which just made it all the more unbearable. For some reason, these two people had not succeeded in bringing forth more than one child, but that one offspring had been enormous. Victor would laugh when he talked about it.

"I ate everything," he said. "And then I made sure to lock up behind me. Little Baby Victor didn't want any competition."

Now his tiny mother caught sight of them and came over to meet them. She allowed them one by one to guide the back of her skinny hand to their foreheads in the traditional greeting of respect.

"I knew that someone was going to die," she whispered

conspiratorially. "Ten days ago a black butterfly flew in and settled on our picture of the Virgin Mary. I prayed that it wasn't him who was being called, but . . ."

She shook her head. That the higher powers had not listened was clearly unfathomable. Then she smiled faintly and revealed a row of beautiful, bright white teeth.

"It's so nice that you've come. Victor's friends are always welcome," she said. "I have plenty of rice, and it's important to eat so we can gather strength for the final nights. The coffin is beautiful. Did you send the money for the funeral, my dear?" She looked at Diana. "Victor has told us so much about you."

VICTOR'S PARENTS AND relatives had already kept wake, kept *lamay* over the coffin for four nights. But according to tradition, there were still four sleepless nights ahead of them. Victor's uncle from Switzerland was on his way home to say goodbye, and they were also waiting for some family from the distant southern islands.

Victor had been placed in a shiny white coffin with cream-colored lining and golden handles. Drifts of yellow roses framed it. The rough wooden walls were painted a bright cerulean blue, and behind the coffin a glistening green satin curtain had been artfully arranged. A gilded Virgin Mary posed in lonely majesty, holding vigil over the flickering candles and gently smoking incense sticks, and beneath the coffin someone had placed a cage with a small yellow chicken.

The tiny living room was already crowded. White plastic chairs had been set out for guests, and the people sitting there were eating and chatting. Most were as sinewy and weather-beaten as Victor's parents, but there were young people as well, in white T-shirts, shorts, sunglasses, and sandals.

Diana walked over to touch the coffin with her fingertips. She had dressed entirely in black for the occasion, but other than that had made no effort. Her hair hung heavy and unbrushed around her face, and she had not put on any makeup to camouflage the dark shadows under her eyes. She looked like a dead woman walking, thought Vincent. Grief had transformed her. The bloom was gone, and Vincent almost felt sorry for Vadim because he was forced to see his beloved grieve for another man.

He bore it well. Was caring and supportive. Brought her water and a small bowl of rice, fresh fruit, and chicken in a strong red chili sauce.

"You have to eat," he said and placed a solicitous hand on her bony hip. "Otherwise you'll fade away completely."

But Diana wasn't listening and left her food untouched on the floor under her chair. She had caught sight of Victor's mother, who had come in to sit with her son again.

"May I see him?"

Diana tentatively touched Victor's mother sinewy arm, and the exhausted gazes of the two women met.

The coffin was closed and without the usual glass window through which the mourners could see the dead person's face. Vincent knew all too well why, but until now both he and Vadim had spared Diana the gory details.

"The embalmers could not get him to look nice," said his mother, and a bitter expression slid across her face. "Those squatters who did it. They are like animals . . . Not even the poorest here would do what they did. Why was he there? Why was he in the slums? He was going to be a doctor."

Diana stepped back as if she had been hit in the face. Her lips were tight and narrow. Outside the men had begun to sing again. "I Will Always Love You." A bit hesitant on the words, but recognizable despite the stumbles. The guitars kept admirable pace. The mosquitoes swarmed, singing around the small yellow light bulbs in the ceiling, and the smell of brackish water from the rice paddies filled the stuffy little room.

Diana leaned into Vadim and rested her head on his shoulder.

"I'm not feeling very well," she said. "I'd like to go home when it gets light."

Vadim stroked the back of her neck and her unbrushed hair, and Vincent felt a sudden jab of pain. As if Vadim's gesture was an echo of what he and Bea had had together a long, long time ago.

He had forgotten. Now he remembered.

They had moved on to Elvis outside. "Heartbreak Hotel" and "You'll Never Walk Alone." The guitar was not as tightly tuned as it had been, or else the player was coming a little unstuck, but he continued with fine abandon. Evening had faded into night, and the sky was pitch black over the fields. No one slept—you weren't allowed to, in here with the dead man. The little downy chicken under the coffin received some cooked rice and water in its cage and stalked about on its disproportionately long orange legs. Vadim couldn't take his eyes off of it.

"A chicken," he whispered. "Why have they put a chicken under the coffin?"

"Because Victor was murdered." Vincent sent Vadim a

measuring look. Funerals must be entirely different where he came from. The rich man's ghetto. Maybe no one was murdered there, or else they had become too urban and refined for the proper rituals.

"But what is it supposed to do?"

"The chicken is there to wake the conscience of the murderer," said Vincent.

Vadim carefully touched Diana's hair.

"Murderers like the kind who shot Victor don't have a conscience," he whispered, still staring at the yellow chicken. Its black eyes blinked at them, and it peeped very faintly. Scraped its feet against the barred bottom of the cage. "People from the slums are animals," said Vadim. "And animals have no conscience."

He rose to his feet with abrupt violence.

"I'm going outside to piss," he hissed. "That chicken is freaking me out. All of this . . ." He gestured with his arms. "I can't stand it. I need air."

VADIM RETURNED HALF an hour later and sank down into the chair next to Diana's. Pulled her close.

None of them slept. They just sat there, Vadim with a hand curled loosely on Diana's thigh. And suddenly there was something about that picture that made Vincent uncomfortable. Something that wasn't right.

He tilted his neck back and stared up at the rusty tin roof above his head. Details from the clinic in Las Pinas City came back to him, but it wasn't Victor's torn body he thought about. It was Commissioner Abiog as he had stood there in the doorway and smoked greedily and impatiently while he waited for them to pull themselves together. A little later he had said something about a red Mazda. Vincent was sure of that. There were many red Mazdas in Manila, but he still couldn't help thinking of Martinez and his greasy grin when he had offered Vincent a lift and a night on the town in his ridiculous red rattletrap.

His thoughts swam away from him. Some men in a corner of the room had begun playing cards, and shouts of triumph took turns with regretful grunts while the cards were slapped on the floor.

At some point Vadim got up and collected three beers for them from an ice bucket outside. They drank in silence, and finally the grey morning light began to seep in through the cracks between the boards of the walls. Victor's mother got up, looking ready to keel over from the many hours in her chair, and began to boil water for coffee.

VADIM AND DIANA left the gathering that morning.

Diana was not feeling well. After just one night the pallor on her face was leaden, and sweat formed a shiny film on her skin. She moaned faintly when Vadim half carried, half supported her down the path between the steaming paddies.

Vincent had decided to stay.

He wanted to escort Victor from the house and see him buried. He had done so few things right in his life until now, but this one task damn well ought to be within his capabilities. Three additional nights and a four-kilometer-long procession behind the hearse. It didn't require thought. It was easy—like it had been for him when he went to school and just needed to do his homework to make everyone around him happy. He knew exactly what was expected of him.

He walked back into the house with a cup of coffee in his hand and sat down. His eyes stung with exhaustion, and it took a while before he noticed that Vadim's cell phone was lying on the floor. He picked it up, wiped it carefully on his shorts and let it slide into his pocket. Then he took it out again and looked at it for a long time before he went outside and began to scroll through Vadim's contacts.

Commissioner Abiog popped up as one of the first on the list. Both his cell and private landline. Vincent breathed in, the kind of inhalation you take before you dive, and called him.

"Abiog."

The voice came without unnecessary polite trappings. Dry and professional.

"Vadim Augustin Lorenzo."

Vincent's voice broke a little. Vadim's voice was deeper than his, but he hoped that the phone's distortion would minimize the difference.

"Yes?"

Abiog sounded impatient, as if he was speaking to a difficult and nagging child.

"I was just curious," said Vincent. "You mentioned that there were witnesses to the murder of Victor Galang?"

"Not to the actual killing. Someone saw a couple of guys run out of the area and drive away."

"And the car . . . ? Do you have any information?"

"A red Mazda . . ." Abiog hesitated. Vincent pictured him

picking his feet off his desk and leaning forward in his chair, maybe giving his secretary a sharp silencing look.

Vincent had to continue with a certain caution.

"Yes, you said that on the day. But has anything further come to light? A license plate or the like?"

Vincent cursed inside at his attempt at jargon. It sounded as if he was in a really bad action movie.

"What can I say," said Abiog coolly. "The witnesses who saw it were idiots, and they didn't remember the number. All they noticed was that the license plate was crooked, and that won't get us very far in this town."

Vincent felt something cold move under his skin, his teeth began to chatter and he almost dropped the telephone on the floor. He fixed his gaze on Victor's coffin. Tried to concentrate.

"Mr. Lorenzo?"

"Yes."

"I'm not telling you anything new here, and you don't sound as if you are quite yourself. Should I be worried?"

Abiog didn't sound worried. He sounded glacial.

VADIM TORE OPEN the door the same moment Vincent stuck his key in the lock.

"What the hell were you thinking?"

His hand closed around Vincent's throat. It wasn't a tight hold, but still enough to push him back against the warm concrete wall in the stairwell. His head rattled like an empty seed pod after the long nights without sleep and the stuffy, endless trip back to Manila. He didn't think he could worm his way out of Vadim's grip, and even if he could have, he probably wouldn't have done so. This had to be done. He had nowhere to run to.

"What are you talking about?"

"My cell phone? Give it to me."

Vadim was going through Vincent's pockets with his free hand, but that was not where he kept it. The phone was buried in the bottom of Vincent's backpack, and for a short moment he considered denying everything and saying that he hadn't found it. That he had no idea what Vadim was talking about. But he gave up. He could lie to most people, but for some reason not to Vadim. Vadim had always been able to look straight through him. Since the first time they met. That had been a part of the attraction.

Vincent grunted and tried to ease the pressure on his neck with both hands. They were both sweating profusely. Vadim breathed through bared teeth. Vincent pointed down at the backpack and Vadim finally loosened his hold so Vincent could bend down and rummage through the contents. Sweaty laundry from the trip to Angeles. Sour underpants and a bag of dried bananas. Vadim's flat Samsung had slipped down to the bottom and had run out of power.

Vadim took it out of his hand and sent him a murderous look.

"Abiog called," he said. "Some guy had used my cell to call to call and ask questions about Victor. I assume it was you?"

Vincent remained standing against the wall. He was having a hard time getting his breathing under control after Vadim's attack.

"It's just that there were a couple of things I wanted to know," he said. "If they had discovered anything, and so on."

"And had they, Vincent? Or are you in the process of solving it all by yourself?"

He gathered his courage. Collected whatever remnants he had hidden somewhere in the hollow place in his chest. He wished he was Diana; he wished he was Victor, or Bea, or even little, intractable Mimi at home in San Marcelino. Why was it that only he, Vincent, had been created so damnably lacking and without a core? He was nothing but a thin and cracking hollow shell.

"Does Martinez still work at your construction sites?"

"Who?" Vadim narrowed his eyes. Retreated half a step.

There was no chance in hell that Vadim could have forgotten the watchman and the job he had sent him to do together with Vincent. He was lying.

"Martinez has a car like the one that was seen out in the road the night Victor was shot. A red Mazda."

"And?" Vadim looked almost relieved. "Is that all? Do you know how many red Mazdas there are in the world? Vincent, my man, regardless of what you think, you're seeing ghosts. Victor was shot by a couple of crackheads. It was just as random as being hit by a bus. Leave it alone. For your own sake. You're killing yourself with this shit."

Vincent could feel that he had begun to shake. It came from inside, just like the time he had thrown up in the operating room, or the time he had been told to squat, naked and with his legs apart, in front of the man who circumcised the boys in their neighborhood. He had been allowed to hold an ice cube against his foreskin until the man waved his hand away with an impatient gesture, grabbed hold of Vincent's member and probingly inserted a rounded bamboo stick between the foreskin and the head of the penis. He had pulled the foreskin down a bit, conferring with himself under his breath, while he drew a imaginary line across the skin with one finger, determining where the cut should be. Vincent was then allowed to press the ice cube over the stretched foreskin once more.

Up until that point nothing had hurt.

Then the man brought his scalpel down in a long cut. The pain was harsh and burning and went on and on while the man carefully cut and scraped his way through all the layers of skin.

He had been afraid to die then.

And he was afraid to die now. He was so terribly afraid of death. He felt as if he was standing on the edge, teetering on the borderline between two worlds. In one world, everything was familiar. Vadim was his friend and Victor's friend and would never harm either of them. In the other . . . on the other side of that line, nothing held true. No rules were unbreakable, no crime unthinkable.

"What's wrong with you?" Vadim's gaze was observant, and still sharp. "You trust me, don't you? Haven't I taken good care of you in all the time we've known each other? Stay with me, Vincent. Together, there's nothing the two of us can't do."

Vincent tried to smile, but his jaw felt wooden. A bit of saliva trickled out of the corner of his mouth, and he couldn't even wipe it away. "I want to go back to San Marcelino," he said. "I think I'll leave tomorrow."

Vadim nodded, smiling faintly.

"Of course you have to go back to San Marcelino," he said calmly. "That's where your family is. I'll help you. Really, I will.

I'll help you, but there's just one thing that you need to do for me first. A trip to Denmark. Business. Can I count on you?"

"ARE YOU SURE that's how you want to do it?" asked Martinez with interest. "Why not use that?" He indicated the Taser with the slice of pizza he was devouring.

"You can't kill people with that," said Vincent automatically, and cursed inwardly for even allowing himself to be dragged into the discussion.

They were still parked at the rest stop. The Land Cruiser was only a few meters away, with the nurse and her husband securely tied to the interior. Vincent had insisted they talk outside of their hearing. He knew that it was unlikely that the two Danes spoke Tagalog, but it still seemed macabre to sit and plan . . . plan what was going to happen, while the victims were listening. Such considerations did not bother Martinez, who had complained about having to eat his food in the cold car instead of the warm one. If it had been up to him, they probably would have stopped at McDonald's on the way, captives in tow. Vincent could never quite tell if Martinez was incredibly cold-blooded or just stupid, but in the end he had let himself be persuaded to make do with half a Hawaiian pizza reheated in the toaster oven of the camper.

Martinez continued to look at the Taser with unfulfilled gadget lust.

"Are you sure?" he asked. "If you do it for long enough? Zing, zing, zing, zing . . . maybe five or six minutes. We could try." He stuffed the rest of the slice into his mouth and offered another one to Vincent. "Do you want some?"

"No, thanks," said Vincent. The smell of melted cheese was making him feel sick. Martinez made him feel sick. He wanted to go home. Not to Manila but to San Marcelino. To Bea and the children—Carlito and the little new one on the way. Vadim had promised, promised that he would be allowed, that this "favor" was the last.

"Simon says," he had said, with a mixture of pity and loneliness in his eyes. "Simon says go home. You're lucky, my man. You know where 'home' is. Off you go, to the papaya fields and Momma's little brown hens."

"What about you?" Vincent couldn't help asking, in spite of everything, in spite of the suspicions that ripped and tore at him, in spite of what Vadim had asked him to do.

Vadim stretched lazily.

"I'll manage. Diana needs someone now. Someone who'll be there for her. My father has spoken to her father. It'll work out. If you don't fuck up, that is. Okay? Promise me that."

"I just don't understand . . ."

"It's the same as with the engineer, okay? The woman is blackmailing me. Making a lot of accusations that aren't true. She's European. Red Cross and all of that. The newspapers will believe her, and I can't risk . . ." For a moment the panic shone so brightly and clearly in Vadim's eyes that Vincent felt an absurd desire to pat his hand and say that everything was going to be all right.

"Are you sure—" he began. Because he was far from certain that Robles had been the asshole that Vadim had claimed he was. What if the same was true of the nurse?

"You're goddamn right I'm sure!" hissed Vadim. "You don't think I'd send you halfway around the world if I wasn't sure?

She's a bluebottle, Vince. One of those flies that lay their eggs in dead animals and spread decay everywhere. Fat, yellow maggots pouring out . . ." His hands made odd cramped gestures in the air, as if both flies and maggots were fully visible to him. "You won't fail me, right? Not now."

"Are you on something?" asked Vincent carefully. Vadim's expensive aftershave was not entirely capable of overpowering the smell of day-old alcohol, but this seemed like more than an ordinary hangover.

Vadim just shook his head.

"Listen, Vincent, my man. I keep your secrets, right? Sweet little Bea doesn't know anything. Your father and mother don't know anything. You'll get a job working for me as a 'health consultant'; all you have to do is rubber-stamp the certificates in front of you so that the health insurance company coughs up the money. You can do that at home in the chicken run if that's really what you want. We'll find you an office. A secretary. A white coat, damn it. Just as long as you promise to come to Manila once in a while to keep the mold from growing on you. I'll keep your secrets—if you help me keep mine. You and me. We'd do anything for each other, right?"

His gaze was desperate, begging. And it was the desperation that made Vincent understand that this wasn't just about a nurse who could tell destructive lies—or truths.

The call to Abiog, the suspicion he had let Vadim catch a glimpse of . . . it had made the abyss open beneath both of them. It was as if they were standing on a glass floor that could splinter at any moment. Vincent could *see* into the abyss. He remembered the argument between Victor and Vadim. Vadim's last desperate cry: "You're my *friend*, damn it!" Victor hadn't answered. He had walked out, and now he was dead. Vincent tried to imagine that it was God's will, that there was a murky but fated connection between the broken bond of friendship and the broken lifeline. It would be easier and less painful than his tortured suspicions. But he knew that if he turned his back on Vadim now, if he didn't pass this new, impossible test . . . the floor would surely shatter, and they would both plunge into damnation.

For Vadim there was only one thing that could outweigh this latest betrayal. Vincent had to take a life—he had to do precisely what he had suspected Vadim of doing. And Vadim wanted proof. Every step of the way had to be documented, photographed, and reported. Vincent knew very well that Martinez wasn't just there as "backup" this time.

He had agreed. Of course he had. Not because he seriously believed in the white coat and his triumphant return to San Marcelino, even though he regularly fantasized about it. It was more because he didn't know how to do anything else when it was Vadim asking and because the consequences of a no were unimaginable.

And so, here they were, he and Martinez, in a freezing cold Danish lay-by, with two captives in the van beside them, discussing how to dispose of one of them. How could something be so absurd and so inevitable at the same time?

"You could run her over with the car," said Martinez, licking cheesy grease stains from his fingers. "That one is heavy . . ." he pointed at the Land Cruiser. "If you aimed for her head, you would probably only need to do it once."

Vincent's disgust took a huge leap up the nausea scale.

"I don't want to talk about it," he said. "I've made up my mind, and we'll do it my way."

"Okay, boss." Martinez grinned and pried the last stray bits of burned pineapple out of the pizza box. "Let's get started, then."

"No. First you have to get rid of the cell phone. The policeman's. They can be traced."

"Does it really matter? In ten to twelve hours we'll be miles up in the air, being served cool drinks by couple of sexy air hostesses."

"Yes, it really matters." Vincent tried to speak calmly and carefully, like a patient teacher to a reluctant student. He had gradually discovered that this worked best. "Listen, it doesn't have to take long. Find one of those diners where the long-range truck drivers pull in—didn't we pass one the day before yesterday? Plant it in someone's pocket or toss it through a side window if you can find one that's open. Or stick it under a tarp; it doesn't matter, as long as that phone ends up someplace very far from where we are now."

Martinez bowed his head and the grin disappeared.

"Will you do it while I'm gone?" he asked.

Vincent tried to keep his face as immobile as possible. To not show his disgust.

"No," he promised because that was what Martinez wanted to hear. "I'll wait until you come back. I'll just drive the camper down to the lake. Here, take the big flashlight, then you'll be able to see the tracks easily." Officially, Vincent was in charge, but he was keenly aware that this state of affairs would only last until he asked Martinez to do something Martinez didn't feel like doing.

"What about the man?"

"Him . . . we'll just dump him somewhere. She's the only one that matters."

Martinez's round moon face took on a calculating, sneaky expression.

"You could also just cut her throat," he said. "Like they do with chickens and pigs, though we don't have to hang her up by her legs first so the blood can run out. We're not eating her, after all."

For a few seconds, Vincent was speechless. His brain was boiling over with pictures he didn't want to see. With pictures that almost made him faint.

Martinez observed him closely. Then he suddenly laughed and gave Vincent one of his usual small, hard punches. By now, his bony knuckles had left a collection of round bruises on Vincent's upper arms.

"Oh, that's right," he said cunningly. "I'm sorry. I forgot that you're not that keen on screams and blood and that kind of thing."

He threw the pizza box into the Triumph's modest backseat—there were two boxes back there already—and hopped out of the car.

"I'll give you a hand with the Danish policeman," he said, "before I go."

How did a person become like Martinez? Vincent wondered. Yes, he had scratched his way out of the slum. Yes, he had probably been abused and neglected. Had taken the blows until he learned to return them and so on. But others from the same background managed to grow and retain a certain amount of conscience and empathy, neither of which seemed to affect Martinez. Vincent's disgust was like a shiny, cold pebble without cracks, without protrusions or crevices where nuances and exceptions could find a foothold. He loathed the man.

But as he got out of the car to follow Martinez to the Land Cruiser, the inescapable question popped up and for some reason took on Vadim's ironic, nonchalant voice: *Vincent, my man. Are you any better?*

BAIT. THEY HAD used him as fucking bait, a fat, stupid grub writhing on the point of the hook. And now they had Nina.

The thought ate away at Søren's insides like pure acid.

He had heard the sound of the Taser, felt her body fall across his. He thought of the searing, paralyzing pain he knew she had experienced. Of the throaty half-choked sound that had emerged from her when she fell over.

Useless, dangerous old man. Dangerous because he had thought he could still be useful. Dangerous because he had thought he could protect her.

Why hadn't he just noted down the number on the Land Cruiser's license plate and left the rest to the local police? To young, intelligent Caroline Westmann and her young and intelligent colleagues? But no. He'd just had to be clever. Had to expose himself like a rank amateur, making it even worse by claiming that he was Nina's husband.

He had wanted to make himself valuable so the parka-man wouldn't just kill him. He had wanted to play the game . . . like the idiot he was. Blind to his own weaknesses. Blind *and* mute, with duct tape across his eyes and mouth. Helplessly bound, with feet trussed together. A fat, stupid grub on a hook. And he had thought *they* were the amateurs here.

Hard hands hauled him out of the camper and dragged him through some form of shrubbery. His heels bumped across the earth, and one shoe was wrenched off. Then he was thrown in the bushes. He heard the two men speak quietly to each other. It sounded as if they disagreed, but it wasn't exactly a fight. A car door slammed, and the Land Cruiser's deep bass engine revved up and accelerated.

Steps approached again. He heard the *riiiiits* of duct tape being torn from the roll. The undergrowth rustled, and he sensed someone kneeling next to him.

"Goodbye, Danish police," said the little stocky Filipino with the soundless laughter, and stretched a strip of tape across Søren's nose.

After the panicked struggle of the first few seconds and several brief blackouts, he realized that he was actually *getting* a tiny bit of air. Not much, but enough to survive if he didn't throw himself wildly around, driving up his body's need for oxygen. The duct tape did not seal off his airways completely.

Calm. Lie still. Don't fight. Lie still and think, *goddamn it.*

Was he alone? No, he could hear something rustle—a foot stirring some dead leaves. The Filipino was still there.

If he discovered that the tape didn't fit tightly, he would make sure it did. A surge of black panic raced through Søren, but he forced himself not to move, not to struggle. He became conscious of the fact that there was a low snuffling every time he took a breath. That had to be stopped. He had to repress his breathing so much that it became invisible and inaudible.

His body screamed for air, but he could not allow it to have its way.

He lay still. Got his abdomen under control. Allowed himself only the thinnest thread of oxygen, the faintest possible connection to life.

A foot nudged him. He came close to releasing a hissing inhalation, but controlled himself. Yet another nudge. Another pause. And finally the sound he had been waiting for: steps on the forest floor, steps becoming fainter as the Filipino moved away.

He gave himself a little more air, but not the large heaving gulps his oxygen-starved organism demanded. Not until a car door slammed—several hundred meters away, it sounded like—and he heard the little Triumph's waspy scream rev up and roar away.

His nose had always been unusually prominent and beaklike. Had it been smaller, he would probably already be dead. As it was, he would survive for a bit longer. The question was whether that was cause for celebration. If he didn't die from oxygen deprivation, there were so many other exciting possibilities. Cold and thirst, for example. Or animals. Birds of prey would gouge at a body if it lay still for long enough. Even if it wasn't dead yet. Foxes? Yes, he decided, also foxes. He wished that he hadn't started thinking about animals.

Stop it, damn it, he cursed himself. *Drop the drama. You can still move. You're breathing. And they have Nina. You're not* allowed *to die.*

He turned his head into his shoulder and rubbed his nose against his windbreaker in the hope of loosening the duct tape strips. It didn't have much effect except to make him dizzy again.

His hands. His hands had to be his first priority.

His wrists were thoroughly taped together behind his back, and purposeless tugging wouldn't improve matters. But if he could loosen the tape enough to get his hands in front . . .

He tried to visualize it. Saw the bound arms as a kind of ring he had to attempt to thread himself through. First force them down round his hips and butt . . . and then what? What about his legs? If he just ended up with his hands behind his knees he hadn't accomplished anything but getting himself so scrunched up that it would be even harder to breathe. Maybe if he had been a super flexible, long-limbed and skinny teenager—but he wasn't.

Did he have anything that might cut the tape?

In his mind he went over the contents of the windbreaker—it was best not to move until he had a plan. Unfortunately, there wasn't a practical little pocket knife. But his car keys. He still had his car keys . . . with their jagged metal edge, almost like a little saw.

He pulled his knees up to his chest, rolled over and got to his knees. The effort made him start to black out and for some minutes he just sat there trying to keep the dark at a distance. Then he began work the windbreaker around so he could reach one of the pockets. He tugged at the zipper with thick, numb fingers and managed to get one hand on the keys.

Again a pause, just to stabilize the oxygen levels in his blood. Then he turned one key around in his hand, so that he could insert the tip in between his wrists.

He could wriggle his hands only a fraction—so little that he might have despaired, had despair been an option. But all that counted right now was to get the key to rub against the tape, a tiny grating, *hrrr-hrrr, hrrr-hrrr,* five millimeters one way, five millimeters the other.

Did it do any good at all? Did it have any effect?

It didn't really matter. He had no better plan.

Hrrr-hrrr. Hrrr-hrrr. Five millimeters one way . . .

And then perhaps a little more. A flickering sensation of hope invaded his chest and abdomen. Yes, there *was* more give. He *had* shredded the tape enough that more movement, a more regular sawing had become possible. He increased his tempo—and then decreased it in order to avoid a threatening blackout. Fuck. He hated the expression "to make haste slowly," but it was the only thing that would work.

Perhaps half an hour had passed. Perhaps an hour. He didn't know. At regular intervals he tried to tear the rest of the tape. It was during one of these impatient, oxygen-intensive attempts that he dropped the keys.

He remained sitting for several long powerless moments. His legs were without sensation because he had been on his knees for so long, his fingers thick and clumsy.

As carefully as possible, he lay down on his side on the forest floor. Groped among roots and prickly twigs for the dropped keys. He couldn't find them. Rolled over on his other side, groped some more. Still no keys.

In pure frustration, he tightened his shoulder muscles as much as he was able in yet another attempt to tear the tape in half. Fought. Tore. Jerked. Until he lost consciousness.

"YOU AREN'T VICTOR."

It might not have been the most intelligent thing she could have said. And definitely not the most important. But it was what came out of her mouth when he removed the tape that until then had prevented her from screaming.

He was *nothing* like Victor. Not even that stupid parka could hide the fact that he was small—no, perhaps not actually small, not by Filipino standards, but in comparison with Victor's height and heft . . .

"No," he said. "My name is Vincent. Victor was my friend."

He reached up his hand and turned on the lamp above the camper's miniature galley. The better to see her? The better to eat her? He didn't look like her idea of the Big Bad Wolf.

"Was?" she said.

He nodded. "He . . . he was killed."

My life is in danger—and so is yours.

"When?" she asked.

"Two months ago."

"So he wasn't the one who . . . on Facebook . . ."

"No. That . . . was me."

"Why?" she asked even though she had pretty much guessed.

To get information about her, to be able to trace her. Just as Søren had said.

He shrugged and didn't answer.

It was pitch dark outside. Big, heavy raindrops thudded one by one against the metal roof of the camper, a slow rhythm with built-in accelerando—the hesitant start of a downpour at the point where things can still go either way.

"Where is Søren?" she asked instead.

"He's okay. Someone will find him, and . . . he's okay."

She could see the doubt in him. His reassurance was more hope than certainty, and the cold spread in her chest. They had just tossed him someplace in the woods, she thought. No doubt still trussed up and blinded. Fury rose up inside her, and she welcomed it.

"What the hell are you doing?" she said. "Do you want to kill him?"

A spasm flitted across his soft young features. He shook his head.

"No. Of course not."

"And you? Were you the one who attacked me?"

Again that . . . shrinking. Like a dog being scolded.

"Sorry," he mumbled.

"What was the point of that? Were you looking for my wallet?"

"No, of course not." Now he sounded almost insulted, as if a simple robbery was far beneath his dignity.

"Why then?"

He didn't answer.

"Would you like a cup of coffee?" he asked instead.

It was . . . macabre. She sat across from the man who had been very close to splitting her skull, and he was offering her coffee.

"What do you want?" she asked.

He pressed a couple of the buttons on the absurdly large espresso machine that took up most of the kitchen's meager counter space. The pale yellow light made the shadows on his face faded and diffuse.

"I wanted to . . . ask you about something."

"And that's why you hit me in the head with an iron bar?"

"No. No, that was . . . It's complicated. You wouldn't understand anyway. But . . . there is something I have to know, and now I have the chance."

She waited. Nothing happened—he just continued to fumble with the espresso machine. A hiss of steam, the scent of coffee. You would think they were in a café.

"Milk?" he asked. "Sugar?"

"No, thank you," she said automatically, then corrected herself. "No, wait, a little milk if you have it." *If you have it?* There was something about his almost pathetic politeness that was contagious.

"Are you planning to let me go?" she asked abruptly. "Am I going to survive this?"

"Of course," he said. "I'm not . . . a murderer."

He raised his dark gaze and attempted to look into her eyes while he said it. He wanted her to believe it, but it had exactly the opposite effect. He was lying. She was sure he was lying.

You're not going to leave us, are you? Ida's pale face, the dread in the glittering gaze.

No, she promised her daughter silently. *I don't want to die. Not now, not here. No way in hell.*

He had bound one of her wrists to the armrest of the bench with a plastic strip, the man who said he wasn't a murderer, so if she wanted to get out of it, she would have to put him so thoroughly out of commission that she would have time to free herself and flee before he came to. She was about the same height as he was, but somewhat slighter. Even though he was clearly no body builder, there was still a solidity to his shoulders and his chest. The physique of someone who worked out dutifully, but not fanatically. It was best not to underestimate his strength.

She took the coffee cup that he handed her. Boiling hot. Excellent. Let her gaze slide carelessly across the interior. Kitchen drawers—knives? Glasses that could be shattered and used to cut . . . Something to hit him with? Not in immediate reach.

"What do you want to know?" she asked.

"You've been to Manila," he said. "You were there when the new apartment building on Paradise Road blew up. Eden Towers. I saw you. You were helping the . . . the wounded."

She nodded.

"That's where you met Victor."

"Yes."

"There was a man . . . an engineer. He . . . he had had his arm almost torn off."

"There were so many," she said.

"But him," Vincent insisted. "You and Victor accompanied that stretcher. But the man died. Victor later said that he was one of the first of the wounded to die."

Nina thought back. To the smells, the sounds, the stench.

She hadn't had a uniform. Not at first, not before she borrowed one when they were finally able to transport some of the wounded to the hospital. The blood from the arm had splashed across her ridiculous tourist T-shirt. I <3 Manila. She remembered that.

"It wasn't the arm," she said slowly. "That's not what killed him. He had internal bleeding and rhabdomyolysis—organ damage we typically see when people have been trapped and had a lot of tissue crushed—and suddenly the heart just stopped. There was nothing we could do."

"Did he say anything?" asked Vincent-who-wasn't-Victor. "About why? That is, why the building exploded?"

More and more details returned. The temporary emergency station under a corrugated tin roof where they had had to place the first of the wounded they had dug out—because there *wasn't* anything but those damn apartment buildings and bare fields, and no one dared stay inside the hastily evacuated towers that were still standing. Volunteers had dragged beds out of the apartments in spite of shrill protests from several owners. The driveway was completely logjammed, it had taken forever to procure sufficient supplies and personnel, and as usual, too many had died who could have been saved.

Then the ambulances had begun to arrive, but it was still too little too late. Conditions at the small hospital nearby had been almost as chaotic as those at the site.

There had been so many children. Many women, and many, many children.

"Was it someone you knew?" she asked.

"In a way. It was . . . later they said that he was the one who had planted the bomb. But that it went off too early, more or less between his hands."

"No," she said categorically. "That can't have been how it was."

"Why not?"

"If he had been that close to the explosion, he would have had completely different injuries. For one thing, his lungs and ears would have been damaged by the blast. There would have been lacerations and impact damage and embedded fragments. And so on. Also, he would most likely have been killed instantly."

"So that wasn't why his arm . . . ?"

"No. He was trapped and crushed when the building collapsed."

Vincent bit his lip—a childish gesture that made him look even younger.

"And he didn't say anything?"

The man had clung to Victor's broad, brown arm with bloody fingers. As if he knew that he was dying, but didn't want to let go.

"Gas. Gas . . ." His eyes, wide open with pain, had clung first to Victor and then to her.

"There's no gas here," she had attempted to calm him, but that had only made him more agitated, and a long choppy cascade of Tagalog had emerged from him which Victor had attempted to decipher.

"I can't tell what he's trying to say." he said to her. "Not all of it."

"Just pretend that you understand," she said quietly. "Give him as much peace as you can." Because she had noted how hands and feet had grown pale and cold, and she knew the man could not be saved, not even if they had had the world's most state-of-the-art hospital at their disposal.

She blinked a few times. The coffee cup she held was no longer burning hot. She drank it as quickly as she could so she would have an excuse for asking for another one.

"Gas?" said the Filipino. "Was that what he said? The engineer?"

"Yes."

"But . . . It was a bomb."

"I don't know anything about that," said Nina. She had, of course, heard some of the first wild rumors about Muslim terror and so on, but after three days, Morten had dragged her to the airport, and they had flown home. The international media quickly lost interest in a very local disaster in one of the world's most disaster-prone areas. After all, no Danes had been hurt . . .

"Explosives leave . . . traces," she said. "They would have found residue."

"Only if they looked," he said absently. "And you don't, if it's more convenient and lucrative not to."

Was that why? Was it because of the dead man and the collapsed apartment house in Manila that she was sitting here?

He was staring straight ahead as if he were in a place very far from the cramped camper's little bubble of light. The rain had become a steady drumming now, noisy and close.

"Could I have another coffee?" she asked and proffered her cup. He filled it without really looking at her.

She wouldn't get a better chance. His attention was miles away.

"Gas," he whispered. "Not a bomb. Oh, Vadim . . ."

She threw the hot coffee straight into his face. He screamed with pain and startlement and leaped from his seat. She grabbed hold of the parka with her free hand and pulled him forward, and headbutted him as hard as she could, the first time in her life she had ever butted anybody. Her forehead rammed into his nose cartilage, and she heard it crunch. Her own abused skull protested, but he came off the worse. To be safe she thumped his head into the table several times before she pushed him onto the floor and planted a foot on his neck.

The kitchen drawer? Could she reach it?

Yes. But there were no knives, just a lot of rubber bands and a corkscrew. Damn it. Could you cut through cable strips with a corkscrew? Unlikely. She grabbed a wineglass, smashed it against the table and sawed frantically at the strip with the sharp, jagged edge. There was no way to avoid cutting her wrist as well. The blood welled up and made it harder to see what she was doing. The Filipino was moaning and stirring.

"Lie still," she hissed. "Or I'll kill you." She had seldom been more sincere.

The camper's back door opened. There stood the other Filipino, the little compact one with the odd grin. His eyebrows shot into the air while he decoded what he was seeing. Then he began to laugh silently and still in some way uproariously.

"Naughty girl," he said and hit her with a flat right hand before she realized she could use the wine glass as a weapon. He twisted it out of her numb fingers and slapped her five or six times in a row. Something popped in one ear, and she was pretty sure it was her eardrum. "Now let's play nicely. Leave my friend alone."

He pulled his still-moaning partner out of the camper. Blood gushed steadily down the man's lower face, and he looked as if he was about to faint. His partner observed him for a few seconds.

"Can I shoot her now?" he asked. "With the Taser? I'm sure it works if you do it for long enough."

"No!" The answer was half choked and bubbling, but definitive. "I'll do it. In just . . . a minute." He looked up at her. "It won't hurt," he promised hoarsely. "It's the best way . . . the most painless . . . I'm really sorry, but . . ."

The rain was pouring down on him, making his black hair stick to his skull. He snuffled wetly with each breath, and his eyes looked glassy and panicked, like those of a hunted animal just before it gives up.

She didn't feel sorry for him. Not even the tiniest little bit.

He shut the back door on her, and came round to the front to pull out something that had been lying under the driver's seat: it looked like a plastic hose much like the ones used for washing machine drains, only longer. Certain premonitions made her spine creep, and they were confirmed when he started the Land Cruiser's engine, rolled down the driver's side window a little, stuck one end of the hose through the gap, and attached it with duct tape. More tape sealed the window shut. She could hear him moving around outside, and thought she knew what he was doing—attaching the other end of the hose to the exhaust.

A few moments later she could smell the first fumes.

SHE HAD STRUGGLED. You could see it from the way she was lying. She had kicked off one shoe and had tried to reach the button that controlled the windows with her foot. It had worked to some degree—she had actually managed to roll down one side window a fraction. The cost was also obvious; the cable strip had cut so deeply into her wrist that you couldn't see anything but blood.

Vincent had to turn away.

"Cut her free," he said to Martinez. "And wrap something around that wrist."

"Why?" asked Martinez

"Because we don't want her blood on us, idiot. What if we're stopped?"

The plan was that they would fly out of Frankfurt—Vadim had arranged for business-class tickets so they could just show up whenever it suited them and board the next flight. But they were still a long way from Frankfurt. And even further from San Marcelino.

He felt strangely empty inside. It had been done now. What he had promised Vadim. He hadn't believed he could do it. He had killed another human being. The rest . . . the rest was just tidying up.

"Take a picture," he said to Martinez and handed him the little compact digital camera. He couldn't make himself do it, but he knew Vadim would expect it.

Martinez expressionlessly snapped a couple of pictures of the dead nurse. Then he suddenly turned the camera on Vincent.

"Say cheese," he laughed.

Click. Vincent held one hand up in front of his face in pure reflex, which only made the grin broader.

"What about the policeman?" he asked.

"Don't worry about him," said Martinez with another glittering grin. "I took care of him." He stuck the camera in his pocket and instead pulled out a roll of duct tape and waved it in the air.

Vincent stared at the tape. And at the naked hand holding it.

"What did you do?" he asked.

Martinez mimed pulling off a strip of tape.

"You blocked his nose?"

"Yup."

"So he's dead?"

"Of course he's dead. Were you planning to let him live? He had seen your stupid mug, and he was a policeman."

"Former."

"That comes to the same fucking thing."

"And then you just let him lie there—with his entire head covered in tape?"

"He's lying in a thicket right in the middle of the forest. It might take days before they find him."

"Maybe. But when they do—they'll also find your fingerprints plastered all over that piece of tape. Unless you used gloves?"

He could see on Martinez's round face that that wasn't the case.

"Fuck . . ." said the moron.

"Go back," said Vincent. "No, wait. Help me get her down to the boat first. And then go back and remove that tape."

HE HAD PARKED the Land Cruiser as close to the lake shore as possible, but there was a slope that you had to navigate on foot. They had already carried the rubber dinghy down. It had been helpful to have something to do, instead of just standing outside the car, waiting for the carbon monoxide to take effect. It might be painless, as Diana had once said, but maybe that was only if it happened while you slept. The struggles of the nurse had made the entire van rock, and he felt like it was taking forever. He had decided to wait fifteen minutes after it grew quiet in there, but ended up turning off the engine after ten. He just wanted to have it over with.

He made Martinez take her arms while he grabbed hold of her feet. He didn't feel like touching the blood-spattered kitchen towel Martinez had wound around her wrist. The light from his headlamp flickered over bushes and tree trunks and Martinez's green raincoat. Then one foot slipped in the mud, and he lost his balance. He had to let go and cling to a tree in order not to fall over completely.

Martinez dropped his end too, pushed the body with his foot and let it roll the rest of the way.

"Martinez, damn it . . ."

Martinez looked up—a bit crookedly in order not to be blinded by the light from Vincent's head lamp.

"She's already dead," he said. "What's the difference?"

Vincent was seized by an abrupt rage.

"Go," he hissed. "Now. What kind of person are you? Do you have no respect at all for the dead?"

Martinez looked at him with an uncertain frown, as if he was really and truly trying to understand what Vincent meant.

"But they're dead," he said at last, as if that was sufficient explanation.

Vincent clenched his fists so tightly that his nails cut into his palms.

"Go," he hissed between clenched teeth.

"Okay, boss," said Martinez, for once without laughing as if it was all a big joke. He began to climb up the slope. Halfway up Vincent saw him tuck a set of earbuds into his ears, and the tinny pop beat from a Kitty Girls song could be heard for a few moments until he reached the top and the rain and the trees swallowed the sound.

But with Martinez gone there was no longer anyone he could off-load the shame and guilt on. He suddenly thought of that damn fluffy little chicken they had placed by Victor's coffin, of its constant pathetic peeping, and of Vadim's face when he heard the explanation for its presence.

To wake the conscience of the murderer.

Did they do that kind of thing in Denmark? Probably not, when it wasn't even widespread among Manila's upper crust. And in any case . . . when he was done, there wouldn't be anybody to bury.

Damn. They should have done the same thing with the policeman. It was the only thing that made sense. Why hadn't he understood that at once?

Because he had pretended that the policeman wasn't going

to be killed. Because he had turned his back and let things run their course. Left the decision to Martinez. So it wasn't on him, but it was anyway. He thought about how once he had not even been able to confess his nightly erections to Father Abuel. Such a distant and innocent time with problems so tiny and banal that he couldn't really understand why they had seemed significant. *Forgive me, Father, for I have sinned. I have killed another human being* . . . No, Father Abuel was never going to hear about that either.

He slithered down the last few feet of the slope and bent over the body. It didn't look as if it had taken any damage from the rough treatment, but the kitchen towel had come loose, and the wrist was bleeding again.

He closed his eyes for a second. *Stop it*, he said to himself. *You can usually manage as long as you're dealing with dead people.*

But dead people don't bleed. At least not as much as the nurse did.

He opened his eyes again. Placed two fingers against her neck and tried to control his own spasmodic shaking long enough to feel it properly.

It was there. The pulse. A faint flutter, from a heart that still beat.

"Our Father, who art in heaven . . ." The words came tumbling out of him without conscious volition. He had the sense that he was already in purgatory. That he had died without noticing, and was now being forced to live through his crime again and again. *How many times do I need to kill her before it's enough?* he asked silently. Should he drag her all the way up the slope and put her back in the car for a while?

No. It made no difference. She was going into the lake anyway, and whether her last heartbeats faded in the car or down there in the dark, cold water made no real difference—except for the fact that he could no longer consider her a corpse.

He took off his parka and swaddled her in it so he couldn't see her face and her bloody wrist. The rain fell heavily on his exposed shoulders, but it wasn't like the tropical rain at home, warm and yellowish—"as if the gods are pissing on us," as his late great-grandmother Evangelina used to say with a cackling laugh. She had become slightly senile in her old age, which had loosened a few inhibitions.

This Danish rain was hard and cold and grey and smelled of forest. He took the parka bundle into his arms and carried it down to the water's edge where they had left the dinghy.

The largest of the camper's gas containers, an orange ten-kilo bottle, was already waiting, with a rope tied to the handle. He assumed it would be sufficient to drag her down to the bottom and hold her there. He had also considered using the even heavier water tank, but then he had realized that a plastic container full of water had pretty much the same buoyancy as the water that surrounds it. He placed her in the prow next to the gas bottle and began to drag the boat clear of the lakeshore. He had to splash a few steps into the lake himself. Holy Mother of God, it was cold, that water. He quickly leaned across the soft rubber gunnel and climbed on board.

The raindrops ricocheted off the surface of the lake—even more violently when a few strokes of the oars brought him out of what shelter the trees had provided. The thin pale beam from the head lamp strapped to his forehead did not light up the lake and the landscape, only the steady, grey rain, like steel hawsers chaining the sky to the earth. Vincent's T-shirt and fleece were soaked within minutes, and he looked over his shoulder. The woods and the lakeshore had already disappeared from view. Fuck. Would he be able to find his way back at all?

How far out did he dare to row? How far was enough? He had seen a sign the first day he camped here, courtesy of the local tourism office. The lake was Denmark's third deepest, it said. Thirty-one meters. That was what had given him the idea. Thirty-one meters should be sufficient . . . but how far did you need to go before it got that deep?

He hesitated. Pulled the black-and-yellow plastic oars out of the water and drifted with the current. Luckily it wasn't windy. The rain fell straight down in spattering cascades.

Here, he thought. That should do it. Here, while he still had some sense of where the shore was. He pulled the oars all the way in and carefully crept over to the parka bundle, very focused on distributing his weight so the boat wouldn't rock too much. He did *not* feel like capsizing now . . . he grabbed the rope and considered how to attach it. The feet? Or neck? In a glimpse he pictured how she would hang there in the lake water, like a big, macabre water plant attached to a rock. It was probably best to use her foot. The other somehow seemed to him to lack dignity, and then he'd have to see her face again.

He grabbed one naked ankle to tie the rope around it.

She moved. He was so unprepared that her bare feet slipped between his hands like a fish he hadn't managed to rap hard enough on the head. While he still sat there, paralyzed by shock, she rolled over abruptly and the boat began to tip. He grabbed at her with his free hand and got a hold of a handful of T-shirt. He wanted to pull her back in, toward the boat's center of gravity, but it was already too late. The gas bottle slid toward the railing; the boat's bottom rose up like a wall and threw them all overboard, Vincent, the nurse, and the gas bottle as well. He had time to suck in one single desperate gasp of air before the water closed over his head.

He tried to scissor kick, but something was in his way. In the flickering distorted beam of the head lamp he saw what was wrong—the rope had become tangled around one of his legs, and the weight from the gas bottle was pulling him down.

He tried to half-somersault in the water in order to loosen the rope. At that moment he felt a tug on his shoulder. A pair of pink legs hooked themselves determinedly around his waist, and an arm closed around his neck. He forced his head round and saw the face of the nurse so close to his own that he could barely focus on it. Only in a dim blur could he make out her expression—awake, alive, and insane—and yet a terror-fueled conviction took root in his soul.

She had come to pull him down to Hell.

WHEN SØREN REGAINED consciousness, he was lying on his stomach on the forest floor with his arms stretched out in front of him. It took a little while before he registered how wonderful it was—*with his arms stretched out*. His hands were free.

It was raining. The shower-proof windbreaker stuck wetly to his back, and the raindrops ran down one cheek and from time to time oozed past the tape so that it bubbled when he breathed.

He rolled onto his side and scraped at the edge of the tape with weak fingers until he could get hold of a corner and pull. First the nose, then the eyes, then the mouth. He sat for a few seconds and breathed freely without sensing much more than that. To breathe in and breathe out, unhindered.

Then he remembered the rest.

Nina. They still had Nina.

He tore wildly and without coordination at the tape that tied his ankles together. When it didn't immediately produce a result, he had to force himself to stop and fumble for the end of the strip. He couldn't see very much, it was dark as all hell, but his fingertips finally found the slight edge they were searching for. He scratched and scraped and loosened another corner.

Finally free, he bundled the tape together and threw it away, completely indifferent to the fact that it might be what the DA would call "an important link in the chain of evidence." He got up, not without difficulty, but in spite of everything he could still move. He felt dizzy and disoriented and had absolutely no sense of where he was, and in what direction the Land Cruiser had disappeared with Nina.

Think. What did he know? What facts did he possess?

They had hauled him out of the camper, carried him at the most ten or fifteen meters, he thought, before they had dumped him in the bushes. Therefore, the Land Cruiser had at some point been ten to fifteen meters from him before it drove off. The ground was wet and greasy and covered by fallen leaves. The Land Cruiser was heavy. It had no doubt left visible tracks, but that was no help whatsoever when he couldn't see. Was there a small chance that the ruts were so deep that he would be able to spot them by feel alone?

He had lost one shoe, and that foot was more or less senseless with cold. Still he bent down and took the shoe off the other foot as well. Brambles clung to his pant legs with stubborn thorns, and he felt the rain sting in several scratches.

Though the Land Cruiser was an off-road vehicle of sorts, it didn't have Caterpillar tracks. It couldn't force its way through shrubbery or across fallen tree trunks. There was no need to go in the direction where the undergrowth was thickest. He turned around and began walking with steps that he hoped were short enough not to miss the rut of a tire track. Then he realized he would have to consider the matter more carefully. He paused. If he met the tracks at right angles, all he would be presented with was a rut the width of the Land Cruiser's tire. Say about thirty centimeters. If his strides were any longer, he could easily step across it without noticing. Thirty centimeters. A foot's length. One foot in front of the other, literally. And if he walked more than fifteen meters without finding anything, then he would have to go back to his starting point. If he could find it . . . Fifteen meters. That was fifty foot-lengths, he calculated. Oh, damn it. It would take him all night. And while he fumbled around here, one foot in front of the other, they had Nina, and . . . and he didn't know what they would do with her. Didn't know *why* they had taken her.

I wanted her to think of heaven. People think too little about that kind of thing while they are still alive.

A deep sound of pain forced its way out of him, halfway between a roar and a snarl. Completely animal-like. Someone had taken *his* woman. Every caveman instinct he possessed yelled at him to hurry, telling him that he should run through the forest, find them, smash them, kill them . . .

If he had known which direction to run in, he would probably have done so, or at least tried.

"Thirty-three, thirty-four, thirty-five . . ."

He reached fifty without having encountered anything that resembled a tire track. Wet leaves clung to his feet, both so cold now that it felt as if they were burning. The best that could be said about the experiment was that he actually succeeded in turning around and finding his way back to his bramble. At least to *a* bramble patch, but he was fairly sure it was his.

Okay. New direction. He turned at what he thought had to be a forty-five degree angle and began again.

"One, two, three, four . . ."

At twenty-seven, he hammered his shin into a fallen tree and fell sprawling on the sodden ground. Momentarily, the pain in his leg overpowered his other miseries, and he remained sitting for a few minutes to massage it. Not a break, thank God, but he could feel a swelling take form under his moving fingers. He fumbled along the forest floor until he found a thick branch he could use as a kind of blind man's cane. He couldn't afford to fall again.

The rain had increased. It pounded the leaves and the forest floor and spattered his ankles with tiny mud blasts for every fallen drop. He was about as wet as a man could get, and the cold was slowly eating its way inward, to the organs that kept him active and alive. Realistically he probably had a couple of hours left, maybe less, before movement became impossible.

When he saw the flickering glow from the flashlight, he thought for a brief moment that he was so weak that he was already beginning to hallucinate. But it was real enough. The light skipped and danced and lit up the falling rain, and now he could hear the crackling, cricket-like sound of music escaping from a set of earphones.

It was the stocky Filipino. *Goodbye, Danish police.* He was headed more or less for the bramble patch, and in a little while he would discover that Søren was no longer there.

Søren ran. Not away from the Filipino but toward him. There was no reason to try to move silently; with that bass line in his ears, the other man would have been unlikely to discover him even if he had been accompanied by a full-sized brass band.

He swung the branch against the exposed nape of the Filipino's neck in a single desperate release of all his restrained caveman impulses. The round head bounced back and then forward with such rag-doll suddenness that for a moment Søren thought he had broken the man's neck. He fell heavily to the ground, and it was clear that the follow-up strike would not be necessary. Søren used it anyway.

It would have been better if he could have rendered the man harmless without taking his head halfway off, he knew that. He hadn't dared. Hadn't trusted his body or his strength sufficiently.

Luckily, the man was fairly robust. He was coming to even as Søren was tying his wrists together with the string from the otherwise pretty useless windbreaker.

Søren grabbed him by the neck and deliberately forced his thumb into the pain center behind the ear.

"Listen," he hissed in English. "You have one chance to survive. Tell me where my wife is. Now."

The man's eyes rolled in panic. His face was distorted by pain, and tears ran down the round cheeks.

"That way," he said desperately jerking his head in the direction he had come from. "Down by the lake. Please, sir. Please don't kill me."

Søren pushed him to the ground again and pulled his limbs into a leg lock that the Danish police were no longer permitted to use. Right now he couldn't care less.

"I have no idea what time it is," he said, with his mouth next to the man's ear. "But you're under arrest."

Then he grabbed the flashlight and ran.

HE FOUND THE Land Cruiser fairly quickly. The back door was wide open, and various inventory had been removed from the galley—the hose for the gas hob dangled, and the water tank had been dumped behind the car—but there was no sign of Nina and the other Filipino.

He stood for a few seconds, staring at the hose that had been led from the exhaust pipe to the window of the camper. Bastards. Evil murdering bastards. His heart gave a cramped jerk inside his chest, and he hammered one hand against the window in frustration and fear. Where was she? Had they gassed her? Was a corpse all he would find now?

Down by the lake, the little one had said. And the rubber dinghy from the Land Cruiser's roof was gone.

Søren let the flashlight's beam sweep across the tree trunks. The lake. He couldn't see it, but he could see a slope with a set of tracks left by someone who had climbed it. He slid down essentially feet first, and sure enough, there it was—the lake. A grey, rain-pocked surface that stretched as far as visibility allowed.

No boat. No Nina. No Filipino.

"Niiiiinaaaa!" he roared as loudly as he could. "Niiiiiiiii-naaaaaaa . . ."

There was no answer.

"YOU HAVE TO wake up now, Nina-girl. There's something I want to show you . . ."

Her head was so heavy that she had to hold on to it with both hands in order to sit up.

She couldn't sit up.

There was a flickering behind her thick, closed eyelids. She knew he was there, but she couldn't see him. Could only hear his voice.

He was lying in the bathtub, and the water was red.

No.

She didn't want to. Didn't want to see that again.

"Nina-girl. Come on."

She felt his hand on her ankle. He took hold of her foot. Why was he holding her foot? If you want someone to follow you, you take them by the hand. She pulled her leg away, and her foot slipped out of his grasp.

He was lying in the bathtub, and the water was red. The blood was flowing from both wrists, and his eyes, still alive, clung to her face.

"Nina . . ."

No. Her entire body jerked. She didn't want to, didn't want to . . . The world rocked wildly from side to side, and she kicked out, waved her arms.

Water. Cold water.

The shock raced through her, but the cold was better, sharper than lukewarm, bloodred bathwater. More real. She opened her eyes. There was a light, a light in the water. She grabbed at it and got hold of something. Fabric. Clothes. Clothes on a person.

The camper. The carbon monoxide. They had tried to gas her. *He* had tried to gas her. Vincent.

She hooked her arm around his neck. Lashed her legs around his body. Clung to him while they sank. Bubbles from the parka hood rose up around them, glittering in the light from his head lamp.

She felt no desire to breathe. It was as if her lungs were paralyzed. She could let herself sink, fall for all eternity.

"Nina-girl. Wake up now."

She ignored him. You don't have to obey dead fathers.

The man, Vincent, twisted in her grip. He tried to bend, fumbling for something with flapping hands. In the light from the lamp she saw why they were sinking so fast. The rope around his ankle. Somewhat farther down, something heavy that was just a shadow. She pulled the headlight off him and let it shine directly on the rope.

You could loosen it, she said to herself. *Or let go of him so he could do it. We could both rise to the surface together.*

She didn't. She just held on. Right until she felt his chest spasm helplessly. She imagined how the water was streaming into his open mouth. He still fought, writhed, kicked. But not for long.

Not until he stopped did she let go.

She hung completely still in the water. A single wriggle loosened the oversized hideous pink jogging pants from her hips. Then she slowly began to rise. She did nothing. Didn't swim, didn't fight, just rose quietly and infinitely slowly toward the surface with the head lamp gripped tight in one hand.

"Nina-girl."

She saw him there in the water, with open still-alive eyes. He stretched his hand toward her, but she didn't take it.

Not now, Dad.

SØREN STOOD ON the lakeshore with an empty twenty-liter plastic bottle in his arms—the camper's water tank, which he had emptied. He had taken off his windbreaker, T-shirt and pants and considered for a few more seconds whether it was really just a form of suicide he was engaged in. Visibility was almost zero. He had tried to direct the beams of the Land Cruiser's headlights out across the lake, but the difference in height between the top of the slope and the water's surface was too great—the beams pointed into the darkness and rain someplace above his head without illuminating what he most needed to see. He didn't know how big the lake was, and to set out without even knowing in which direction it made sense to swim . . . It amounted to a form of madness. But he wasn't sure he wanted to live with the consequences of his mistakes if he didn't find her. If there was still hope, if there was even the tiniest chance that she was still alive . . .

He had tied a length of blue nylon rope around the bottle, more or less like you tie a ribbon around a package. The flashlight was lashed to the top of the bottle. He hoped it would hold. The other end of the rope he had tied around his waist, with a few meters' slack between himself and the bottle. He began to wade into the lake water. He was so wet and cold already that it actually felt warmer than the air.

As he was letting himself slide forward to start swimming, he thought he saw . . . something. He rose abruptly again, found the bottom with his feet and stretched to his full height.

There.

A tiny glint of light, a vulnerable spark that disappeared, came back, disappeared, came back, with each flat slow ripple of the lake.

"Niiiinaaaa!"

Still no answer. He might be swimming toward a murderer, he was well aware of that. It could be V. But if it was and if he was alone . . . Søren began to swim with long, solid strokes. The bottle bobbed along in his wake, and he could feel the little tug on the rope around his waist with every kick.

Ten strokes. Then head up and treading water, to be sure he still was going in the direction of the light. Ten more strokes. Ten more.

It wasn't a boat; that much he could see. It was a person. A person floating in the water, unmoving and silent.

Ten strokes. Ten strokes.

It was her.

She was floating on her back, face up. Dead people don't do that, he tried to tell himself. But if she was alive, why wasn't she swimming? Why was she just lying there?

Five strokes, six strokes . . . and then he could finally touch her.

"Nina." He barely had enough voice to get her name out. Did she react? He pulled her close, grabbed hold of her face with one hand. She looked up at him, eyes alive.

But her pupils were enormous, wide and unfocused. She didn't try to answer him, and when his fumbling fingers found her pulse, it was so slow that he thought at first he had lost it again.

"Nina . . . Nina, wake up. Help me a little."

Her lips moved, but there was no sound.

He had to face the fact that she was incapable of holding on to the plastic bottle. He managed to get one of her arms across it, but he had to tie her on, and then he had to hook himself to the rope to make sure the bottle didn't just tip under her weight.

Now he was grateful for the Land Cruiser's headlights. Their beams gave him a direction, a marker to swim toward. He forced his stiff and exhausted legs to scissor, but he didn't have the strength for the faster, more exhausting crawl.

He didn't think much. Not even about how she had survived—only about getting them both safely to shore.

THERE WERE LIGHTS around her. Lights and voices. A mask was pushed down over her face, and she tried to push it away.

"It's oxygen," she heard Søren say. "You need it."

Oxygen. That made sense. She lay still and let them do it.

The light stung her eyes, but it also reminded her that she was alive. Even the pounding, hammering headache that felt as if it was squeezing her brain out through her eye sockets, even that was better than nothing. Not to feel was to die. And she wanted to live.

She closed her eyes, raised one hand slightly and fumbled blindly. He grabbed it. His hand was cold as ice, but that was another thing it was possible to live with.

Better than nothing. *Much* better than nothing.

LATER SHE FOUND out that he had dragged her all the way to shore, up the slope and back to the Land Cruiser. He had driven her directly to the hospital because he didn't have a cell phone and it was faster than trying to get help any other way.

They had given her pressurized oxygen. She remembered it floatingly, unclearly, as if it was something that had happened to someone else. Almost twenty-four hours had passed before she stopped hallucinating. None of the ghosts were her father's, however. She wondered whether she had left him there in the cold, dark waters of the lake. She wasn't sure.

She floated in and out of sleep, dozing among flickering illusions on the border between dreams and wakefulness.

During one of the lucid moments, she found Caroline Westmann standing by her bed.

"I know you're tired," she said. "But I just need you to confirm the following: Was it Vincent Bernardo and Ubaldo Martinez who exposed you to carbon monoxide poisoning?" Westmann placed two photographs on her covers. One was an oddly smiling portrait of Vincent, the other a more neutral identification photo of the other Filipino. Her pulse gave an involuntary skip and jump at the sight.

"Is that Martinez?" she asked.

"Yes. Was he one of them?" Caroline Westmann's gaze hung on hers like a dog waiting for a treat.

"Yes," she said.

"Thank you!" The detective sergeant beamed with satisfaction. "That's about all we need for now. Get better!"

THE NEXT TIME she opened her eyes her mother was sitting there looking at her.

"Are you awake?" asked Hanne Borg. "Really awake?"

"Yes," she said. "Can't you tell?"

"You opened your eyes earlier, but I couldn't get you to answer."

Unresponsive. Not a very promising sign.

"I'm okay now," she said, even though she wasn't sure. Carbon monoxide poisoning could do ugly long-term damage, even if you survived the acute phase. Heart problems. Brain damage, other organ damage. Some issues only surfaced over time.

Oh, damn. She didn't want to be a disability case.

While she had been struggling to get the Land Cruiser's window open, to get air, to get oxygen, she had thought only of surviving. She knew now that two things had kept her alive—the thin stream of fresh oxygen-rich air that had come in through the not-quite-closed window, and the fact that modern cars were equipped with a catalytic converter that cut down on the carbon monoxide in the exhaust. When the two Filipinos had opened the door and dragged her out, she had been partly pretending to be unconscious. It was the roll and tumble down the slope and the final loose-limbed fall that had turned off the last of the lights.

It could so easily have been permanent.

"Where is Søren?" she suddenly asked. He had been there at the beginning, but . . . that was a long time ago. Several awakenings ago. That she had seen him . . .

"He's been admitted too," said her mother. "Relax . . . It's pneumonia. He's being treated. He'll be fine."

"Mom, he . . ." She couldn't figure out how to continue. Didn't know what it actually was she needed to say. Something about holding on, something about there being someone . . . that there was someone now who made sure she didn't go down. Literally. Someone who could hold her, hold on to her, someone who knew what it was like in the war zone and still wasn't . . . wasn't desperate.

"What do you want with him?" asked her mother. Not unfriendly, just as a clarifying question. "To love and obey? Cohabit? Or is he just a temporary solution? What are you thinking?"

"Mom! That's none of your business."

Hanne Borg smiled faintly.

"Do you remember what I said about being impatient? That is, when you're not quite sure how long you're going to remain on the planet?"

"Yes."

"I also like clear answers. It's faster."

"But . . . I don't know. We . . . have to figure it out ourselves."

"Okay. Thanks for the update."

"The kids. Are they still with you?" She had no idea what day it was, how much time had passed. Was it still half term?

"Yes. I can bring them with me—if you promise not to stare at them with open eyes without saying anything."

Nina considered it.

"No," she said then. "Let's wait until I'm released. It can't be much longer." She hoped.

Ida and Anton. The longing to see them, to touch them, to inhale their smell was intense and almost animal-like. A mother primate and her young. She knew that she still had two children who were afraid of losing her. It would take a long time to convince them that she wasn't going to leave them, not today and not tomorrow. That she was planning to sink her hooks into them and into life—and, yes, probably into Søren too—and hang on until she was old and decrepit and had reached what was so poetically called "the end of her days." It had to be possible, even for her, if she tried hard enough. And something *was* different.

The life she had saved—her own—had not come without a cost. Another human being had gone down. She had sent him into the deep in order to be able to rise again herself. Her will to survive had been stronger than his.

A therapist would probably enquire whether she was feeling guilty. But she'd lived with that survivor's guilt since she was twelve years old. Practically her entire life. It was what had driven her into the war zone, led her to embrace danger and disaster. Paradoxically, she was feeling calmer and lighter than usual. As if she had left something down there in the lake's icy darkness, with her hallucinations and her ghosts, and the dead man.

"I'm not doing it again."

It wasn't until she saw her mother react that she realized she had spoken out loud.

"What aren't you doing?"

She couldn't say it with one word. Not even with many. She lifted one hand in an unclear gesture.

"It." *Damn it*, she thought. *Now she'll probably think I'm losing it completely.*

But her mother understood. She could read such awkward, incomplete Nina code with no difficulty at all. Beneath the chemo-induced fatigue, a clear relief was spreading.

"Good," she said simply.

WHEN HER MOTHER had left, Nina carefully got out of bed. The sun was shining outside the window, so it was day, anyway. Some day or other. She should have asked while she'd had the chance.

The floor behaved normally this time—she remembered how it had heaved and swayed when they had helped her to the toilet the last time—and she poked her arms through the sleeves of the hospital robe on the hook by the door. Tied the belt. Considered slippers. Couldn't find any and decided not to care.

Pneumonia. That would be T Ward, probably. Good, it wasn't far then.

"SHITTY WEATHER," TORBEN growled, rubbing a towel across his smooth shaven skull. "Snow in November. What's up with that?"

"It's December tomorrow," Søren reminded him, as if he was hired to apologize on behalf of the meteorologists.

"Yes, okay. It's still too early."

It was, you had to admit, unusually awful weather. Large grey-white globs of wet snow—even with the best of intentions, no one could call them flakes—fell heavily and unremittingly on Søborg and the rest of Copenhagen. The bicyclists slithered along on the bike paths, half blinded by the slush, and el-train wires were falling by the dozen all over the regional network. The rage level of the morning traffic was almost tangible.

Torben threw the towel on top of his ubiquitous gym bag and pointed at the guest chair.

"Sit down, damn it. Do you want some coffee?" He let himself drop into his own deep, well-upholstered executive-style chair.

"No, thanks," said Søren.

"Okay."

Torben frowned, moved his pad a few inches to the left, looked at the telephone.

"Are you sure?" he said.

"Yes. I just had some."

"Good. But I need something to keep my strength up. Just a second."

Torben grabbed the phone.

"Pernille? Have you fired up the coffee works? Good. Would you mind bringing me a cup? Black, please. Nasty morning. Thank you."

Søren waited quietly and calmly. He had rarely seen Torben in this uncomfortable, bush-beating state. His friend and boss was not normally a man who avoided hard decisions or found it difficult to express his views.

"Well," said Torben. "How are you feeling? Lungs more or less back to normal?"

"More or less," said Søren.

"What was all that about, anyway? Something to do with the Philippines?"

"Yes. Some months ago there was a violent explosion in an apartment building right outside Manila. More than four hundred people were killed. Terrible story."

"Terror?"

"No. It was as simple as shoddy construction work. When the authorities finally started an independent investigation, the whole operation turned out to be rotten to the core. Safety requirements had not been followed, the materials were substandard and had been used incorrectly . . . it appears that a gas line had been leaking for a while, so that a gas pocket had developed in the foundations. The damage from the explosion was all the more devastating because of the flaws in the construction, and because the cement that had been used was of inferior quality. An entirely avoidable disaster, not a terrorist bomb, as the first official version had it. The three remaining towers have now been leveled."

"Tragic," said Torben tersely. "But how the hell could an apartment building explosion in Manila get my group leader abducted and half-killed?"

Søren smiled dryly.

"Well. That was mostly Nina's fault. And mine."

"How so?"

"Nina was there. In Manila, that is. She joined the rescue effort—they were in dire need of people with the right qualifications."

"And she just can't keep her nose out of things that don't concern her . . ."

Søren acknowledged that evaluation with a small nod.

"There was an engineer who had apparently been trying to persuade the owner and builder to fix the mistakes. He was seriously wounded during the collapse and died shortly afterward. Nina was among those who tried to save him. She and another volunteer heard his last incoherent words, and that was apparently enough to make them a threat. Vadim Lorenzo, the owner, is the son of one of Manila's movers and shakers and was obsessed with keeping his good name untarnished. Or at least, only somewhat tarnished. A bit of a playboy, they say. So he sent a couple of cowboys to eliminate her. Luckily they weren't very professional, but . . ." He had to suppress a flashback of Nina's face, Nina's eyes, as she had floated in the water with him not knowing whether she would live or die. "It was bad enough. A little too close."

"And the two . . . cowboys?"

"One drowned. Vincent Bernardo. The divers managed to find the body, and he was sent home to Manila in a coffin about a week ago. He has a wife and child, I've heard. A pregnant wife and a child, in fact."

"He should have thought of that before," said Torben mercilessly.

"Yes. I don't feel sorry for him either. Maybe for her. He wasn't your typical hired killer. The other one, Ubaldo Martinez, I was able to arrest, and we have most of our information from him. Frankly he is not all that bright. He ended up boasting of all his connections, clearly thinking he could scare us into letting him go. He is in custody in Viborg now, and there's very little doubt that we can get him for attempted murder."

Caroline Westmann was whistling as she worked, tying up the last loose ends of the case. He was happy to let her have every last bit of gratification it might afford her, and any points it might give her in the promotion lottery.

"And the young building tycoon from Manila? Can we get him?"

"Too late for that . . ."

"Meaning?"

"They found him yesterday at the bottom of his penthouse swimming pool with three diving belts around his neck. Twenty-one kilos. More than enough."

"Suicide?"

"It looks like it. There's no note, but there was no one else in the apartment, and it didn't look as if anyone had been there. Except . . ."

"What?"

"The housekeeper said she had opened the door to a young woman who had a present for Vadim Lorenzo. A young pregnant woman."

"Are you suggesting it was . . . What was his name . . ."

"Vincent Bernardo. Vincent Bernardo's wife? We can't say, and in any case, she left again right away. She was merely allowed to place her present on a table in the kitchen."

"And what was the present?" asked Torben impatiently.

"A cage. A cage with a small yellow chicken in it."

"Bizarre. It's not their Easter or anything like that, is it?"

"No. They pretty much celebrate the same holidays we do."

"I don't see the relevance."

"I don't either. But in any case, nothing suggests foul play. He might just have taken the easy way out, what with a trial and the scandal and so on hanging over his head. Not so very strange."

"Oh, I don't know," said Torben. "Rich man's son in Manila? That kind usually manages to come up smelling of roses."

"Not this time, though."

"No. Not with twenty-one kilos of lead around his neck."

Silence descended. Torben carefully placed a pen on top of his pad.

"Oh, hell," he said. "I might as well get it over with."

There was a knock on the door, and Torben's assistant Pernille came in with the coffee tray. There were two cups—she had apparently been informed that he was in a meeting. This was not an informal chat, in other words.

Søren and Torben sat looking at each other while she placed cups and coffee pot on the table. Only when she had disappeared again did they continue.

"Are you firing me?" asked Søren.

"No," said Torben. "No, damn it. You're still one of our best interrogation experts. And a damn sharp analyst and all of that. But . . ."

"But you can't use me as group leader anymore."

"I'm sorry. But for your own sake . . ."

"And for the department's. You don't need to say any more."

"Yes, I do! This isn't easy, and you deserve better. But the shrink says it would be best for you to be transferred, and that we risk driving you permanently into the ground if we don't do it. So when your sick leave is over, I'm transferring you to Analysis, and we'll just call on you now and then when we need you to lead an interrogation. As of tomorrow, you no longer have operative responsibilities."

"Thank you," said Søren and poured himself a cup of coffee after all.

"What?" Torben looked at him in total confusion.

"I know it was a difficult decision."

"Damn it, Søren. Would you please stop that?"

"Stop what?"

"Stop pretending it doesn't matter to you. We've known each other much too long for those kind of games."

Søren smiled.

"But it really doesn't matter."

"That's a damn lie."

"No." He looked directly at Torben and hoped his friend could see the calm in him, the strange new equilibrium he had found. "Honestly. It's fine. I need to get better. We both do."

"You . . . and Nina?"

"Yes. Me and Nina."

Torben stared at him as if he had gone insane.

"How did it go?"

Nina was sitting in the kitchen when he got home, wearing a big, bulky red sweater and a pair of red felt boots he had bought for her because she always complained that her feet were cold here. The house was from before the energy crisis, so the insulation wasn't first-rate. Her tolerance for cold was also not what it had been.

"As expected," he said. "I'm now an ex–group leader. Put out to pasture with the Analysis boys, with occasional guest appearances as an interrogation expert."

She got up, took his face between her slender, cold hands and kissed him. She tasted of peppermint tablets and faintly of cinnamon.

"Cinnamon rolls?" he asked when he could breathe again.

She smiled sheepishly.

"I can't help it," she said. "You're the one who keeps buying them."

"Because you keep eating them. Those aren't even real cakes; I only have them because my nieces like them."

She kissed him again. He felt the heat of it through his entire convalescing body.

"Are you tired?" he asked carefully. She had been with her physiotherapist while he had been in Søborg. The carbon monoxide poisoning had left her with balance problems and certain other issues which had, her chronically optimistic therapist maintained, a good chance of disappearing entirely over the next six months if she didn't neglect her training. They were carful not to call it brain damage. That sounded so permanent.

There were frustrating days. Days when she dropped things because she was tired. Days where she was angry and miserable because she had forgotten something important, or because she couldn't concentrate on reading a book. Days when he had to remind her that it was early days yet, and that Rome wasn't built in a day.

"I don't give a shit about Rome," she had screamed at him two days ago. "I just want to be able to walk without falling down!"

Today was one of the better days, he could see. She laughed at him and poked him in the chest.

"Are you looking for consolation sex?" she asked.

"Is that on offer?" he enquired hopefully.

"Only if you promise to pick up another bag of cinnamon rolls afterward."

THEY LAY TOGETHER, she with her shoulder tucked into his armpit and her head on his chest, he with his right arm closed around her waist. He could feel the muscles in her abdomen rise and fall under the warm, naked skin.

"Are you really okay with it?" she asked without raising her head.

"Yes. I think I actually am. I'm not looking forward to saying goodbye to the group, but . . . they'll survive. And so will I."

She let one index fingers follow the contours of the scar she had given him.

"*We're* the survivors," she said. "You and me. The others are just amateurs."

His right arm pulled her in and held her more tightly without any conscious decision on his part. Life and death were separated only by a single breath. But she was right. At this moment in time, they were both alive.

She slid from his grasp and propped herself up on one elbow.

"So if you aren't *actually* traumatized and depressed," she said, "where are my cinnamon rolls?"

Acknowledgments

THERE IS NO St. Francis College of Medicine in Manila or any Eden Tower complex on Paradise Road, or any road in Viborg called Cherry Lane. Our Viborg Hospital doesn't have much in common with what today is called Regional Hospital Viborg. Here—and in a few other respects—we've let fiction reign. We hope that the story feels realistic and plausible despite these deliberate inaccuracies. If we've succeeded, it's in no small part due to the many people who have generously and tirelessly offered their knowledge and experiences, to those who have read and listened and provided valuable insights on the text, and to those indefatigable friends and relatives who continue to support us in what we do. A HUGE thank you to:

Bernadette and Ernest Camarillo
Ruchell and Jensen Victorino and their entire big family
Carmelita Diamante
Dr. Crislyn Joy Sandigan Mendoza
Dr. Joey Tabula
Hans Jørgen Bonnichsen
Lone-emilie Rasmussen
Bibs Carlsen

Jorgen Liboriussen
Lotte Krarup
Esthe Kunz
Lisbeth Møller-Madsen
Erling Kaaberbøl
Eva Kaaberbøl
Gustav Friis
Kirstine Friis
Henrik Laier
Inga Friis
Henrik Friis

As usual, each author would like to point out that any errors and unintentional inaccuracies are entirey due to the shortcomings of the other.

Continue reading for a preview of Agnete Friis's novel

What My Body Remembers

"Can't you get him to shut up at night?"

Rosa came to stand next to me on the gallery and took out a cigarette. Her hair was platinum blonde, if one were kind enough to ignore the ten-centimeter band of liver-pâté roots on top. Her skin was pink and chronically pocked, a skin condition from half a life of alcohol and too much sun. Her color combination reminded me of rainbow ice cream melting in the sun; chocolate, vanilla, and strawberry. The cheap stuff they dished up at Bakkegården when it was time for a party.

"He's got nightmares. He can't help it," I said flatly.

We'd had this conversation hundreds of times before, practically word for word, but Rosa had no sympathy for social aberrations of this kind. Her life—as I had come to know it in the two years we'd lived in the apartment next door—was little more than an endless row of repetitions. Morning coffee with the husband at eight, shopping at Netto at ten, rye bread with meat and raw onions at twelve. Thereafter, two hours on the sofa with an indefinite number of Kodimagnyl and Valium swimming in her blood. Cake, coffee, and TV at three. Dinner with the husband at six. Some kind of fried meat, potatoes, and cooked vegetables. Then more TV, more coffee, and a stack of smokes. Washing was done Monday. Lotto Wednesday and Saturday.

"It's not normal for a child his age," she went on.

I was inclined to agree with that, but didn't say so out loud. Alex's nightmares were undiluted terror and, according to Doctor Erhardsen, most common amongst preschool kids. Alex was eleven, almost twelve.

"And what do you suggest I do about it?"

Rosa wrinkled her nose in disapproval and looked away.

"He keeps us up, for Christ's sake. And Jens has to be fresh for work in the mornings." Her voice was tobacco-rough, no trace of a smile. "If your son were a dog, we would've had the super put him down."

Dry laughter.

The walls of our concrete apartment complex were thin as eggshells; after eleven, anything going on next door always felt like a blatant lack of consideration.

Rosa coughed, smacked her chest with a flat hand and sighed dramatically.

"Have you been to see Erhardsen about that?"

She nodded.

"It's the lungs. I've got to keep taking the pills."

"That's not what I meant," I said, clapping her on the shoulder. "I meant that thing you've got stuck up your ass. It's been there for quite a while."

"Shut the fuck up!"

She choked a smile, and I turned my back to fish a hand-rolled smoke out of my jeans pocket. I kept them in an old King's pack, so they smelled traitorously like the real thing, but tasted all wrong. When I needed nicotine, I had to smoke three of the hand-rolled before I could feel the same lull in my bones that a single King's could deliver. But it was still cheaper, and it was seldom that I smoked for the sake of the nicotine. The smokes were a habit; something to do with my hands, an excuse to stand on the gallery and look out over the other apartment blocks. We all need something to apply ourselves to. Even the apes at the zoo are made to pick sunflower seeds out of coconuts with a stick so they can sense the meaning of life. I know this, because when we went to see the apes for Alex's seventh birthday, the zookeeper was kind enough to explain it to us. The habitual activity with the seeds makes the chimps happy, he said. They're also fond of smashing cardboard boxes, snapping twigs, and throwing shit at the other apes. Actually, I was envious of them. It seemed like a much more meaningful occupation than the kind of crap those idiots from Welfare had me doing.

The wind was blowing from the east today, bringing the sour smell of exhaust fumes and warm asphalt from the parking lot with it. I leaned over the railing, just far enough to feel the pull of the deep drop.

"You've got to get him to stop screaming," Rosa mumbled behind me. "He's too old for all that."

"Okay," I said, without looking at her. "I love you too, Rosa."

I could hear her disappear into the apartment next door and lock the door behind her.

We were a fragile alliance, Alex and I; a freak and a skinny eleven-year-old boy. I was the only family he had, and he was mine, and although we'd spent the last eleven years in numerous apartments amidst various people on the dole or early pension with phobias about earth rays, allergies to electricity, and aches and pains in mysterious parts of the body, we still stuck out like pubic hair on the pussy of a porno star. I had no friends to speak of. In fact, there was only Rosa, and my friendship with her was, well . . . complicated.

Officially, Rosa had been diagnosed with a pelvic girdle disorder after the birth of an oversized diabetic boy some twenty-three years ago, when Rosa had been declared unfit for work. Unofficially, it was an open secret that both Rosa and Jens had been stone drunk up till about three years ago. The social authorities' forcible removal of their son, Michael, was one the most spectacular stories in the history of our apartment block. Rosa had left the five-year-old Michael in the care of the dead-drunk Jens while she herself went grocery shopping: beer for the adults, rye bread, liver pâté, and milk for the boy. On her way back she was overtaken by the fire brigade, and back home a small gathering of residents were stood on the tiles under their fifth floor window, where Michael was sitting watching the world go by, his feet dangling in thin air. The firemen managed to break down the front door before Rosa arrived with the keys, and afterward there was a screaming performance when Michael was brought down from the window and driven away. Jens had apparently slept through the whole thing, leaving Rosa to sob alone on the couch in a haze of alcohol.

For my own part, I had only known her sober, and she was one of the most respectable people I had ever met. She didn't smile very often, but she was honest. She did her best not gossip about other people, which was rare as life in space here in Ghost Town.

The heavens opened in the same second I caught sight of Alex. He came running through the crash of warm water with his arms stretched out wide, as if he were flying. The steam stood off his scraggly frame and his dark fringe clung to his forehead in jagged tufts.

I leaned out over the railing and whistled to get his attention. He smiled when he saw me and a moment later I could hear him rhythmically banging the banister, all the way up from the bottom of the staircase. He didn't like taking the lift on his own. He was afraid it would get stuck, or crash, and there was a permanent stench of piss from that shiny-black blotch in the corner. He was a sensitive child; his nerve endings were frayed. The child psychologist said was something he'd inherited from me, but I don't buy it. When I see myself at age twelve, I see an angry forbidding girl, crew cut with small beady eyes.

Alex let his fingers run along the rails of the banister till he got right up next to me.

"Are you hungry?"

He nodded and we went into the kitchen, where I buttered a couple of slices of toast-bread on the mottled kitchen counter. At one time, the surface had presumably been meant to imitate marble, but now it resembled what it was: worn, yellow plastic. I wiped the crumbs off the counter with a cloth, swearing under my breath. It smelled foul, stiff with dried porridge. The washing basket in the bedroom was overflowing and I desperately needed a twenty-kroner coin for the Laundromat.

"Do you want to go to the park with me?"

I put a hand on the back of his damp neck, but he pulled away from me. This was new.

"It's pouring," he said. "Can't we wait a while?"

"Nope, we can't. It's the perfect weather for collecting cans. We'll have the whole place to ourselves."

I went into the hallway and rummaged in the cupboard for my raincoat and Alex's yellow windbreaker. It was too big, bought on sale. You could draw it tight round his face so only his olive-skinned nose poked out the front.

He shot a skeptical glance at the mirror.

"I hope we don't fucking bump into anyone we know."

"Don't swear."

"And I hope we get there before Sveske."

Sveske was a scavenger and can-collector and lived on the stairway opposite ours. He was a cute little tyke, as long as you didn't come on his turf—then all hell broke loose. The words that came out of his mouth were so filthy that even the bigger boys kept their distance when he lost his temper. Sveske usually collected the empty bottles and cans on the eastern side of the apartment block—and in the park, of course. But the park was fair game, a common expanse of grass—it was simply a question of first come, first serve.

We went down to the little stream together, each with our own plastic supermarket bag from Aldi. My flip-flops slipped on the wet grass and I had difficulty keeping up with Alex, who jogged on ahead, his hood still pulled down low. There was thunder in the clouds, and the rain was heavy and warm.

Splash.

Alex landed in a puddle right next to me, both feet planted close together, and muddy water splashed up over my legs.

"You little brat!"

Alex laughed, and ran, sprinting ahead for all he was worth in his flapping galoshes, but I caught up with him in large strides, tackled him, and deftly brought him down onto the muddy grass. I'd have to wash his clothes by hand, but as long as it didn't cost me any coins for the Laundromat machines, it was worth it. We were soaked, but he was grinning from ear to ear. He wrinkled his nose.

"There's got to be duck shit in the water," he said, pointing down to the stream, where the ground was marshy, clogged with the last couple of days' rain. Shiny water covered the lawn and a few clucking ducks waded about in the newly created biotope.

"Sissy."

I tore off one of his galoshes, got up, and swung it triumphantly over my head like an Olympic hammer thrower.

"Come and get it."

But Alex stayed where he was, his smile had disappeared. The transformation was so complete that at first, I thought he was taking the piss.

"Stop it, Mom. You're acting like an idiot."

I followed his gaze and saw a flock of elder boys with school bags slung over their shoulders making their way over the grass towards us in impossibly slow motion. One of them cast a velociraptor-like glance in our direction without seeming to fix on anything in particular. Then they went along their way, cajoling each other in broken voices and high-pitched whoops.

I looked at Alex, who got up swiftly, half-turning away from me and pretending to study something important in the space between his feet.

"You can't just rip off my galoshes in the middle of the park," he said, angry tears choking his voice. "Now look what you did!"

He grabbed his gumboot and shoved his foot into it furiously. Then he picked up the Aldi-bag he'd lost in the heat of the tussle and steered straight for the next trash can and bench.

I remained standing for a moment to look after the group of boys, who were now on their way up the path to the concrete blocks, but I didn't recognize any of them. Or rather, I didn't think I did. The bigger kids from the complex all looked the same: enormous, tent-like hoodies with denim jeans and chunky shoes in winter. Huge T-shirts, shorts, and the same chunky shoes in summer.

Alex fished a beer can out of the garbage with two fingers while I waded through a puddle and followed the gravel path to the next bench. Bingo. Two empty soda bottles and one mineral water. Just twenty minutes more, a trip to Hvidovre Square, and there would be enough coins for a cycle of washing at the Laundromat and two cupcakes from the bakery.

I waved my loot over my head in Alex's direction and he waved back. The gang of boys appeared to be forgotten, but he still pulled his yellow hood down over his eyes and turned his back when I tried to send him a smile. I recognized that look of shame; till now, we'd been a good team, Alex and I, but he was starting to look at me with a stranger's eyes. Not all the time, but more and more often, and eventually he'd desert me altogether. I could feel it, as I fed the empties into the automat outside the Netto store, and I could feel it afterward, when we went to the bakery. That measured glance, which saw me from the outside: Ella Nygaard, 28-year-old woman on the dole. The thin legs sticking out of a pair of denim shorts, feet stuck into a pair of pink flip-flops scavenged from the Red Cross's clothing container.

We walked home in silence.

In the foyer to our apartment block I checked our mailbox.

The letter I found lying in there was narrow, skimmed milk-white, and covered in postage stamps and markings. Tiny imprints of Buddha in orange overalls, elephants, and colorful flowers, all bunched together with my name and address.

The plastic bag of cupcakes fell out of my left hand and landed on the cement floor with a soft thump. I could hear Alex pull up behind me, and I told myself that I could get through this, if I just concentrated on thinking logically, I could talk my body back to calm.

A faint buzzing sensation in my hands I carefully folded the letter, slipped it into a stack of advertisements and carried the little package to the garbage shaft. I could feel a pain in the index and middle finger of my right hand. It was always the same pain, which followed in the wake of the initial shuddering. I stretched out my arm and supported myself against the grey speckled wall. I tried to breathe deeply, into the pit of my stomach.

In and out. In and out.

It was a technique I had learned from Doctor Erhardsen that was supposed to dampen the fear. Not that it had ever had that effect on me. When the fear came, it washed through me like ice water and the breathing exercises were no more effective than dams built of fine beach sand. Everything was destroyed and washed away. Breathe out. Breathe out.

I felt the familiar shuddering like a faint, inner hum. It felt very distinct, as if someone had stuck a vibrator in my chest and was slowing turning up the pitch. If I had made it up to our apartment, I might've been all right. The right dose of cheap vodka is a good trick to take the edge off just about anything: one glass filled to the brim, and then—if you have the patience—one more that's big enough to steady your hands.

"Mom?" Alex had picked up the bag of cupcakes from the floor. He was watching me intently. "Is it bad? Is it . . . ? Do you need to lie down?"

"I just need to get upstairs," I mumbled, but kept standing where I was. My legs were no longer cooperating.

Residents coming into the building were staring now as they passed. I tried to meet their gaze, but occasionally I had to kneel down to avoid losing my balance altogether. My arms and legs were shaking and soon the vibrator would be on full throttle. The world surged and closed in on me. Strangely enough, I rarely lose consciousness. On the contrary. My senses open up, registering each and every painful, ugly detail. The filthy grooves between the tiles on the floor, the surface of the rough walls that looked like a contagious, greyish rash, the stench of the industrial detergent, the piss, and the wet cement exploded in my forehead. I pitched over, taking a couple of kids' bicycles with me as I fell, then my hands came crashing down after me onto the floor.

It hurt. There would be grazes and bruises afterward. There almost always were.

In some skewed way, the cramps that followed reminded of the time I gave birth to Alex; the sense of muscles moving me, rather than the reverse. My teeth scraped against one another and my body arched into a shuddering bridge. A separate, sudden jerk smashed my head down into the tiles. My head rang.

Alex was kneeling beside me. I could see him out of the corner of my eye, but I couldn't turn towards him. His eyes were was calm and dark as he carefully lifted my head onto his lap and stroked my forehead.

"Has someone called an ambulance?"

A man was bent over me, looking into my eyes. He was old as Methuselah; he had bony shoulders and an enormous Adam's apple in his red, scabby-scaly neck. But his eyes were kindly, mild and brown. I tried to smile.

"Don't worry about a thing, Ella. We'll take care of everything, as usual," he said, pressing my cramped hand tightly to his chest. "Rosa and I will take care of Alex till you get back."

Other Titles in the Soho Crime Series

STEPHANIE BARRON
(Jane Austen's England)
Jane and the Twelve Days of Christmas
Jane and the Waterloo Map
Jane and the Year Without a Summer

F.H. BATACAN
(Philippines)
Smaller and Smaller Circles

JAMES R. BENN
(World War II Europe)
Billy Boyle
The First Wave
Blood Alone
Evil for Evil
Rag & Bone
A Mortal Terror
Death's Door
A Blind Goddess
The Rest Is Silence
The White Ghost
Blue Madonna
The Devouring
Solemn Graves
When Hell Struck Twelve
The Red Horse
Road of Bones
From the Shadows

The Refusal Camp: Stories

CARA BLACK
(Paris, France)
Murder in the Marais
Murder in Belleville
Murder in the Sentier
Murder in the Bastille
Murder in Clichy
Murder in Montmartre
Murder on the Ile Saint-Louis
Murder in the Rue de Paradis
Murder in the Latin Quarter
Murder in the Palais Royal
Murder in Passy
Murder at the Lanterne Rouge
Murder Below Montparnasse
Murder in Pigalle
Murder on the Champ de Mars
Murder on the Quai
Murder in Saint-Germain
Murder on the Left Bank

CARA BLACK CONT.
Murder in Bel-Air
Murder at the Porte de Versailles

Three Hours in Paris
Night Flight to Paris

HENRY CHANG
(Chinatown)
Chinatown Beat
Year of the Dog
Red Jade
Death Money
Lucky

BARBARA CLEVERLY
(England)
The Last Kashmiri Rose
Strange Images of Death
The Blood Royal
Not My Blood
A Spider in the Cup
Enter Pale Death
Diana's Altar

Fall of Angels
Invitation to Die

COLIN COTTERILL
(Laos)
The Coroner's Lunch
Thirty-Three Teeth
Disco for the Departed
Anarchy and Old Dogs
Curse of the Pogo Stick
The Merry Misogynist
Love Songs from a Shallow Grave
Slash and Burn
The Woman Who Wouldn't Die
Six and a Half Deadly Sins
I Shot the Buddha
The Rat Catchers' Olympics
Don't Eat Me
The Second Biggest Nothing
The Delightful Life of a Suicide Pilot

The Motion Picture Teller

ELI CRANOR
(Arkansas)
Don't Know Tough
Ozark Dogs

GARRY DISHER
(Australia)
The Dragon Man
Kittyhawk Down
Snapshot
Chain of Evidence
Blood Moon
Whispering Death
Signal Loss

Wyatt
Port Vila Blues
Fallout

Under the Cold Bright Lights

TERESA DOVALPAGE
(Cuba)
Death Comes in through the Kitchen
Queen of Bones
Death under the Perseids

Death of a Telenovela Star (A Novella)

DAVID DOWNING
(World War II Germany)
Zoo Station
Silesian Station
Stettin Station
Potsdam Station
Lehrter Station
Masaryk Station
Wedding Station

(World War I)
Jack of Spies
One Man's Flag
Lenin's Roller Coaster
The Dark Clouds Shining

Diary of a Dead Man on Leave

RAMONA EMERSON
(Navajo Nation)
Shutter

AGNETE FRIIS
(Denmark)
What My Body Remembers
The Summer of Ellen

TIMOTHY HALLINAN
(Thailand)
The Fear Artist
For the Dead
The Hot Countries
Fools' River
Street Music

(Los Angeles)
Crashed
Little Elvises
The Fame Thief
Herbie's Game
King Maybe
Fields Where They Lay
Nighttown
Rock of Ages

METTE IVIE HARRISON
(Mormon Utah)
The Bishop's Wife
His Right Hand
For Time and All Eternities
Not of This Fold
The Prodigal Daughter

MICK HERRON
(England)
Slow Horses
Dead Lions
The List (A Novella)
Real Tigers
Spook Street
London Rules
The Marylebone Drop (A Novella)
Joe Country
The Catch (A Novella)
Slough House
Bad Actors

Down Cemetery Road
The Last Voice You Hear
Why We Die
Smoke and Whispers

Reconstruction
Nobody Walks
This Is What Happened
Dolphin Junction: Stories

NAOMI HIRAHARA
(Japan Town)
Clark and Division

STAN JONES
(Alaska)
White Sky, Black Ice
Shaman Pass
Frozen Sun
Village of the Ghost Bears
Tundra Kill
The Big Empty

STEVEN MACK JONES
(Detroit)
August Snow
Lives Laid Away
Dead of Winter

LENE KAABERBØL & AGNETE FRIIS
(Denmark)
The Boy in the Suitcase
Invisible Murder
Death of a Nightingale
The Considerate Killer

MARTIN LIMÓN
(South Korea)
Jade Lady Burning
Slicky Boys
Buddha's Money
The Door to Bitterness
The Wandering Ghost
G.I. Bones
Mr. Kill
The Joy Brigade
Nightmare Range
The Iron Sickle
The Ville Rat
Ping-Pong Heart
The Nine-Tailed Fox
The Line
GI Confidential
War Women

ED LIN
(Taiwan)
Ghost Month
Incensed
99 Ways to Die
Death Doesn't Forget

PETER LOVESEY
(England)
The Circle
The Headhunters
False Inspector Dew
Rough Cider
On the Edge
The Reaper

PETER LOVESEY CONT.
(Bath, England)
The Last Detective
Diamond Solitaire
The Summons
Bloodhounds
Upon a Dark Night
The Vault
Diamond Dust
The House Sitter
The Secret Hangman
Skeleton Hill
Stagestruck
Cop to Corpse
The Tooth Tattoo
The Stone Wife
Down Among the Dead Men
Another One Goes Tonight
Beau Death
Killing with Confetti
The Finisher
Diamond and the Eye
Showstopper

(London, England)
Wobble to Death
The Detective Wore
Silk Drawers
Abracadaver
Mad Hatter's Holiday
The Tick of Death
A Case of Spirits
Swing, Swing Together
Waxwork

Bertie and the Tinman
Bertie and the Seven Bodies
Bertie and the Crime of Passion

SUJATA MASSEY
(1920s Bombay)
The Widows of Malabar Hill
The Satapur Moonstone
The Bombay Prince

FRANCINE MATHEWS
(Nantucket)
Death in the Off-Season
Death in Rough Water
Death in a Mood Indigo
Death in a Cold Hard Light
Death on Nantucket
Death on Tuckernuck
Death on a Winter Stroll

SEICHŌ MATSUMOTO
(Japan)
Inspector Imanishi Investigates

CHRIS MCKINNEY
(Post Apocalyptic Future)
Midnight, Water City

MAGDALEN NABB
(Italy)
Death of an Englishman
Death of a Dutchman
Death in Springtime
Death in Autumn
The Marshal and the Murderer
The Marshal and the Madwoman
The Marshal's Own Case
The Marshal Makes His Report
The Marshal at the Villa Torrini
Property of Blood
Some Bitter Taste
The Innocent
Vita Nuova
The Monster of Florence

FUMINORI NAKAMURA
(Japan)
The Thief
Evil and the Mask
Last Winter, We Parted
The Kingdom
The Boy in the Earth
Cult X
My Annihilation
The Rope Artist

STUART NEVILLE
(Northern Ireland)
The Ghosts of Belfast
Collusion
Stolen Souls
The Final Silence
Those We Left Behind
So Say the Fallen

The Traveller & Other Stories
House of Ashes

(Dublin)
Ratlines

KWEI QUARTEY
(Ghana)
Murder at Cape Three Points
Gold of Our Fathers
Death by His Grace

KWEI QUARTEY CONT.
The Missing American
Sleep Well, My Lady
Last Seen in Lapaz

QIU XIAOLONG
(China)
Death of a Red Heroine
A Loyal Character Dancer
When Red Is Black

MARCIE R. RENDON
(Minnesota's Red River Valley)
Murder on the Red River
Girl Gone Missing
Sinister Graves

JAMES SALLIS
(New Orleans)
The Long-Legged Fly
Moth
Black Hornet
Eye of the Cricket
Bluebottle
Ghost of a Flea

Sarah Jane

JOHN STRALEY
(Sitka, Alaska)
The Woman Who Married a Bear
The Curious Eat Themselves
The Music of What Happens
Death and the Language of Happiness
The Angels Will Not Care
Cold Water Burning
Baby's First Felony
So Far and Good

(Cold Storage, Alaska)
The Big Both Ways
Cold Storage, Alaska
What Is Time to a Pig?
Blown by the Same Wind

AKIMITSU TAKAGI
(Japan)
The Tattoo Murder Case
Honeymoon to Nowhere
The Informer

CAMILLA TRINCHIERI
(Tuscany)
Murder in Chianti
The Bitter Taste of Murder
Murder on the Vine

HELENE TURSTEN
(Sweden)
Detective Inspector Huss
The Torso
The Glass Devil
Night Rounds
The Golden Calf
The Fire Dance
The Beige Man
The Treacherous Net
Who Watcheth
Protected by the Shadows

Hunting Game
Winter Grave
Snowdrift

An Elderly Lady Is Up to No Good
An Elderly Lady Must Not Be Crossed

ILARIA TUTI
(Italy)
Flowers over the Inferno
The Sleeping Nymph

JANWILLEM VAN DE WETERING
(Holland)
Outsider in Amsterdam
Tumbleweed
The Corpse on the Dike
Death of a Hawker
The Japanese Corpse
The Blond Baboon
The Maine Massacre
The Mind-Murders
The Streetbird
The Rattle-Rat
Hard Rain
Just a Corpse at Twilight
Hollow-Eyed Angel
The Perfidious Parrot
The Sergeant's Cat: Collected Stories

JACQUELINE WINSPEAR
(1920s England)
Maisie Dobbs
Birds of a Feather